FROM G[illegible]
TO T[illegible]

by St[illegible] [illegible]aylor

An Old Dogs Publishing Paperback

First published in Great Britain in 2023 by Old Dog Publishing
5 Hogshill Lane, Cobham KT11 2AG

1st Amazing Edition 2023

Printed with love by
www.dcslondon.com

TH JAM

You CAN teach an old dog new tricks

Danny DC   PjH
Mr Bingley   KP   Lilith Isaac Aquilina
Fiona Day and Alex Dewing. Moira and Gary Loveridge

THE MAN RESPONSIBLE

I am now 58 and retirement has thankfully arrived.

I have thought about doing a Suffolk based part/sectional autobiography (of sorts) for a while and my inspiration came originally from Giles Smith's brilliant book Lost In Music (which I have read three times) and more laterly Pete Paphides excellent Broken Greek.It was Roger Osborne not John Wark though Pete!

Hopefully my brief attempt will appeal to those who grew up in an era of contrasting/exciting music styles,and proper football. If you weren't into Glam/Punk/Mod or footy I wouldn't bother.

It helps if you lived in or have experienced life in East Anglia. If not prepare to be enlightened!

From this I have produced a Suffolk schoolboy's memoirs for the period 1970/1983. I attended the same High school as one Ed Sheeran. A loose desperate claim to fame as 35+ years elapsed between our respective attendances.

This is a journey through Glam, Punk, Mod Revival, Post Punk together with sporting anecdotes and reference to the times in terms of television, films, prevailing attitudes and football related issues.

At no point in the following text will the words 'awesome or 'epic' be used apart from on one justified occasion. Spot it if you can.

The account would not be authentic without reference to, and occasional use of the Saaaarfolk accent. It is a truly unique and often unfathomable phenomenom (often included in brackets) speak them out loud, you'll be with it by the end. These are not spelling mistakes!

Cards on the table :
I don't like The Beatles.

Always more of a Monkees man myself. It seems as though to get any 'street Cred' it is a necessity to like The Beatles. Whilst they are pleasant enough how can I take seriously a band comprising four lads from Liverpool with no discernible interest in football. Weird, very weird. Suffice to say I would take 'What Am I Doin' Hanging 'round' over 'Penny Lane' any day of the week. I can't deny that without The Beatles there would probably have been no Jam but I'll turn a convenient blind eye / deaf ear to that one.

I can't stand Monty Python.
I hope the increase in level of dislike is duly noted.

Predictable 'cult' humour born from a 'you've got to like it' prog rocker/student perspective. Hippy based 'trend comedy' rooted in the late 1960s. Not remotely funny and certainly not for me.

I have never seen a Star Wars film.
I am very proud of this fact. I simply do not get the on-going fascination (a bit like Harry Potter). If we were talking the original Star Trek Series (with Bones McCoy, Zulu and Scotty- who looked remarkably like Bernard Cribbens) you may be talking but the Blakes 7 style unbelievable sci fi shit that is Star Wars leaves me cold. Sorry.

Rugby Union.
Don't get me started on this one!

I have a complete and utter abhorrence of this sport and all the upper class baggage that goes with it. Hemispheres my arse. A virtual chapter of derision follows later.

That should have alienated half of the potential readership.

If you're still with me (and I'm sure already that many are not) let's get on the steamer.

The following events took place at time when, thankfully, there was no such thing as social media (not sure Ipswich has it even now). Today a total reliance unfortunately utilised largely by an illiterate, grammatically inept Chav following.

Back in the 1970s McDonalds/Nando's/Domino's had not brain washed the country. As for home delivery that was about as likely as Spurs winning the league or someone making a claim on their 'essential' Scotch Guard protection policy. The world was a better place for it. People communicated face to face, by phone or by letter. How quaint.

All chapters (and some sections within) have a title followed by a loosely related song reference. These give a broad clue as to what follows within the chapter. No names are given in association with the song titles which may be from the Glam, Punk, Mod or Post Punk eras (never rock or disco). It's up to you to place the song title with the artist?

As the book is part school based the chapters are interspersed with the occasional test (including an oral) and a chance for you naturally to compare, contrast.

In addition at the end of every chapter is a 70s/80s teaser. No googling. Answers follow at the end of the book.

I would strongly suggest that prior to reading this short account ask 'Alexa' (or similar electronic device) to play 'Days' (that changed the world) by Tom Robinson.

In five minutes this song satirically and brilliantly portrays the changes from the demise of glam/prog through the punk era to the reality of middle age against a backdrop of prominent figures and events of the times (Rock Against Racism and Live Aid included).

It is a brilliant composition and very apt with regards to this offering.

This should have provided Mr Robinson with a top twenty hit (he cynically claims to have one of these per decade) and a number of DJs picked up on it but to no avail. It remains an undiscovered gem.

Worth re-visiting this track at the end of the book.

Note. Originally entitled From Glam To Whaam at the publisher's suggestion this was altered to reflect my obsession with The Jam as I had no Wham ties.

Cast yourself back to the heady 1970s and re-live the days when music thankfully shifted away from dinosaur rock and artists didn't feel the need to 'feature' anybody, TV shows were unique, penny sweets ruled the newsagent's shelves (Black Jacks eight a penny until political correctness took hold, changed the name to Aniseed chews and reduced the allocation to four a penny into the bargain) and, commentators were true legends.

Marathons were Marathons, Opal Fruits were Opal Fruits and Tab (complete with the pretty pink cans) were way ahead in the emerging world of Diet Colas. Cereal boxes contained free choking hazards (still have my Dr McCoy badge), Mousetrap was viewed as a game of technical wizardry and 'losing' your five pence Sunday school collection money allowed for convenient 'finding' and financing of a Milky Way and tube of Love Hearts. Happy days.

Finger V sign sew on patches were widely seen on the back pockets of high waist banded flared jeans accompanied by belts advertising the likes of Cinzano and Swan Vestas, Iced lolly sticks carried jokes, a Troll was something that appeared in the chronicles of Narnia and Nestle's adverts blatantly declared in a true sexist way that girls could not manage big chocolate bars.

It was a time when quantity ruled the roost over quality (at least amongst the youth). No-one would choose a Nestle Golden Cup bar if there was a Waggon Wheel lurking in the wings. The same can be said for 1970s Monster Munch. Hunks of roast beef flavour corn snack in a monster sized bag. Contrast this with the pitiful 2023 version which contain a mere nine hunks per bag.

Some naff 70s/80s institutions still endure today. Reid Recruitment's cringeable ad has a permed youth dancing on and off buses and across town squares before arriving at the office. He is the double of one Bruno Martelli that Kids From Fame Star Maker.

A packet of Embassy Number 3 set your parents back forty pence, a Kellogg's variety pack was the definition of luxury (together with a Ghia on the driveway), a tenner was enough for our Dad to fill the car up with Four Star, Big D peanuts gave the lecherous pub clientele the chance to strip nut bags off the blonde bikini clad model on the classic hanging card display, bag by bag gradually increasing the extent of flesh exposure and county lines were localised bus routes rather than the Chav controlled drug networking that we see today.

At football matches adolescent young males in white lab coats sold limited refreshments (Kioras, Mars Bars and Aztecs) to the first couple of rows of fans from a plastic tray suspended from their necks with a sash. Tough luck on those more than four rows back. Half time scores were theoretically displayed on an alphabet board which remains as confusing now as it was then.

Forget the bleak aspects of the seventies and banish the long established stubborn remnants of Prog Rock to the bins of the sparsely furnished early seventies Whistle Test studio. Re-live the exciting fresh beats that were Glam, Punk, Mod Revival and Post Punk.

I

A Brief Background boring, necessary and brief

Goodbye To Spain / Take Me Back 'Ome

I was born into an RAF Services family in Wegberg, West Germany.

There then followed Geoffrey's (my dad) RAF European Tour which at this time amounted to Wegberg (West Germany) to Hatfield (Doncaster) via Hemswell (Lincoln).

Geoffrey was being posted here, there and everywhere leading to family movement/upheavals left right and centre but I was too young to be affected by this.

You may have noticed Spain does not feature in Geoffrey's placements but a play on the Slade song title was again too good to miss. Goodbuy To Deutschland doesn't have the same ring!

Geoffrey was a Navigator and his postings took him initially across Europe and then across the UK.

As noted above the early days is always the boring section of any book. I will cover briefly in a summary format. Five years in little more than five pages.

Wegberg West Germany:

I was born here at a hospital either on or close to the RAF camp. I am sure the Germans were delighted to have to welcome a UK RAF base so soon (in relative terms) after the Second World War. I am not sure what the arrangement was that led to this scenario but one can only assume it was based on an on-going level of distrust with our new ally.

From a personal perspective this gave me the attractive potential option of dual nationality which in my deluded mind would be useful in determining whether I should play football for England or West Germany and led me to an on-going attachment to Germany, from a football perspective that I hold to this day..

In April 1972 when I was seven the West German team (inspired by Gunter Netzer) beat England 3-1 at Wembley in the European Championship quarter final first leg (they did it differently then).

Naturally I was not unduly upset and took an instant liking to the Germans attractive green away shirts (this would come back to me later in my Gooner loving years).

In my early days at primary school I got my mum (Franny) to dye my red footy top black so as to look like West German goalkeeping legend Sepp Maier who nearly always wore a black shirt but on occasion light blue. Amazingly in July 2003 Arsenal signed a near look alike in one Jens Lehmann and he was German into the bargain. He even wore black on occasions.

The dyed shirt also served to double up as an All Blacks top as I was strangely attracted to that team (at a time of limited live sport coverage) and a certain player called Sid Going who from memory looked a bit like Ralph Coates. God knows why. My rugby hatred had not taken its firm grip on me at that stage.

To be honest to call the dyed shirt black is a little generous. It was at best an off-set dull brown but it did for me at the time.

On our return to the UK Geoffrey was based at RAF Scampton in Lincolnshire and we lived in a village a few miles away called Hemswell.

A small detached bungalow with sizeable back garden and meadow to rear sited on a single track road leading to a detached 1960s derelict house to which my brother and I were strangely drawn to even at dusk (and on our own!!).

That house scared the shit out of us but we couldn't resist it. What was even more unfathomable was why, at the respective ages of six and four our strict parents allowed us to access this property on our own.

Little more remains in the memory other than bawling my eyes out on the first day at Primary school when I failed to secure a miniature second hand grand piano at the school jumble sale.

Hatfield Doncaster

Fast forward to UK location two. Luckily we fast forwarded out.

God knows where Geoffrey was stationed at this time but we ended up on a grim 1960s housing estate in a suburb close to Doncaster called Hatfield. A bland detached two storey property with wrap around side/back garden with pretty rough sweary neighbours either side who hung over the fence and infringed our privacy.

I could sense that my parents felt uncomfortable living on an estate that resembled the residential enclave inhabited by Bob and Terry in Whatever Happened To The Likely Lads.

Little of note remembered other than:

A small two storey parade of shops opposite with housing above which included a launderette and a Newsagents which (in the build up to November 5th) sold two varieties of Bonfire lollies, both with hard dark red sticky toffee style coatings on processed long-life apple base. In addition they sold yard lengths of delicious red liquorice. That's 0.91 metres.

No wonder the local dentist was inundated.

My other recollection is dislocating my shoulder showing off to my mum on an icy incline outside the primary school.

That's about it.

Luckily our respective spells at these two ' Northern' locations were brief.

Faggots, Chips and Gravy and 'them' Northern accents didn't sit well with me or the family at the time (although the Suffolk one was to follow) and I was never going to follow the likes of Lincoln or Doncaster in football terms although funnily enough three years later when visiting one of Geoffrey's ex RAF colleagues who was into his footy, and attended the 1966 World Cup Final, I attended my first ever football match. A midweek encounter between Lincoln City and Doncaster Rovers no less under the floodlights at Sincil Bank.

How appropriate.

In 1970 Geoffrey landed a role at Volvo Concessionaires stationed (in RAF terms) at Raeburn Road Ipswich latterly within eyeshot of the newly constructed impressive Orwell Bridge. Over the next 15 years he would rise imperiously from what was effectively a sales clerk/representative role to become the Managing Director, all off the back of his one educational qualification - a mere college of proceptus . Don't ask!

According to my mother (Franny, not her real name) he also had the gift of the gab or 'flannel' as she called it. This saw him through many tight spots and helped with his career opportunities.

It must have been quite a change for Geoffrey as he had spent the best part of fifteen years venturing across Europe with the services and now he was to be stationed permanently at Ipswich's main Volvo distributor.

He had absolutely no experience in this sector. His past had been dominated by navigating and to be fair these compass based skills were probably very useful given the extraordinary size of the Volvo car compound at Raeburn Road.

With Geoffrey's job came what at the time was a non- taxable perk. The company car. At a time when Petula Clarke was imploring us to put a Chrysler Sunbeam in our lives Geoffrey was entitled to the exciting angular Swedish Volvo (although once their emphasis on safety became apparent the exciting image was replaced by one of dour placidity, consistency and reliability).

Geoffrey did produce some classics in our early years. On one occasion we stopped at a restaurant/ service station (Darts Champ Eric Bristow was also dining there at the time).Geoffrey ordered roast beef with horse radish sauce.

It arrived. He applied the sauce and took a mouthful before retreating violently back into his seat. He called the waiter over and uttered the famously embarrassing words ' excuse me but this is sauce tartar'. Myself and Sid hid our faces in embarrassment. At least say tartar sauce. Mr Bristow was unaffected.He was probably too busy smothering his healthy full English breakfast with Chav Sauce (aka ketchup).

As he went steadily up the career ladder the cars became more and more impressive and were replaced on an almost six monthly basis.

At this stage my knowledge of Suffolk was non-existent (but I was only six years old on arrival). What I was soon noticing (apart from the accent) was that in Ipswich Town FC Suffolk had a club and manager who were starting to turn a few heads.

The Manager Bobby Robson was appointed in 1969 and would stay at the helm until 1982 steadily building the foundations of what would become a startlingly good side by the mid 1970s.

Okay the impact of excessive finance in those days was negligible but their rise was still about as unexpected as seeing a beaming Nicholas Newton Henshall Witchell face on a day of breaking Royal scandal or a picture of health and fitness leaving a McDonalds 'restaurant'. In summary it was a new beginning for us on all fronts.

Aside: At A level results time why do the TV/Media insist on TV coverage of the bright sparks and their celebrations rather than the reactions of your average Joe and why the mock surprise?

Q1: Music.
Mud's hit Dynamite (written by Chin/Chap in 1973) was allegedly turned down by which Glam band of the time?

II

A New Beginning 1970

I've Changed My Address / I'm Stranded / Safe European Home.

Geoffrey's role in Ipswich meant a property in relative proximity was a necessity.

I remember nothing of the property hunt but we ended up settling on The Post Office in a village called Coddenham (8 miles North of Ipswich) and by default Franny had to take up the position of post mistress. I have no recollection of her undergoing any training.

Surely you couldn't just buy a post office and run it from day one (retail, savings, pensions etc) without any guidance. Her only training related to the impending decimalisation.

I think in general terms training was on the job from her loyal assistant Sheila. Either way a Post Mistress she was.

Coddenham:

The village essentially encompassed a grocer's shop -Gudgeons (Spar departed in 1975), a Post Office/Stationers (ours), a pub (The Dukes Head) and Coddenham Country Club (tied in very strongly with the village footy team) which regularly hosted discos and also had table tennis and snooker facilities at ground level together with doctor's waiting room/surgery where the annual Cricket Club AGMs were held and many of whose patients came courtesy of the Club above.

We latterly lived on the site of the former Spar and were part involved in the construction of the house when the builder went into administration mid contract in the hot Summer of 1976.

There was also a village hall, a church, Coddenham Hall (a country mansion set in vast park land) and a recreation ground, the home of Coddenham FC (under the management of the Flint family entourage) and Coddenham Juniors Cycle Speedway Team (a very Suffolk phenomenon) plus a Cricket Club.

The school had long gone and youngsters were ferried by Bickers Buses (run by the 1960s World Scrambling champion who had their bus depot and workshop in the village) between Coddenham and the school at Stonham Aspal which, in reality was a classier village.

More later.

'No Elvis , Beatles or The Rolling Stones' declared Joe.

He obviously had never set foot in Coddenham and why should he have. Aside from all the crusty old rock infused rustics we had Suffolk's answer to Elvis. Step forward - John Tweed. (see below). Our very own Shaky.

What can I say?

This was to be our base for the next 14 years. A wonderful village but centred firmly and inescapably in the past with a very insular rural community.

This was a new scenario for us. One of stability. We were no longer the RAF travellers.

Essentially the village was split either side of the recreation ground into what was in broad terms the more manual sector at one end and the more middle class clientele at the other end. (Weekend Vs Terry's All Gold in Chocolate Box terms). Harsh but true.

Certain families 'stood out':

The Tweeds

Based at the more manual end of the village this family included male offspring in the form of David and John plus daughter Louise. I have no recollection of the father.

Like all council kids they were the first on to the clothing trends of the time. John being resplendent in the black high waist band, side pocketed, pinstriped, flared pavement sweeper monstrosities accompanied by black and white sandwich panel wide soled Spoon brogues which were the in thing at the time. Flapping lapels and collars were also the order of the day giving rise to a real health and safety issue should a sudden strong gust of wind catch hold and whisk the assailant over the hedge rows into the surrounding fields.

As noted above John Tweed saw himself as Coddenham's answer to Elvis and he would strut his stuff to the old rock n roll crap that was ceremoniously belted out at Coddenham Country Club.

He was older than the rest of us (upon reflection arguably too old for the upcoming youth club setting). He looked like a cross between David Essex and Chachi from Happy Days giving him a perceived right of passage with the young 'chicks' at the burgeoning Youth Club (within reason). Before long there were Village Youth Club Discos (JB Sounds) and John would step, spin and swivel earnestly to the sounds of Tavares, the Bee Gees, Showaddywaddy and other disco tunes. When Elvis departed this earth John evolved seamlessly via Summer Lovin into John Travolta and ultimately into The Ole House occupied by one Shakin Stevens.

The Flints

Again from the more manual end of the village. Mr Flint was an Articulated Logistics Technician (lorry driver) for Brush Aggregates, a company who shifted stone/concrete about the county and were based in the neighbouring village of Hemmingstone.

This was the age of the emerging CB Radio (the rudimentary forerunner to paging and mobile phones). He had acquired the nickname Pebbles obviously a play on his surname and quite funny as he worked in the aggregates industry. Very impressive if the rustic community based this nickname on both factors but my suspicion is that it was based purely on his surname.

If this family did one thing to excess it was to believe firmly in their own self-importance.

Example. We youngsters spent the best part of two months preparing diligently for the annual bonfire on November 5th

This involved the arduous time-consuming gathering of branches/timber from a steep wooded glen by the farmer's ploughed field that we were allowed to use for the celebration.

The fire was built by ourselves (no concern for health & safety/ possibility of collapse) on the field opposite the recreation ground. It was a long slog.

On November 5th all the respective parents and their families dutifully turned up with their regulation metal lidded Family Circle/Peak Frean tins containing a selection of Astral and Standard (how appropriate, they were shit) fireworks.

These were commandeered at the entrance by The Flints who in their wisdom announced that in the interests of safety they would need to be 'in charge of the display,' and by default let off all the fireworks. They were ahead of the game with regards to Health & Safety.

Amazingly they were given free reign.

Suffice to say up-market Stonham Aspal (the neighbouring village with the school and classy football stanchions), had the full works .

An organised managed official display complete with Hot Dog and Soup vendors, fenced arena with entrance fee on the gate. In essence a Flint free event.

But were we jealous? Yes. Intensely.

Once again in fashion terms the Flint's offspring seemed to be at the front of the queue as new trends took hold although Paul Flint early acquisition of a pair of DMs (at the start of the DM craze that continues to this day) did back-fire a little as his were the 'workman's version.

Essentially this meant they lacked the surface sole stitching around the perimeter, which was deemed crucial, thereby leaving the boot looking a bit naked. As with all brown DMs at the time they had to be deeply polished into a deep russet cherry red.

He was also the first to acquire the new Admiral England strip in 1975 complete with red and blue trim down the white shirt arms, cuffs and collar, red and white trim on the blue shorts, red and blue trim on the white socks and an alluring, addictive smell.

If I am honest seeing him in one inspired me to save to acquire.

Mrs Flint (Pebbles' wife) insisted that when she withdrew money from his Post Office account that the proceeds included at least one £50 note. 'Pebbles likes to look big' she declared! To be fair in the mid 1970s a £50 note was seriously big tender but you have to question the small minded logic!

More importantly Pebbles was the Manager of Coddenham FC.

Coddenham FC

To be brutally honest they were crap and that is being generous. Pebbles was appointed to address this situation.

Playing on the recreation ground pitch which sloped from top side to bottom by about 15 degrees they were a motley collection of overweight middle- aged plasterers, electricians, post men, farm labourers combined with a token sprinkling of youth.

They wore tatty off-colour irregularly faded orange shirts in the early years until Pebbles upgraded the strip to a far more professional looking red shirt with vertical dark blue and white stripe).

Pebbles would stand on the touchline in his all in one blue overalls and 'coach' the team with such tactical wisdom as 'let him know you're there boiy' or 'get it into the box'. He was no Bobby Robson.

They changed in the small wooden pavilion and worst of all they were extremely mean with the use of their goal nets. There is nothing more exciting to a footballer (of any standard) than rattling a ball into the upper reaches of the goal frame and watching it ripple down the net. This was enhanced further if the goals had a decent set of stanchions (unfortunately Coddenham had boring teardrops at the time, latterly removed altogether to leave peg backs).

Just for the record in the 1970s all professional teams (and many amateur) had stanchions. They ranged from the common or garden teardrop to the more exotic angular version.

Of course, Stonham Aspal had the latter. They were always perceived (mainly by the jealous Coddenhamites) as having the best of everything from football teams, to schools, to shops to fireworks displays, houses and they were extremely protective.

Although they had the best stanchions in the area by a country mile apart from StonhamAspal FC no-one else was allowed access to them or get within 50 metres of them.

Amazingly about fifteen years ago I was back in the area visiting the parents in law and I decided to drive across to Coddenham and then Stonham Aspal for old time's sake.

My youngest son decided he would come (presumably to humour me) and when we got to Stonham Aspal I took him to the football pitches.

Unbelievably those dreamy stanchions were still there (complete with nets). We had a football in the boot so I said to him 'do you fancy a quick kick about in those nets'? He wasn't that fussed. I was.

I forced his hand and we nipped back to the car grabbed the football and ventured forth. Literally within three minutes we were accosted by a villager who rather abruptly enquired 'what ya doin? Them psssts are nart for yuwesin' boiy' or, to you and me hands off our stanchions. Clearly the football posts remain, even after all these years, a sacred no-go area.

My opinion of Stonham Aspal and its residents as a result remains unaltered.

A Final Stanchion Aside:
With regards to professional teams the top three stanchions (in my opinion) in the 1970s were:

3rd. Hampden Park. A fine extended arched affair (unfortunately with square posts which St Etienne claimed cost them the European Cup in the early 70s when a shot deflected off the woodwork at an uncanny angle). Only criticism the nets were a bit tight.

2nd. Stamford Bridge. I may hate Chelsea but I loved their 1970s stanchions. A small/moderate sized club with a mighty fine stanchion. Angular and with a 12" vertical base. Once again the nets were a trifle tight.

1st. Wembley. Pure perfection. A perfectly arched stanchion and nets that rippled gloriously whenever a goal was scored. I remember only one cup final goal that looked poor.

That was when, in 1978 when Ipswich's ROGER OSBOURNE (not John Wark Mr Paphides) scrambled a close range effort in following a monumental defensive error by Willie Young although I am undeniably biased on this one given my Arsenal leanings and my residency close to Ipswich at the time. To be fair Man Utd's deflected second against Liverpool was probably worse.

In actual fact I remember going to the rec just after that final (I was a glutton for punishment?) and all the young joyous rustics taking the piss out of me 'one Roger Osbourne, there's only one Roger Osbourne'. Fact was most of them had never heard of him prior to the final. Bloody glory hunters.

Just for the record West Ham and QPR had the worst stanchions. Narrow and vertical with small angled corner pieces coupled with a narrow-gauge net. They were horrendous but in my warped mind at least when QPR played West Ham we had a stanchion derby of note as they were so rare.

Nowadays stanchion derbies don't exist due to the bland standard nets on display covering all clubs. The only unique derby we did have in 2019/20 was The Eyebrow Derby which occurred when Everton played Fulham and Carlo Ancelloti and Scott Parker locked eyebrows!

Sad but true if you asked me to name the stanchion type for any club in the top two divisions from that period I could do it nine times out of ten.

Even Subbuteo jumped on the stanchion band wagon with the 1978 World Cup Edition.

Two days that brought tears to my eyes.

England 1 Scotland 2 4th June 1977

Not because Dalglish's winner didn't even touch the net, the final score or the fact that Scotland had secured the Home Internationals Trophy for that year , oh no it was the way the flare attired Scottish savages invaded the pitch and tore down those beloved stanchions. Wembley should have counted itself lucky that damage was limited to the goal posts and minimal turf theft.

Luckily the expansive flares hadn't caused any friction burns to the turf. But would those stanchions ever reappear?

Thankfully the answer was yes albeit with a dark blue rather than a dark green stanchion.

Unfortunately little did I know but the stanchion's days were numbered.

England 1 Switzerland 1 Euro 96 8th June 1996

The horror commenced as the teams walked out. The stanchions had gone. The score was by the by. The lack of stanchions was not.

When the teams walked out onto the pitch I stood up in a crowded golf club lounge yelling 'where have they gone' to the bewilderment of all around me. I was devastated.

Gone were the curvy saggy netted legendary supports and in their place were the hideous standardised European based vertical pole monstrosities which had first appeared in The World Cup in West Germany way back in 1974.

It was the start of a UK wide takeover by the bland stanchion.

All individuality had gone.

No More Stanchion Talk (at least for a while) but I would advise googling a few or watching ITV 4's Big Match Revisited to see where I am coming from.

Back to Coddenham:

Coddenham FC II.   Time For Action

On the subject of nets (don't want to bore you) the club would carefully erect the nets before the match and remove them immediately after thereby leaving a paltry ten minutes at half time when we could run onto the pitch and belt the ball in a few times (even this was frowned upon).

Largely as a result of this the idea was put forward to form Coddenham Juniors FC. A chance to play footy (in 'an official capacity) and the prospect of goal nets for 90 minute + period.

Not surprisingly the idea had to be vetted/approved by The Flints. Approval was granted by Pebbles, the team was created and shock of shocks not only was the captain Paul Flint but his brother Adrian was the goalkeeper.

We were also given the privilege of wearing the men's red striped shirts and I swear that on many occasions washing from the previous adult match had not been seen to given the stale beefy odour. This ran a close second to the times I used a communal box when playing Cricket for Coddenham CC. .

We were pretty good and played over the next two/three years building quite a reputation as a talented team.

Fact. A member of the Flint Family at time of writing was still involved with Coddenham FC (Now Coddenham Athletic) Assistant coach no less!

Coddenham Cricket Club ('Bawled 'im')

This was a completely different scenario from the football club. It was run by a sound rustic elderly couple John and Marge P. The team it has to be said was a pretty countrified array of characters with a wide age range but all were friendly and amenable.

The season would start with the AGM in April held in the Doctor's Surgery waiting room beneath Coddenham Country Club. Players would sit in the perimeter seating and John and Marge would conduct the proceedings which always included election of Captain and Vice Captain for the season , announcement of any new players and details of club finances and donations made.

Geoffrey would always get a mention as he contributed generously every year.This almost certainly cemented places in the team for myself and Sid.

We would be ferried to and from matches by Laurie (a genial rustic plumber) in his beige Morris Marina. We would try our best to influence his music tastes by bringing along cassettes by the likes of Stiff Little Fingers, Boomtown Rats and the like as he was very much a Dire Straits (Coldplay of the time) man. We made no impression. The Vice Captain in Thatcher terms was not for turning.

The ages in the team ranged from the opening bat/skipper who must have been close to sixty to me, the precocious thirteen year old who thought he was a bit of a bowler.

The fact was that I was a standard middle paced left arm over, length and line merchant who literally bored the batsmen into submission.

We had no consistent batsmen of note. It didn't matter if you batted at number eight if you scored in excess of ten runs the chances were that you would be opening the batting the following week.

One of the special features about village cricket is always the teas.

Certain away matches would be noted as must plays on the basis of experience of the tea provided the year before.

These would be the classic rural spreads with trays/plates sitting on checked table cloths open to you to select whatever you wanted and come back for more.

Our lifts with Laurie were often shared with a player called David G who had a Roy Hodgson style speech impediment. As we got into the car within minutes he would be drooling on about the last weekend's teas (particularly if we had missed a cracker) . On one occasion he came out with his classic ' it was a hell of a spwead last week. They had fish paste wolls' declaration.

For the record David G was no cricketer (although he thought he was) and often would spend the past part of 15 overs scratching about for 8 runs or so and then wondered why there were audible sighs of relief and forehead slapping when he returned to the pavilion amid muted reserved applause.

Glorious teas were certainly not the order of the day with regards to Coddenham home games.

Coddenham played out of the village at a school in Claydon. There was a large sports hall in which we could get changed. There was no kitchen. Tea was brewed off site and transported.

As a result an old white tea urn (which looked like it was commandeered from a prisoner of war barracks) was used to house the warm muddy fluid portraying itself as tea. The tea would hence sit cooling in this old rusty urn from about the 30th over mark (40 over match) and would be at best tepid by the time that tea was taken. In addition the bland uninspiring Coddenham tea comprised two Mother's Pride white salad cream sandwich quarters, a cup cake and a biscuit (semi sweet). Supplementary helpings were not an option although the luke- warm tepid muddy coloured tea/rust cocktails were readily available.

Quite frankly it was hugely embarrassing and many Coddenham players would literally cower away in the Sports Hall when this fare was presented to the opposition.

Added to the above we weren't very good, lying in league J in alphabetical terms. To put it bluntly that was league 10. Hardly John Player League standard.

Although out of the time bracket for this book I vividly remember on the day of Live Aid in 1985 my girlfriend turned up at the dreaded Tea Time to watch the rest of one of our cricketing debacles. She was dressed in a Jay Astonesque short white and blue Summer dress and blue high heels. I have no recollection why. One of our romantic dinners perhaps!

One of the younger team members Ally (a classic rustic) took one look at her turned to me and muttered 'Croist boiy, is that your Missus? I bet she rattle ya cawnkers'! He had obviously been makin his mind up. Priceless!

Coddenham Youth Club Life Begins At The Hop

The club's creation was born out of a general display of disgruntlement and isolated petty vandalism by the youngsters of Coddenham.

A meeting was convened at the home of The Tweeds to discuss the pros and cons with the youths under the governance of Mrs Tweed. The meeting culminated after these discussions with Mrs Tweed standing up and posing the all - important dramatic question to the assembled 'now you do want a youth club'?

No we just wanted to kill thirty minutes sitting around your uninspiring living room chatting for the sake of it. Of course we wanted a bloody youth club!

The said club duly arrived.

It was in many respects a bit Heath Robinson. Warped timber- based pool table, full size table tennis table (a little rocky but nothing that a few carefully placed beer mats couldn't address), board games skittles, marbles, Rubic's Cubes, a serving hatch selling own brand soft drinks, colas and snacks plus the most vital piece of equipment. The old navy blue Dansette.

This gave us the chance to air our latest punk offerings to the youth of Coddenham. A chance to show them that there was more to life than Elvis, The Baron Knights, Darts and Quo.

The Club was run by a kindly rustic gent one Mr H.

He would set the gear up every Friday night and ensure there were volunteers on duty to man the refreshments counter and oversee the bedlam.

The Dansette was a godsend, however, it was antiquarian with an origin unknown. As for the stylus to say it was rudimentary is an understatement. The damage it was inflicting to our beloved vinyl is best forgotten.

This concern paled in comparison to the opportunity to blast out confrontational/rebellious songs such as Frigging In The Rigging, The Modern World (album version) and on occasion Bodies to the unsuspecting adults on duty.

To be fair we also blasted out the commercial non sweary Punk tunes of the time and enlightened the sheltered country folk to the likes of Pretty Vacant, All Around the World, Something Better Change and Peaches etc.

Every month a competition night was held and without blowing my own trumpet too much I tended to win the Table Tennis and Pool on a fairly consistent basis securing me a can of own brand Pop and a bag of crisps per success.

Largely as a result of these competition nights the Youth Club took steps to cobble together a Table Tennis (now apparently called Ping Pong) team and a Table Tennis match was arranged against local ' professional' team Gosbeck.

I played quite well beating two out of three of their players and ran the third extremely close. Luckily I didn't beat him as apparently he was prone to bursting into tears.

They obviously noted my performance and within weeks an illegal approach was made for my services despite my existing contract tying me to Coddenham

Youth Club! I am over emphasising this a touch. No envelopes bulging with cash were forthcoming.

Weekly matches for Gosbeck then took off and we were transported to away matches in the back of the organiser's transit van quite literally. There were no seats in the back. We just rolled around on the rusty oily steel floor often to the sounds of Manfred Man's Davey's On The Road Again!

Not very safe and certainly not the best preparation for a table tennis match.

As usual the team were all rustic country boys.

I clearly remember on one occasion I was down in the dumps as things were not good with my girlfriend. One of the players in team sensed I wasn't on my game and he sidled up to me after one of matches and whispered 'what's the ma''er boi? Trouble with ya Fukks'?

I had absolutely no idea what he was on about. It was the Suffolk accent kicking in again but then it dawned on me he meant folks!

A poor night was compounded by Arsenal going out in the semi- finals of the Milk Cup to Man United 2-1 following a 2-4 first leg home debacle. The curse of the Green shirt?

Then there were the Youth Club discos provided on a monthly basis by JB Sounds. This comprised of a man of seriously pensionable age with a twin deck and four coloured lights.

Although he had two decks I am pretty sure that one was there purely as back up to the other in the event of breakdown rather than for use in unison such was the age and limited technology on JB's deck and the pregnant pauses between tracks. Seamless track merging was not the order of the day. The 'lights' merely aided him in positioning the stylus on the record.

Studio 54 it was not.

JB's play list was rooted in the 60s and supplemented by 70s disco and old school rock. Whilst this delighted the John Tweed's of this world it was an abomination to us in the punk fraternity.

We soon realised that there was an opportunity to bring a selection of our own records along for a proper speaker enhanced airing and we grasped that chance.

I clearly remember that we attended one of the discos dressed in Johnny Fingers style pyjamas adorned with a liberal coating of punk badges and safety pins. We pogo'd to the punk tunes that we managed to get aired by the non-plussed grumpy old git JB.

On another occasion I remember dancing in my tight black Rebs Jeans (courtesy of Jean Jeanie Ipswich) to Ant Music and tapping a short pool queue on the deck Adam style, a la promotional video, whilst doing so! How cool.

Getting JB to play obscure acoustic Jam B Side Innocent Man was perhaps a step too far (an undanceable second-rate Foxton tune) leaving me self- consciously mooching about in isolation on the dance floor going puce into the bargain with other attendees sitting around the permitter of the hall bewildered. Never did a track last so long! My Brucey obsession held no bounds.

The Silver Jubilee Celebrations June 7th 1977

Apparently a day when the nation was to come together and party for the Queen like it's 1999 or rather 1977 just like the Pistols did on the Thames.

Needless to say our friends up at Stonham Aspal did it in style.

Similar to the Bonfire night celebrations they had an organised fair, a street parade, street vendors purveying hot dogs, burgers, candy floss and possibly Go Go Girls. Compare that to Coddenham.

We had what can best be described as a rudimentary fete on the recreation ground with your standard tombola, skittles and put the football through the tyres plus fancy dress parade. Soccer AM eat your heart out.

From a positive perspective this meant that Coddenham FC had had to be coerced into putting up the football nets (albeit only in one goal) to stop the numerous misdirected shots from the general public entering the field of the slaughterhouse behind the goal.

For us it was a double whammy. You either won a prize (choccy bar or something equally non- descript) or you had the satisfaction of seeing the football ripple down the netting. Win win.Suffice to say many a two pence was spent on this.

In the evening Coddenham as a village had arranged for a Disco to be held in one of the open sided farm barns (you know the ones steel framed and covered in hazardous asbestos) at the top of the hill.

From memory I think the services of JB sounds were once again engaged. The associated rudimentary rust rendered BBQ was sited at the barn door where some farm hand was employed to ' flip them burgers boiy'.

Stonham Aspal doubtless had drafted in a full blown Night Club arrangement with Champagne and croupiers but again I may be being unduly cynical.

Scouts (Why?)

Not an activity that would have appealed to either me or Sid but the parents in the village decided it would be 'good for our development' to attend the local Scout Troop which was held four miles away in Needham Market. It would give us the chance to develop our knot tying skills.

There were about eight of us from Coddenham who attended on a Tuesday night and a mini bus plus driver was hired from Bickers to ferry us to and from Needham Market.

The main attraction for us was that the Scout hall was sited down a narrow track in Needham which had a Fish And Chip shop enroute and as a result the pennies were saved in advance of the Tuesday night return journey home.

The driver (from Bickers) was strict and when the subject of chips was mentioned he refused permission to eat on the bus . Consequently we used to sprint around to the chippy after scouts to pick up the goods and stuff them down our throats before the bus arrived.

On the many occasions when we didn't have the necessary finance we would still go in and ask for 'scraps'. To all intents we were the out of town village vagrants.

Scouts not surprisingly was pretty dull. We were split into three 'patrols' all of which had a leader (brother Sid was one). We did a bit of sport, a bit of hiking and a bit fund raising which included ' Bob a Job' week which loosely translated equated to Kunta Kinte style slave labour.

We once spent two hours cleaning out some villager's two cars internally and externally and received the princely sum of £1 per car between us! It involved an awful load of back breaking bending over and over reaching. Luckily the gentlemen concerned showed no Savillian tendencies at least we didn't notice any.

Camps were, however, another story.

The first of these took place about ½ a mile away from the Scout hut in Needham Market presumably as a trial run.The field extended down to an open railway line and much of the time was spent placing coins on the line to see if we could get the trains to cut them in half.

The high spot was the tuck shop and the open vat of ice cold orange squash into which we pitched our used beakers to offset the Summer heat.

Health and safety was not a consideration for such camps.

A new boy latterly joined the scout group. Let's just call him Chappers. This took the numbers up to a level where a new patrol was possibly needed and would need to be named.

Being the wit that I was I suggested they be called Pansies to which the scout leader cut me down immediately with the comment ' naturally you will be the Patrol leader then'. A top response. I felt humiliated.

Chappers was young ,unassuming and instantly bullyable. Shamefully we didn't hold back.

On a scout camp near Great Yarmouth in the Summer of 1977 we diverted off a trek to go and see The Spy Who Loved Me (Chappers included). This included a scary character called Jaws.

We returned to camp and a plan was hatched to scare Chappers. Just prior to tent curfew Sid and me ventured out to the cookery store and acquired some tin foil. We then returned to the tents via the cess pit which we carefully covered with a selection of leaves and soil masking the variety of fresh turds and luke warm piss within..

Sid carefully arranged the tin foil over his teeth Jaws style and we waited until dark at which point, when Chappers was asleep we burst into his tent armed with torches shining across at Sid's foil clad face whilst he growled in Jaws like fashion. Chappers was distraught.

He yelled and terrified ran out of the tent into the murky surroundings soon finding himself ankle (possibly knee) deep in the rancid contents of the cess pit. 'How we laughed'.

Not surprisingly the scout leaders got wind of these antics resulting in some form of punishment on the camp site. Something along the lines of vegetable peeling and denial of access to the Tuck Shop. In Enid Blyton terms we were frightful and I am deeply ashamed of our antics. If you happen to be reading this Chappers please accept my unreserved apologies but it was undeniably good fun.

We were ejected from the scout troop for good about six weeks later when something upset the Coddenham fraternity on one of those Tuesdays and the night ended up with us jumping up and down on the boot of the scout leader's Ford Escort RS.

The chip shop days were over.

Although village life was good there were obviously periods of boredom.

Kicking a ball around the rec, playing cricket up against the fence or paddling in the River Jackass which ran through Coddenham could only hold the attention for so long. This was particularly the case during the long six week Summer holidays.

However, for all kids around at this time we did have a range of classic TV shows to fall back on and a re-acquaintance is needed. This usually comprised Robinson Crusoe followed by The Flashing Blade and rounded of with the utterly dreadful English offering Why Don't You.

At this point I must dip back chart style into the shows that helped you through the long hot summer holidays of 1976 (and many before / after).

TV TIMES

The Top Ten TV offerings in the 70/80s

In Top Of The Pops terminology some shows were bubbling under Follyfoot*best known for the sobbing Dora, Steve and motorbiking farm worker rebel Rod, Banana Splits*classic 1960s drug crazed programme including 3 shows- Arabian Knights, Three Musketeers and the one everyone forgets Danger Island.

The Monkees*again classic 1960s mayhem from the only warranted manufactured boy band. (Cowell take note).

Tucker's Luck famed spin off from Grange Hill starring Tucker, Alan and Tommy together with evil skinhead Passmore (RIP) portraying depressing life albeit in the early 80s.

Let's not forget there was plenty of crap too bubbling nowhere near the surface. The likes of Rent A Ghost (Master Meeker / Claypole) and Michael Bentine's Potty Time spring to mind.

The chart : Reminisce fondly. Alternatively reach for the google button.

10. The Singing Ringing Tree.

Baffling and disturbing it featured a distressed young lady, an evil dancing dwarf and a tree that not surprisingly rang and sang.

I trust the creator was sectioned.

Limited excerpts can be found on You Tube.

9. Top Of The Pops.

OK naff poncey miming it may have been but for many this represented the only audio/visual access to the first wave of punk bands. I was always concerned that they would fade out tracks by the likes of The Jam and The Stranglers well before the end and this was often the case.

Memorable amongst other things for Hugh Cornwell wearing the Whale Oil Beef Hooked T shirt and Jean Jacque the Fuct Ford logo shirt during Something Better Change. Michael Grade clearly blinkered at the time.

An appearance generally ensured a climb up the chart the following week(unless you happened to be the brilliant Magazine who managed to drop out of the top 40 following their appearance with Shot By Both Sides).

Amazingly The Jam appeared three times promoting the single David Watts but the single failed to rise any higher than 25. Baffling.

The Clash stood their ground and refused to appear. Whilst this was to be commended to some extent on occasions it backfired. Legs & Co dancing to Bank Rober complete with black and white stripey prison outfits and masks being a prime embarrassing example?

8.The Double Deckers.

Produced by The British Independent Film Company this was a strange show with a very catchy tune (recently covered by Eater punk legend Andy Blade on a solo album). It involved a group of kids including Brains, Doughnut , Scooper, Sticks, Spring, Billie and Tiger residing on a stationary red London bus in the yard.

I actually have no idea what it was all about or what the gang achieved but there was something about it and it did give a first screen outing for Brinsley Ford in the role of Spring. He would later front the cutting edge reggae band Aswad.

7. Robinson Crusoe.

Surely no one of my age can forget this black and white classic. The music is legendary. Starring Robert Hoffman the series was produced in France and recorded in the mid 1960s but it was shown repeatedly in the 1970s so again qualifies. A little of the magic faded when it became known that it was filmed not on a remote Caribbean Island but on Gran Canaria! *

6. The Flashing Blade.

Another dubbed classic with a riotous theme tune (you have to fight for what you want).

Based broadly on the French/Spanish war and the siege of Casalle the actors appeared suave, sophisticated and daring . Produced in the 1960s it was shown repeatedly during the 1970s.

The clumsy over-dubbing was on a par with the Calgon dishwasher ads and some of the acting as wooden as Ian Botham's Revitive ads but a nine year old was blind to this indiscretion. It was riveting stuff.

5. Hammer House Of Horror.

We are not talking films. More the TV Series. Some were throwaway, others were gruesome, spine tingling and ultimately memorable.

Two Faces Of Evil featuring the man in the yellow waterproof fisherman's jacket standing in the pouring rain on the country road when the car hits him and The House That Bled To Death where the gas pipes in a detached residential home eject blood across the kids birthday party spread live long in the memory as does the haunting theme tune and imagery of Hammer House itself on the opening credits.

Cracking stuff.

4. Wait Til Your Father Gets Home.

Essentially the forerunner to The Simpsons and Family Guy. Approximately half of the 24 episodes had no canned laughter the remainder did.

It featured the trials and tribulations of Harry Boyle (voice over by Tom Bosley of Howard Cunningham Happy Days Fame) and his family including fat Alice, financially alert infant Jamie and lazy loafer unemployed Chet.

The real star was neighbour Ralph who (with his team of vigilantes) guarded the neighbourhood and was obsessed with infiltration from the likes of 'Commies, Pinkos, Blacks and the Yellow Peril hey, hey, hey?'. His words not mine. A one- off neighbour as individual but far more radical than Neddy Flanders.

Politically incorrect on all levels but utterly hilarious.*

3.Shoestring.

What can I say about this one? The creators were clearly geniuses.

Being set in the late 1970s at a Radio Station there was always a cross section of generally good music in the background (Blondie, Elvis Costello spring to mind).

The concept of a radio based 'private ear' was delivered in episode 1.

A detective (Eddie Shoestring) based in Bristol on Radio West taking calls from concerned locals and solving a variety of crimes including exploding electronic games, jealous Radio West security guards, domestic violence and drug dealing band related shenanigans (the latter being an episode called Find The Lady where Toyah played Toola and performs Neon Womb on some dodgy pier just outside of Bristol prior to losing all her street cred with narration of The Teletubbies and marriage to Robert Fripp). For the record Gary Holton and Christopher Biggins also made appearances in this one.The show ran for two series . It was fantastic.

More were planned but Trevor Eve had had enough (not wanting to be typecast) so the writers turned their attentions to Bergerac. Enough said.

*Note box set now available for both series after music copyright issue resolved.

2.The Tube. (Post Punk's own Old Grey Whistle Test).

Just what was needed at the time (the early 1980s), hence the placing at number two.

It was in essence a cutting edge version of The Old Grey Whistle Test based on current music trends rather than boring crusty old outdated prog rock performed by bearded public school musos and compared by much of the same. Bob Harris 'interesting and compelling track from Bachman -Turner Overdrive there to get the programme up and running'. Really?

Although The Old Grey Whistle Test improved a little in the late seventies after the arrival of Annie Nightingale with performances from the likes of The Jam, The Damned, 999 and The Vibrators it was still essentially rooted in rock and on rather late for the school fraternity.

The opening Tube show for the new anarchic channel 4 was on Friday 5th Nov 1982. The opening band were Toy Dolls, appropriate as they were from the North East and the studios were in Newcastle. The show finished with a brief 30 minute set by THE JAM. (also appropriate as Olga the lead singer of Toy Dolls was a huge Jam fan).

It was their last ever live TV performance and followed a floundering pre gig interview by Muriel Grey with Paul Weller although he was as usual awkward and none too compliant to be fair.

I still vividly remember watching this through tearstained eyes and wondering why there was a girl with massive bins (possibly the sister of Eddie The Eagle) at the front of the stage beaming with delight. Did she not understand that this band were splitting up?

The show was compared by Jools Holland and Paula Yates who complimented each other well. It featured numerous quality live acts in addition to The Jam including The Stranglers, The Cure, The Icicle Works, Big Country, Killing Joke, Tom Robinson, The Damned and Toy Dolls.

Apparently Half Man Half Biscuit were offered the chance to play on the show but declined as it clashed with a Tranmere Rovers home match .Probably true as they played home matches on Friday nights to avoid clashing with Liverpool and Everton.

After five series the show was pulled following numerous uses of expletives particularly by Joolz Holland at what was a children's peak viewing time.

It was great while it lasted.

Britain's Number One

1.Randall And Hopkirk Deceased

We are not talking the shoddy Vic Reeves/Bob Mortimer remake, we are talking the legendary 1960s partnership of Mike Pratt and Kenneth Cope. Made around the same time as The Avengers and The Prisoner this was based on a pair of private detectives resplendent in sharp sixties suits.

In the first episode Marty (Kenneth Cope) is mown down by a car and killed but he returns (white suit and wig worn the wrong way for the first few episodes) as a ghost figure and only Geoff (Mike Pratt) can see him.

Often corny, some of the editing is crude and there are numerous errors (doors changing colour in different scenes and the shadow Marty's ghost often being seen) but the popularity of this series grew and grew over the years.

It ran for just 26 episodes and was filmed largely in the area around the Elstree Studios BorehamWood and the Home Counties. It retains significant cult status to this day. *

Mike Pratt was clearly a fun character on and off the screen. He tragically died from cancer aged 37.

His son Guy Pratt (who lives down the road in Hove) is an esteemed bass session player who started with 1979 Southend Mod Revival band Speedball and over his career has played/toured with the likes of Pink Floyd , Icehouse, Madonna, Roxy Music, The Smiths, Echo And The Bunnymen. More importantly he has worked on the last two studio albums by The Members.

All in all this was one great father and son combo all things considered (ignoring the Floyd aberration) !

*denotes available on DVD/Blue Ray box set. I have them all.

Whilst on the subject let's also not forget the range of loosely 'competitive' sport related shows that ran in the 1970s and early 1980s. They were essentially split into three categories.

Junior . We Are The Champions (not that Queen crap).

Adult Amateur/Comical. It's A Knockout.

Professional – Superstars.

The classic junior show We Are The Champions was hosted by Ron 'away ya go' Pickering.

Set in a school in a different region each week (Oswestry sticks in the memory) three schools would take each other on in a variety of field events culminating in the pool free for all and concluding with the classic 'Away Ya Go' cry and chaotic pool scenes at the end. Absolutely no Health & Safety considerations. This was kids having competitive based fun. It was allowed then.

Sadly Ron passed away in February 1991. Surely as the coffin was lowered into the ground someone somewhere must have uttered the words Away Ya Go' as a parting clarion all..

Then we had what was effectively the adult version of We Are The Champions in It's A Knock Out hosted by the legendary (at the time) Stuart Hall and Arthur Ellis with Eddie Waring covering the boring, dull, repetitive Marathon.

This was very similar with the significant exception that the contestants were hindered by ungainly costumes, masks and gloves etc and were often attached to elastic, swinging on ropes or skating through slime to make their tasks nigh on impossible.

The winners of the UK Heats then competed in Europe under the title of Je Sans Frontiers.

Sadly and embarrassingly my perceived attachment to all things German reared its ugly head again when with one Je Sans Frontiers episode I remember fervently cheering on the Germans from Munstereifel against the UK's market town qualifier!

Finally there was the professional version.

Superstars.

The original anchor man/presenter would have looked more at home as a Chemistry Undergraduate for Kings College Cambridge on University Challenge such was his professor like demeaner. Step forward one David Vine.

Strangely enough he was also the mainstay of the solitary Snooker show, the BBC's ridiculous one- off frame show Pot Black which was shown on a 30 minute Thursday night slot prior to the snooker explosion in the 1980s.

Superstars swept the nation in the mid-seventies and involved both current and past sportsmen.

The likes of Kevin Keegan, Henry Cooper, David Hemery, Brian Jacks and John Conteh would take on each other in the British shows and latterly European stars would also compete (including the likes of Bjorn Borg) with strenuous gym activities, cycling, obstacles races, shooting, Javelin etc.

It is completely unfathomable to think such stars could risk serious injury and some did (notably Keegan re the bike incident and Stan Bowles literally shooting himself in the foot, not good for a footballer!) competing in shows like this whilst still being actively involved in their own professional sports. Amazingly it was permitted in those days. Let's not forget that Leeds' Duncan McKenzie was also busy jumping over Mini Coopers at the time!

Darts and Snooker were in their infancy then and served to give great confidence/reassurance to the alcohol dependent overweight slobs in the UK of their sporting potential as a high proportion of the competitors for both were cradling a pint or a fag (or both) over a bulging waistband as they portrayed their 'art' on the television screens.

Bill Werbeniuk allegedly drank a standard thirty pints of lager a day during his playing peak and was only barred from the game when he tried to move onto Beta Blockers on medical grounds. Alex Higgins was also similarly regularly inebriated (allegedly) during games. No wonder Steve Davis was viewed as boring in comparison and who can forget the 1982 Lada Classic and the first televised 147 by Davis. That look of bewilderment on his face when he secured perfect positioning on the final blue with pink and black on their spots was not one of tension, more a realisation that sinking those final three balls was going to land him a fucking Lada.

As for darts? A pie eyed Jocky Wilson was regularly seen battering the best of them at dingy smoke- filled locations such as Jollees Cabaret Club in Stoke or The Lakeside in Surrey. Bearing in mind the sponsorship hold that companies like Embassy, Guinness and John Player had on these 'sports' it is hardly surprising that heavy drinking and smoking were deemed natural behaviour and openly portrayed across our TV screens and much on The BBC!.

Contrast the above with the complete raft of shite we have to put up with on TV these days. Reality and dumb down crap across the board (largely associated with ITV and their offshoot channels). Shows often based on a mix of thick chavs lying around a pool or isolated in a remote house swearing at each other.

Essex oiks talking you through their 'real lives', tearful mothers guiding their daughters as to which 'gorge' wedding dress to choose and the 'sowshall media style current affairs' programmes such as Steph's Packed Lunch. Avoid the lunch Steph.

All are aimed at the mindless middle aged mother/chav brigade and interspersed with adverts centring on bingo, loans (at extortionate rates), gambling (with a 'do it responsibly' caveat') aimed at your average lucid betting shop punter. To be fair the concern of the chav for their peers understanding of their illiterate mutterings has to be admired. So much so that they always quantify with 'do you know what I mean' which is very considerate.

Whilst on this subject you have to question the 'wisdom' of David Cameron when he felt it suitable/logical to put the monumental economic decision regarding withdraw al from the European Union to the great British public a high proportion of whom think that taking up loans at up to 900% APR makes good financial sense. Spoons boss take note!

APR stands for Annual Percentage Rate NOT Additional Pint Revenue.

Derek's cheese and tomato sandwich/parsnip jam making Sun Life liaisons with neighbour June seem to be on a permanent re-run. Namewise it's suspiciously reminiscent of that shit seventies sit-com. Debbie McGee harps on about funeral costs when marrying into the upper echelons of The Magic Circle surely has seen her sorted and as for that 'my lot know how to party' chap he seems to be the face for funeral plans, intruder alarms and gold bullion.

Those twenty minute Optima Mattress adverts imply that the definition of a loving couple is a pillow fight. Forget the offer of a free pillow most of the sexist daytime viewers would trade that for a 10 minute romp with the featured blonde.

Finally there's the raft of inane lottery ads where moronic (often Northern) chavs are paid about £80 to dance about uncontrollably on screen pretending they've won a fortune? Utterly cringeable.

From a comedy perspective I see nothing amusing in the likes of Jenny Éclair. Merely a digitally enhanced Sue Pollard? Bring back Ted Bovis. All is forgiven.

In no way am I bitter but to qualify for 'celebrity' status these days it seems you need to be:

Sweary

Continually speaking in upspeak (all statements are by default questions)

Smothered in tattoos (whether male or female)

Illiterate (with the ability to add 'you know what I mean' after every other sentence).

Talentless

'Fick'

During the riots in Britain about 5 years ago (allegedly caused by another chav related incident with the police as usual entirely to blame) day after day the uninitiated British public took it upon themselves to loot shops etc in the name of justice. The government were at a loss as to how to stop it.

Surely this could have been solved by sending a simple instruction to the Government advising them to contact ITV with a view to screening 24 hour re-runs of Big Brother/Love Island/X Factor/Essex. I guarantee the chavs causing the mayhem would have ceased rioting and returned to their pits to watch this shite providing Deliveroo could supply regular deliveries of McDonalds and' Peatzza')! Bring back Morecombe & Wise, Mork & Mindy,

Arthur Negus, even Mike Yarwood. All is forgiven.

University Challenge has been mentioned. Why was there no Polytechnic Challenge? Were the BBC worried about the potential nature of the specialised subjects from 'The Universities Of Life'? The life, times and drug taking (alleged) of Keith Richards possibly?

One thing that has remained worryingly consistent from the 1970s to the present day is Captain Birdseye. Not only is he is still cruising the Atlantic Ocean with a crew of ten year olds boys but perhaps, arguably more worryingly, why, when he has this wealth of fresh Atlantic fish at his disposal does he insist on feeding these young lads processed fish fingers. It's beyond comprehension.

I am not a film buff of any description but in my opinion there were five 'great' 'films' in the 1970s subject to interpretation:

Dr Who. Spearhead From Space.

I'm cheating here as originally a four episode John Pertwee tea time classic but later released on DVD so I'm bending the rules and counting it.

Quite simply the most frightening of all the Dr Who productions. In essence blank faced shop dummy mannequins were created and programmed to kill. The hands dropped away to reveal a gun. They patrolled the country under the nestene consciousness looking for spearhead modules and some of the scenes were pure terror (dummies smashing their way out of shop front displays in Ealing, attacking the old lady in her country cottage etc etc).

Such was the impact that the government of the time actually held a debate in parliament to decide whether it should be withdrawn from the day-time viewing schedule!

Never Too young To Rock.

This 'starred' Mud, The Rubettes and The Glitter Band and in all honesty had no real story other than a mad professor driving around Britain in a detector van trying to gather together glam rock stars to perform in concert together for the kids who should not be deprived of this pleasure merely due to their age. Worth watching if only for the songs performed and the Arlsford Timber sponsored wooden acting.

The Monkees Head.

A drug infused psychedelic affair which effectively served to kill The Monkees off as a commercial entity. Knocks spots of that Yellow Submarine film by some Scouse band.

Fascinating viewing and very much of the time.

Slade In Flame.

Lambasted at the time by the critics (and indeed fans) for being far too dark a portrayal of the shady side of rock and roll it is now viewed justifiably as a classic.

Once again it did the band no commercial favours although some of the more melodic tracks which came out of it such as Far Far Away and How Does It Feel remain classics.

The acting of the Slade boys was pretty good (with the possible exception of Don Powell), the storyline is believable and at the time it was described as a film of grim reality. The expected glitzy glam spectacle it certainly was not.

Quadrophenia.

Rightly revered as a cult classic and served to bolster the commerciality of the mod revival movement (albeit briefly) in 1979.

The tale of the disillusioned Jimmy and the excitement of mod night clubs, pill popping and ventures to Brighton captured the period brilliantly. The actors incredibly included Lesley Ash, Toyah Wilcox, Sting (rather wooden), Phil Daniels, Timothy Spall, Ray Winstone and Mark Wingate. What a debut for film director Franc Roddam. Whatever happened to them?

We should not forget that in the 1970s all the viewing public had to entertain them was based on the output of a mere three channels, BBC1, BBC and ITV. That was until 2nd November 1982 when (after nearly two years of parliamentary deliberation) Channel 4 was launched.

The introduction of this channel was viewed by many in the middle classes as an affront on society (my parents included). It was almost television's own Punk moment.

My parents steadfastly refused to watch the channel (and kept this up for about two years) implying that it was mindless and serving of the less switched on in society. This stubbornness was not limited purely to TV and Channel 4. Another example was the tea bag.

This idea was becoming more and more popular in the 1970s but my parents continued to buy the small red oblong Typhoo Tea box and steadfastly brew pots of tea well into the 1980s.

There was no such thing as grabbing a quick cuppa in the Taylor household it was a full blown military operation as challenging as putting a cover on a duvet after a couple of lagers.

Back to Channel 4 and the opening edition of The Tube. This epitomised everything that my parents disliked about Channel 4 with cocky young presenters and a disillusioned looking studio audience in the post punk regalia. It was alternative as the comedy of the time.

Luckily they were preparing tea on the opening night when The Jam graced our screens for their last ever TV appearance and I was able to watch the band in all their glory uninterrupted for the last time albeit through tear stained eyes.

The Suffolk Accent.

No, not a film but a concept that needs some explanation.

You may have noticed that spellings on occasion above have been rather strange. This is deliberate and serves to project the Suffolk accent/dialect.

The Suffolk accent is a strange beast. It either involves the abrupt shortening of the word concerned or an elongation/enhancement of a vowel.

Examples: For

- For Ipswich read Eerswich
- For Church read Chuch
- For Road read Rud
- For Cream read Crayum
- For Cheese read Chayuz
- For Post Office read P'st Arwfice
- For stones read stuns
- For Folks read Fukks
- For Stowmarket read St'maaarket (a place near Eerswich where John Peel resided)
- For Felixstowe read F'lxxstoo
- For Town read Towen (The Towen for the football fraternity).
- For pocket read Paark't
- For Coffee read Corrfee

I trust it is making sense.

Computers are referred to by Suffolk folk (Fukk) as Compooters. Apparently this medium only arrived in the county in about 1990 together with Indian Restaurants!

Actually that's a bit unfair as Compoooter Studies was an option in the Sixth form in 1982 but it did involve using a computer processing unit the size of a horse box. Not that many Computer Studies places were taken up by the sixth form students.

This was not due to lack of interest more the logistical nightmare caused by the size of the CPUs plus the associated monstrous bulky screen units which impacted greatly on the availability of classroom space thereby restricting the number of students who could physically fit in and further their skills with this cutting- edge technology!

Suffolk was (and remains), overall, a very slow, one paced agricultural community. I can appreciate the benefits now but at the time it became very restrictive and by the early 1980s (to use the words of Jake Burns) 'I gotta gotta get away'.

Book Test 1. Can you handle the Saaaarfolk Accent ?
Read the following paragraph out loud to see if you can

a. Successfully imitate the Saaarfolk accent.

b. Understand it.

A fictitious conversation between two typical young, reserved, rustic Suffolk villagers.

Maaartin:

' Oi Cliyuv. Are you gowen up the towen t'night t' see M''tluff?

'They're on at The Gomaarnt'.

Cliyuv:

Yeah, a bit laa'er boiy'.

'F'sst I've got to go down the r'd to the P'sstt Arfice to get me mum her cheyas and baked beyans as she's 'avin' beyans on t'sst tonoight'.

Maaartin:

'You'd better make sure you've got enough powends in ya paaaarket'!

Cliyuv:

'Too roight boiy! Tell you what I'll catch ya in The Crowen later.'

Maaartin:

'OKaay. Oi'll get you a point of laarger and liyum in then'

Cliyuv:

'Cheers boiy. See ya in a mernit then'.

Translation

Martin:

'Oi Clive. Are you going up the town tonight to see Meatloaf?' (God forbid).

Clive:

'Yeah. A bit later boy'.

'First I've got to go down the road to The Post Office to get my mum her cheese and baked beans as she's having beans on toast tonight.'

Martin:

'You had better make sure you've got enough pounds in your pocket!' (Suffolk humour).

Clive:

'Too right boy. Tell you what I'll catch you at The Crown later.'

Martin:

' Ok. I'll get you a pint of lager and lime in then.'

Clive:

' Cheers boiy. See you in a minute then.'

With my spell check over-heating I think enough is enough but this was the continual dialect we had to contend with during our extended spell in Suffolk.

Aside 1: The word 'the' was once deemed to be the most commonly spoken English word. Due to the curse of the Chav this is no longer the case with 'like' taking the mantle' You know what I mean'?

Aside 2: In the 1970s sitcom Bless This Sexist House Sid's son Mike Abbot was responsible for unexplainable crimes against both fashion and hairstyles. Unbelievably in comedy terms George & Mildred was a cut above Bless This House.

Slade Fact.

Many put Slade in the Merry Xmas Everybody box. Although a festive single above others it did not reflect the talent of this band. They actually released no less than 57 singles but infuriatingly many of the quality offerings such as Do You Believe In Miracles and Universe failed to break the top forty. Unfathomable. This band remain a cut above the rest in Glam/Rock terms.

Q2: Snacks .

In 1975 Smiths released a crisp based product range called Horror Bags.

How many varieties were there and can you name them?

Badges

III

Stonham Aspal. The Primary School Years. 1970/76

All I Wanna Know / Senses Working Overtime/ Do You Know/ I Don't Trust You

This was the school that we would attend from age six to eleven. No interruptions, no excuses.

Certain aspects frightened me. The Head being the main one. Anyone who has the total respect of your parents is naturally one to be extremely wary of.

Mrs S was a harsh forthright head mistress who lived a mile from the school and drove an angular dark blue Saab. A model which was a reflection of her demeanour. Geoffrey and Franny loved her approach and thought it would do wonders for our respect and sense of learning/responsibility (see petty crime chapter later).

At this stage in life neither myself or Sid could not swim and this issue plagued me for the next couple of years. The school had an outdoor pool which although not horrendously deep was very green, very cold and very very unpleasant. A legionella hazard if ever there was one given its infrequent use and limited maintenance.

For months I flailed around the pool clinging desperately to any tombstone shaped polystyrene float or tyre inner tube which came by trying desperately to stay above surface level whilst all manner of irritating reprobates surrounded and taunted me for my inadequacies.

Very gradually my confidence built to the extent that one day the teacher deemed I was ready to attempt the 25 metres (two lengths of the pool) albeit via an ungainly doggy paddle. The remainder of the class stood poolside to watch my unstylish rudimentary foray.

I started confidently enough but after 20M tiredness kicked in and, with paws tiring, I completed the last 5 metres in a downward trajectory suffering uncomfortable water intake peering through the cloudy green mass. I emerged knackered cold and distressed to muted applause and laughter from crowd around the pool. Mark Spitz I was not. To be honest I could feasibly have walked the last 5M such was the deep green shade of the water. No-one would have noticed.

My fondest memory of the swimming pool was not actually the pool but the small brick changing room. The satisfaction of sitting there wrapped in a sundried hot towel slowly regaining muscular movement and the ability to speak again was bordering on heavenly.

Every year the school held its main fundraising event. The Christmas Fayre, usually on the last Saturday in November. Why they could never at least extend the date into the early part of December was baffling. A date in December would at least conjure up a degree of anticipation for the approaching festivities. Illogical Captain.

On one occasion the top class were given the task of designing a Christmas Fayre poster and for the only time in my life my extremely limited artistic skills were rewarded when I won the competition with a design showing a football match between Bell Town United and Parcel Rovers complete with goal mouth scene including a cracking set of angular stanchions!

We (me, Sid and village buddy John B) would cycle from Coddenham to Stonham Aspal (about 4.5 miles) for the fayre and the privilege of lapping up squash and crisps/biscuits in the dinner hall (a nice change from the suet puddings and ginger stodge regularly served as part of the compulsory school dinner fare) and play silly kids games at this annual event. In addition there were the standard asides such as bagatelle, guess the number of Dolly Mixtures in the jar, Tombola, Lucky Dip etc.

Why anyone would pay ten pence to dip into a bucket to claim a cheap mystery item valued at five pence (usually Fizzers, Refreshers or Trebor Mints from memory) when you could take your ten pence and select twice as much of exactly what you wanted from the sweets on offer in the school hall was beyond me but the one game which hooked us year on year was the darts.

For ten pence you would throw three sets of fairground style darts. The main prize was for the top scorers from three darts and some pretty serious parents vied for this title with some even arriving with their own detachable flight arrows. The other challenge was to score under 21 with three darts (all had to score). If you achieved this feat you won yourself the choice of an Aztec, an Ice Breaker, an Old Jamica , a Texan (in the latter years), a Marathon or a Fry's Chocolate Cream bar. It was frustratingly difficult to achieve especially with darts like those.

Once again unless you secured yourself two wins out of the three sets of darts you would be out of pocket bearing in mind most of the above retailed for about 5p from about 1975. You were better off taking your 10p to the school dining hall but In terms of raising revenue for the school it was fruitful.

The Christmas Party

Unlike the Christmas Fayre the party outrageously took place in December in Stonham Aspal village hall (opposite the school and close to the church). All pupils were instructed to bring two foodstuffs to the party (one savoury one sweet) making it a very economical event for the school.

A rudimentary disco was laid on (no not JB) and in December 1975 (my last party) I can clearly remember dancing (or rather manic kid rushing) in the hall to the sounds of Mud's Tiger Feet and The Cat Crept In (the latter a blatant Elvis vocal style rip off by Les Gray as indeed was Lonely This Christmas). It was to be another 4 years before The Jam released their own party classic 'Eating Trifles'. Oh the wit of the rustic fraternity.

As for the party food the middle class kids dutifully arrived with the responsibly sourced sensible healthy wholemeal crackers for cheese, the salad sandwiches, sausage rolls, carrot sticks, Celery, fruit and if you were lucky the odd homemade cup cake.

Thankfully the 'social' fraternity could be relied upon for the ' Social Snacks' . The iced gems, crisps , Wagon Wheels, Kipling Cakes and Angel Delight. Authentic unhealthy processed party food crap infused with E numbers. All this was displayed on long tables.

The games and disco would begin but all eyes would be on the tables with a view to securing a seat close to the Wagon Wheels, the Club Biscuits or Iced Gems.

At a set time (usually following British Bulldog) the kids were asked to sit up to the table and a mass scramble/bundle would ensue based on access to the crap foods. British Bulldog the sequel.

The instruction to eat savoury first was wilfully disregarded resulting in mass scoffing and table barging. It guaranteed year on year a manic end to the party proceedings. The formula never changed.

Milk Monitors

I had a couple of dodgy mates at the School the main one being Des H. Somehow by the time we were in the top class we had gained enough trust to become 'Milk Monitors'.

In those days the school took daily delivery of crates of quarter pint mini milk bottles. In our role we had to pierce the silver top (occasionally the extra creamy Gold top heart attack inducing version) with the narrow red straw and dish them out to the classes. Often there would be a few bottles over and these would go to those who wanted more. There were never enough to satisfy demand. We got to know the greedy kids so we hatched a plan.

There were always a number who left dregs in the bottle. We decided (behind the scenes) to take an empty bottle or two and fill up with the dregs/remnants of the half-drunk bottles to create further quarter pints for distribution to the gutsy greedy few.

Not happy with that at the end of our dedicated 'service' we would go out to the front forecourt of the school to stack the empties in the crates. Opposite the school was a grand church with accompanying church yard and the temptation to lob glass bottles over the churchyard wall onto the gravestones was irresistible. Amazingly we held our Milk Monitor posts throughout the final year of primary school.

Like all primary schools at the time we had the legendary drinking fountain. This was essentially a vertical stainless steel water fed tube above which was sited a perforated petri dish with a stubby feeder in the centre. A small side handle controlled the water flow. All manner of kids with a variety of colds and viruses slobbered over the spout. In addition cleaning was infrequent and conducted by the overall clad caretaker using hands which had previously been engaged in the removal of 'pineapple chunks' from the urinals or possibly a bit of personal Izal action.

We were also not averse to other minor pranks including self-invigilating our 5 Star Award scheme which naturally led to over exaggeration. An eleven year old hurling a cricket ball over 75M was of Olympian stature but it was not questioned.

We also took great delight in accessing the unlocked basement boiler room which was full of the caretaker's tools, fuels and obviously the two main boilers. It was warm and cosy down there especially in the Winter months and many a playtime was spent in the Boiler Room as it was never locked.

Down there we discovered two sacks which contained some old netting and obviously (due to my goal nets obsession) we brought this to the attention of the teachers. It was our chance to have goal nets attached to the football goals and this was eventually accomplished. No stanchions, simply tie on and drag back jobs. Naturally questions followed from the teachers as to how we had discovered the nets. I have no idea how we wriggled out of that one.

Des H was essentially a bit of a thug or a ' ruffian' as my parents put it (in the same way that they called burgers rissoles). He was also a Jehovas Witness. I had no ideat what this meant. All I knew was that it gave you the undisputed right to snub morning assembly. That was my kind of religion. Why did Christianity lack this flexibility?

Glam Influenced Grooming!

It was around this time that male grooming products were being heavily advertised and I found myself being drawn in. I favoured hairspray, in particular Falcon and Black Knight which were being heavily advertised at the time. Why I took to these products I have no clue but probably I fantasised about having a hairstyle similar to those being portrayed by Messrs Connolly, Tucker and Powell and being drawn in by the naff advertising of the time. The hairspray certainly gave it a refreshing odour for a kid who only washed his hair once a week but as for style enhancement. No chance.

Parental control meant this was unattainable so why anyone would want to effectively set a Co Op barber induced fringeless bowl cut in place with spray I have no idea. My Glam hero at the time was Dave Hill. This was not surprising given the similarities in hair style. Mine was not a style of choice but it kind of matched Dave's. Suffice to say it lacked the super yobbish flowing rear locks. Sid's hero was Marty Christian of The New Seekers. A strange choice and strangely repeated in the late 70s when he opted to follow Bram Tchaikovsky as opposed to the commercially vibrant Motors!

The other was aftershave heavily promoted at the time by a politically incorrect type-cast young Asian chap in white robes chopping planks of wood in half with his bare hands to a cry of Ahh So. In my teens I progressed to Blue Stratos (the 1970/80s Insignia) and I am still desperately seeking an outlet that sells that lovely light blue stick deodorant of theirs.

The Glam awakening. Cum On Feel The Noize

My first singles 1973:

Thanks to Popswop Magazine I had been alerted to the phenomenon that was Glam Rock. I still have the annual from 1973 which includes pop star's favourite recipes (Donny Osmond's was a cheese sandwich!). Apart from Popswop what attracted me to the Glam scene?

It has to be said that whilst we often quote Punk as being the necessary reaction to the dirge that was/is prog rock credit must be given to Glam as this can be interpreted as the first real challenge to prog.

Most bands deemed it essential to queen it up a bit and a degree of femininity was an essential ingredient for many of the groups concerned. This was evident with regards to Bowie, Bolan and of course The Sweet. In Steve Priest this band had the ultimate pouting lipstick clad rebel who occasionally complimented this with Hitler moustache and Nazi regalia.

This kind of image naturally provoked an outraged parental response, the spark which ignited an allegiance that any self-respecting youngster would be looking for.

I was intrigued by The Sweet and their singles (Co Co, Little Willy and Alexander Graham Bell aside) were incredibly catchy. However, it was Slade who really grabbed my attention.

No femininity as far as they were concerned. These were four growling yobs from Wolverhampton who had come up the ladder the hard way. No Chinn/Chap compositions were delivered on a plate for them. Holder and Lea composed all of the band's tracks (the odd cover version excepted).

Of course I wasn't aware of this at the time and it probably wouldn't have influenced me in the least but the important thing was that these lads were young, long haired, rebellious and couldn't spell which was great as neither could I. The dream package for any young lad.

Latterly I learnt that Geoffrey's boss at Volvo Concessionaires was Trevor Chinn the brother of one Nicky Chinn. One half of the Chinn/Chap song writing duo. How many glam rock Sweet, Mud, Suzi Quatro guest list passes could that have acquired if I had known at the time. The relevance was lost on Geoffrey and Franny. An opportunity missed.

As so it was that the purchase of singles began.

I had missed the boat on Slade's previous two singles which had both made the top spot (Cum On Fee The Noize and Sqweeze Me Pleaze Me) as I was too young to be trusted to buy records then. By 1973 this changed.

Single One.
Slade. Mr Friend Stan b/w This Town.

Arguably the first Slade single with a title spelt correctly (although the Ns were reversed). To my dismay unlike the previous three singles it failed to make number 1 (stalling at 2) probably because this was a more melodic piano based track.

It served me right as I was a little late to the table and failed to secure a picture cover. This was viewed as sacrilege in years to come.

Single Two.
Sweet. The Ballroom Blitz b/w Rock n Roll Disgrace.

An absolute humdinger of a track but once again it failed to reach the top stalling at number 2. Again I was late to the party and failed to get the picture sleeve so poetic justice once more.

In those days I was arguably as bad as the rest with my assertion that any track worth its salt had to get to number 1 or it was a failure.

It later occurred to me that chart positioning more often than not had absolutely no bearing on the quality of the product and was largely influenced by bland TV promotion , the Radio 1 play list mentality, a gullible (easily brain washed) market and the British tendency to lap up crap novelty jokey singles (Housewives were the main culprits often being exposed to an unhealthy amount of daytime radio one).

I give you Mr Blobby, Grandma We Love You, Jive Bunny and Matchstalk Men and Matchstalk Cats and Dogs as prime examples. Current day tripe like X Factor, The Voice and Britain's Got Talent continues propagate this scenario and for this we have to thank Mr Nasty himself . Cowell.

How this fraud continues to brainwash the 'great British public' continues to amaze me. About as genuine as those heavy -weight boxing press conference/weigh ins.

Cowell owes his wealth to one person, Tony Hatch who in 1973 became the baddy on panel show New Faces. At the time this was revolutionary and at least Hatch was in addition a talented producer/arranger. Cowell is merely a Tony Hatch clone and a poor one at that.

Single Three.
Hudson Ford Pick Up The Pieces b/w This Is Not The Way To End The War (or to die).

I know I was young but this was an illfounded dip into prog rock. Although quite a catchy track (as was the B side) it certainly did not fit into the Glam envelope.

Added to this was the major disappointment to this nine year old child that it got nowhere near number 1 (stalling at number 8) so it must have been crap. On reflection it was.

Once again no picture sleeve, merely a drab beige company issue paper effort which, matched the lacklustre nature of the band and product .

To be fair the band had emanated from The Strawbs who were quite well renowned and had had a pretty catchy hit the year before , Part Of The Union which did actually make number 1 .It must have been good!

Those were my first 49p single purchases (at the time full price not Woolworth's bargain bin). For albums the sensible parents pushed me and Sid towards the better value Top Of The Pops / Hot Hits type compilation albums many of which involved the services of rank session musicians.

You were usually guaranteed a Big D style scantily clad female on the cover often partaking in a sporting activity (blonde over the pool table or bikini clad over the tennis net type thing) but the music was at best second rate. Geoffrey and Franny were not on our wavelength. They claimed that you couldn't notice the difference. You could. A more sexist range of album covers than Hot Hits I defy you to find.

I retain a great love for Slade and Sweet (Hudson Ford got the boot with the follow up single releases of Burn Baby Burn and Floating In The Wind neither of which appealed remotely).

Stupidly I sold all three to a guy two years older than me called Nigel. Why Slade and Sweet?

I suppose you could say I was inadvertently 'Making Plans For Nigel' in terms of his future music taste. I just hope he was wise enough to stick with Slade and Sweet ('we only want what's best for him')

Apologies for the other one Nigel.

This was all a bit of a mystery to my mum.

Not reckoning with Slade's rebellious nature she could not fathom the spelling on Slade singles but she loved Noddy's sideburns and Brian Connolly's feather cut curve fringed blonde hair although both bands were seen as 'a bit girly' in that classic parental method of pigeonholing.

Bless her, at Christmas she made both me and Sid two patches each for the front pockets of our matching dark blue corduroys .

They were fluorescent green with a dark blue stitching. Mine read SLADE and SWEET respectively. Sid's Read NEW SEEKERS and MUD. I think I got the better deal.

No official logos or anything (parents never understand that) but to be honest she had no chance given that I had missed out on the picture sleeves as the singles were firmly wedged into the Top 10 by the time I had woken up and purchased.

When I see glam footage now on You Tube or TOTP 2 the crowd holds my attention not the bands.

Why do they persistently clap out of time, why are so many dressed by the wardrobe department of Man About The House and why do so many appear to be a couple of bricks short of a wall? Retrospectively thinking maybe there is a link.

Christmas 1975 saw the School put on a pantomime/show based loosely on Dick Whittington.

Being a bit shy I garnered minor bit parts but this did include a slot in an entertainment show on a ship where our glam group mimed to My Friend Stan dressed in an array of glitter tops, flares, hats and long haired wigs.

Naturally I (despite my Dave Hill infatuation) was Noddy, the main man, Kev L was Jim Lea (uncannily he actually did look like him), Des H was Dave Hill (same intitials) and Steve G was Don Powel and banged on upturned litter bins with his hands! We were Slade.

In our dreams.

Due to the love of Queen sweeping the nation at the time we considered changing our chosen track My Friend Stan to Bohemian Rhapsody (John B's brother had a copy, he was a Queen obsessive) at the last minute.

I remain puzzled as to why this last minute substitution was ever considered. Queen for Slade? What was wrong with me? Was I really showing signs of being swept away by the Queen mania of the time? Unforgivable.

It should never have been considered under any circumstances. In my opinion Queen have only produced one single of true merit in Seven Seas Of Rhye. Still a classic, unlike this over pretentious pompous bullshit.

Luckily we were only allotted about a 90 second slot. This effectively made the decision as it would have barely covered the dull piano backed Freddie based vocal intro let alone reaching anything resembling a chorus (although it didn't have one) and as for performing like Freddie! Stan it was.

A copy of the school photo copied 'programme' remains to this day in the possession of Franny. Luckily video recorders were a mere pipe dreamat the time. I remain mightily relieved.

Chart 1. My Top 10 Glam Singles 1971-75

10. Wizard. See My Baby Jive Far superior to their Christmas ditty.

9. Suzi Quatro. 48 Crash. A real stomper.

8. 10cc Rubber Bullets. Stretching it a bit in terms of glam but a classic.

7. T Rex. Twentieth Century Boy. My first realisation of Mark Bolan. Never really followed it up.

6. Bay City Rollers. Bye Bye Baby. One of many catchy releases.

5. Pilot January. Narrowly pips Magic. Both great.

4. Mud Rocket. The best of a fine Chin Chap written batch.

3. The Glitter Band. Goodbye My Love. So much better without the paedo.

2. Sweet. Fox On The Run. Timeless, addictive and classy.

1. Slade. How Does It Feel? Pure melody. A skillful band in all respects bar image.

Slade's melodic stuff was wonderful but actually led to their downfall. It could easily have been Far Far Away, Everyday or the lesser known Nobody's Fool as all are quite brilliant.

With regards to the top two both Slade and Sweet could have filled the top 10 on their own such was the range of classic material that they had. Chinn Chap obviously take a great deal of credit for the hits of this period although the Sweet track I have chosen was their first self-penned A Side.

The 11 plus selection process.

A controversial yet necessary system which essentially determined , based on a couple of exams bestowed on an unsuspecting 11 year old, whether you were cut out for an academic or manual future.

I could not afford to bugger this one up as I had absolutely no prowess in the manual/DIY field. A trait I hold to this day.

Was I really from academic stock? Geoffrey's College of Proceptus and Franny's solitary Art A level would suggest not.

I was in danger of falling It's A Knock Out style between two stools. Fortunately I scraped the required grade but unbeknown to me and partly due to the School chosen by Geoffrey and Franny this would lead to trials and tribulations in trying to keep up with my academic peers in the years to come.

More later in The Grammar School chapter.

1971 FA Cup Final. Arsenal v Liverpool

The Footy / Arsenal obsession begins. Glory hunter, moi?

This is the first FA Cup Final I remember watching. Amazingly the League Cup final was not screened live in those days and if your team made it to Wembley you would be relying on Grandstand updates from Tony Gubbaor latterly Bob Wilson perched behind a goal to keep you in the picture with what was going on or second half only commentary courtesy of Sport on 2.

Unbelievable.

The first 90 minutes were uneventful and ended 0-0.

What a bonus. This meant extra time and in these days of extremely limited live TV football coverage this was in the 'special treat' category!

Geoffrey had grown up in North London and on alternate weeks he would go to Highbury and White Hart Lane . Times have changed..

Over the early years thankfully I locked on to Arsenal. This was probably due to the impressive Cannon badge rather than a poncey Cockerel certainly not the Cup victory. That's what I'm sticking to.

However, this was formally endorsed following the 1971 Cup Final where a longhaired layabout called Charlie George cemented himself in my heart by grabbing the glorious winner against 'The Scouse Hub Cappers'. I was hooked.

Contrast this with my tears the following year in the final of 1972 when a clown called Geoff Barnett (more about him later) was in goal for Arsenal due to injury to Bob Wilson and The Gunners failed to show up losing the final 1-0 to 'Dirty Leeds'.

Little did I know that that would be the last major event for Arsenal until the Cup Final of 1978 and the less said about that the better. And yes I cried.

Geoffrey also had a fondness for Man City and Sid adopted them as his team from 1971.In the early days at least I appeared to have got by far the better of this deal.

However ,in recent times given the advent of all the excessive cash in the game this has served to distort the distinction between genuine big club and small rich clubs such as Chelsea.

Citeh have found themselves at the top of the pile largely due to the vast amounts of cash injected into them by a country of questionable morals. As a result Citeh have made great in-roads into my (Arsenal's) once privileged position in trophy terms.

The media still seem to be blown away by Citeh. They are not mind numbingly brilliant they just happen to have used huge finances to buy two first elevens both capable of winning the league. I can accept this given their persistent level of under achievement in the previous 15 years.

Back in the 1970s it was proper football. There certainly were some characters and many had doubles. Not only did Geoff Barnett strongly resemble Keith Harris (minus Orville) there were others with uncanny resemblances:

Player	Club	Double
Gary Shaw	Aston Villa	David Van Day Dollar
David Geddes	Ipswich Towen	Mike Nolan Bucks Fizz
Terry Mancini	Arsenal	Grumble Weed Graham Walker
Frank Worthington	Leicester City	Any 'dodgy dealer' from The Sweeney.

Tony Curry	Sheff Utd	Gunter Netzer West Germany
Billy Bonds/ Frank Lampard Snr	West Ham	Chaz And Dave
Gary Stevens	Brighton & Hove Albion	Radio 1 DJ Gary Davies

These characters were not aloof from Joe Public. Many a time the players would socialise in the pubs with the supporters after the match rather than merely leaving the ground in a self-obsessed head phoned bubble of spoilt materialism and self- importance. The game is so detached from the fans now that I have lost much of my passion. Where are the characters of the calibre of Tony Adams? Apparently on Strictly.

A one club legend who would give it all for the cause, not tolerate shirkers in the team and then adjourn to the boozer for a skin full.

Aside. Plenty of chocolate references above and below but one of life's mysteries is that a Mars Bar which is a third of the size of the standard Mars bar is deemed to be 'Fun Size'? Truly warped logic in any kid's eyes.

Q3 Chocolate.
Frys produced a range Cream bars in the 1970s.
What were the four main types?

Author's Note:
Following extensive research I have finally solved the mystery of origin of those kidnapped Football Collection figureheads!

Yes they were a giveaway with every £10 of Petrol but Esso were not the culprits.

It was actually Cleveland, a name that I can only vaguely remember, and this was their only dip into football having previously issued the heads of Kings and Queens!

The collection came out in 1971 and was entitled Joe Mercer's Great Britain Squad (he was caretaker manager of England around this time). It comprised 16 'legends' largely sourced from England and Scotland. The reason for this issue remains unclear and seems pointless. Am I missing something?

For the record Esso took over Cleveland in 1973 presumably to maintain their monopoly on football related giveaways!

The Action Man alternative

A classic set of wheels

IV

It's not big and it's not clever. Life and Crimes 1971/1980.
I Fought The Law / Thick As Thieves / Young Criminals/ Ay Oh, Let's Go.
Largely due to Geoffrey's Services background our upbringing was strict. There were limitations particularly regarding sweets to the extent that myself and Sid would happily try to develop coughs or colds to secure a couple of Strepsils or Zubes!

On the subject of medical ailments when I was about nine I endured a serious period of constipation and experienced the crudest of remedies. Senokot was not a twinkle in the GP's eye in those days and after about three weeks of 'non- production' in which even the reliable black German Rye Bread failed to work its magic the parents called the local GP to the house and explained the predicament.

I am fully aware of the term 'ripping the shit' out of something but I had no realisation that this was a working practice. This G.P. fella took me up to the spare bedroom, covered the bed in newspaper , applied lubricant to my backside (steady) adorned some narrow rubber gloves and then quite literally ripped the living shit out of my arse.

I howled like a wolf but the problem was solved. I was rewarded by my parents with a Thornton's fondant cream filled chocolate mouse as I lay there amidst the warm debris of my rectum. Wrong on so many levels today but this actually happened. My arse sang for days.

In the early 1970s the likes of Texaco, BP, Shell would entice drivers to fill up with £10 of 4 star at their garage by offering inducements. This could range from the classic seventies exotic tropical tumbler to a range of football based collections.

During his services and early Volvo days Geoffrey used his car quite regularly and as a result petrol was readily purchased and in 1970 the World Cup Silver coin collection and associated display board had already been acquired and completed.

Esso followed this up in the early seventies with the domestic football crest collection (covering Divisions 1 and 2 and selected Scottish). With the petrol being readily acquired once again both me and Sid had soon filled our respective display cards.(retained to this day).

Soon after a new Marble Head figurine collection was released (again Esso) to honour what I think was broadly speaking 'Football Legends'. This portrayed such luminaries as Gordon Banks, Pele, Franz Beckenbauer, Gerd Muller, Geoff Hurst, Bobby Moore, Eusebio etc. They were head and shoulders only about 1.5" tall in marble coloured yellow plastic on a flat felt bottomed base. We had acquired about four of the figurines and signs were ominous with regards to completion of the set as Geoffrey was now essentially settled at his Ipswich base and no longer travelling the country in a sales capacity.

In the early days at our new school I had noticed that one Mark B was in possession of the full legends collection and was openly flaunting it. This didn't seem very fair.

His father was in the farming community and this must have entailed numerous visits to ports such as Felixstowe to acquire fertilisers and the like plus extensive use of farm machinery. Geoffrey's car use by comparison was by now a limited 8 mile commute.

Either way Mr B obviously used a variety of vehicles extensively and a healthy petrol/diesel consumption resulted leading to plentiful acquisitions of the much desired figurines.

To add insult to injury Mark B was no sportsman. He didn't even like football! I passed this news to Sid who (suitably enraged) instructed me to kidnap the set on the first occasion that Mark visited the toilet and to deposit it in the class stationery cupboard. I duly obliged. I was the fall guy in this operation.

Not surprisingly this resulted in cries of dismay/sobbing from the said Mark B on the return to his desk. Luckily the dinner bell went at that stage. Never had my chocolate semolina tasted so bland.

On return to the classroom the teacher lined us up and demanded answers. I couldn't hold it together and with quivering lip I explained where the collection was and tried to justify my actions.

Luckily the school took it no further. The same cannot be said for the next incident.

On occasions two people from the top class would be entrusted to go to the staff room to collect the massive dictionary. One day this duty the task was allocated to me and Des. We arrived in the empty staff room and clocked a handbag on a chair. Without thought from either me or Des we looked inside found a purse and started shovelling the loose change into our hands.

Suddenly a staff member appeared and ordered us to wait outside the staff room whilst she got the Head. Panicking we deposited the cash behind some books on shelving in this area. The Head returned and we were made to explain ourselves. The handbag belonged to the head dinner lady Mrs M.

We claimed we were merely looking through the bag but naturally this was dismissed instantly. We had no cash on us but a stiff staff reprimand was metered out.

We had to apologise face to face with Mrs M and it was decided that we would serve a two match suspension from the school footy team (we were the Keegan/Toshack striking combo). This was deemed suitable as apparently no cash had been taken. Pretty light on reflection.

For the record in the next two matches the goals dried up and the team was defeated.

The scenario was unfortunately relayed to our respective parents. Mine were horrified. I'm not sure Des's reacted in the same way but then again he was a ruffian!

Without a hint of remorse we returned later on the day of the theft to the bookshelf area to recover the coinage from behind the books as leaving it there would have deepened our predicament if discovered. We had no alternative.

Step by step we were heading towards the inevitable. Full blown shop lifting.

Myself and Sid familiarised ourselves with this trait by conducting a trial run. The setting for this was none other than Franny's Post Office shop! We figured that this was ideal with the point of plunder on our own doorstep.

To be honest there was little of attraction in the Post Office as the stock largely amounted to end of pier style nick-nacks. The likes of Whimsey china animals, maths rulers/protractors and exercise books etc.

As it was a non-food outlet there were obvious limitations in terms of stock range and attraction. We were desperate for Franny to stock Football cards but because at the time these came with a slither of Anglo Bubble gum in the packet it was deemed a foodstuff and as a result she could not stock them.

What we were left with was the incredibly trite Animal card series range. Produced by The Totally Square Company these were packs of 5/6 cards housed in a green packet with a charging Elephant on the front. They were undeniably aimed at the non- sporting fraternity The kind who would willingly choose Animal Magic over Football Focus.

Unbelievably it was these cards that we stole on a periodic basis. Unfathomably we shoved the green packaging under our bunk beds. Clearly geniuses at work. We conducted this crime safe in the knowledge that neither of us were remotely interested in the behaviour/habitat of African Elephants or Vietnamese Pot Bellied Pigs.

Not surprisingly Franny soon sussed that the stocks were dwindling despite the lack of any physical sales and our cover was blown formally on the occasion of a bit of periodic housekeeping. We hadn't thought this through.

The sorting office at the rear housed our private catering box of crisps and can tray of Barr Cola which Franny acquired from the local wholesaler Chumleys (later taken over by Nurden & Peacock). With Colditz style planning and precision plus extensive use of carefully timed coughs to mask the noise, we periodically pillaged and escaped to the nearby woods to consume.

Unfortunately the theft and shoplifting seeds had been sown. The natural development down our 'criminal path' led to the next incident. The unlawful acquisition of goods in Ipswich. Grown up shoplifting.

Myself, Sid and John B (who later became a policeman) decided we would take the Bickers bus to Ipswich one day with the sole intention of lifting a few goods from the shops.

The wheels of ill-gain were set in motion when John B needed to raise funds for the bus fare. He did this by stealing a compass from his dad and flogging it to Sid. There was to be no turning back. The theme for the day had been set.

We cruised around shops such as WH Smith and John Menzies gleefully pinching whatever came to hand (pens, compasses, sweets you name it). Towards the end of the morning we alighted on Woolworths. It all started to go seriously wrong. I think a couple of the cheap out of chart singles were successfully bagged but it was the 1lb bag of chocolates mis-shapes which were my downfall.

A somewhat ill-thought move I grabbed the rustling bag and tried to shove it up my jumper/ jacket. I dropped it twice before pouching but as we attempted to leave the shop a hand alighted on my shoulder and the classic ' would you like to come with me?' line followed.

We were taken to a ground floor office behind the scenes and a blonde store detective, sitting cross legged behind a desk, systematically took items from our bags and monotonously posed the question 'nicked?' to which the answer was invariably yes.

We didn't even try to explain the pre- trip compass shenanigans. We were in far too far. The police (not the band) were summoned and we were driven away through the Woolie's car park and deposited in the cells at Ipswich Police Station to await the mortified parents. Their unrestrained disgust and bafflement was etched across their faces.

In hindsight the Cops let us off relatively lightly with a subsequent visit from them at the post office. All a bit LAPD for the village which led to extensive localised curtain twitching as two policemen parked up outside the quaint building. Had the Black Panther struck again? Six weeks Summer holiday slave labour on the parent's allotment duly followed.

This was in effect a double punishment. Not only hard labour under the unforgiving Summer sun but following that compulsory vegetable consumption on a daily basis.

Speaking of The Black Panther this related to a series of crimes being committed in the early 1970s by an assailant nicknamed The Black Panther. I admit that it troubled me intensely.

He started by robbing remote sub post offices up in the North of England. The level of violence increased attack after attack and lives were lost. It culminated in the kidnap of a Coach Company heiress Lesley Whittle and her resultant death in a drainage system in Bathpool Park Staffordshire.

Having recently moved into a village post office in the early 1970s I was cacking it and was convinced that he would strike in Coddenham, a mere 180 miles from the area where the crimes were being committed. An unlikely round trip for a minor sub post office raid by anyone's standards.

Many a night I would be in bed and hear a noise from downstairs and would lie rigid in my bunk bed waiting for the door to open and The Panther to strike!

Meanwhile our register of crime expanded with incidents including:

The pilfering of Geoffrey's silver shilling collection.

Gudgins (The Grocers) strangely became suspicious of the daily purchases of either one hundred 1p Monster Chews or fifty 2p Sherbert Lollies a day by two boys who up to that point had barely spent more than a few coppers on the odd bubblegum. Franny's purse was also accessed on the occasions when it's weight equated with a generous amount of silver coinage within.

Firing stones from a catapult directly at cars and hitting the windscreen of a passing sky blue Austin Avenger (shattering it). This cost us the princely sum of £37 to replace.

I feel a whole lot better admitting my indiscretions and getting them off my chest but as quoted by many a primary school teacher both then and now it was neither big or clever.

Please don't view us as East Anglia's answer to The Kray twins. We weren't all bad. We were from a good stable, dare I say it, middle class family background and we had principles drilled into us. We just didn't take kindly to them.

We attended a Methodist Sunday School which was strange given that we were not Methodists. The Methodist Preacher was our neighbour hence it was a marriage of convenience. I admit that on occasions we did 'lose' our collection money on the grass bank outside the chapel only to miraculously find it a few days later allowing for a visit to Gudgins shop for scoffs but at least we went.

We also collected the money on carol singing nights without any hint of pilfering. Our patchy reputation had clearly not been recognized by the village community at that stage however I can confidently state that each year we diligently called at every house in the village and dutifully placed all proceeds, commission free, into collection tin amid the off-key wailing of the carol singers.

Chart 2. THE CHART OF SHAME

As a record purist I am still actively hunting down old Glam/Punk/Mod Revival singles to fill the gaps. This can involve a bit of 'peg on the nose' Charity shop involvement as there are some hidden gems out there. You have to wade through serious piles of throwaway shite to unearth it.

Certain acts appear rather more frequently than others in the battered racks irrespective of the number of records they actually released. This gives me the opportunity to compile:

The Charity Shop Top 10. (singles based)

Bubbling under are the likes of Cliff Richard, U2, Elaine Paige, Peter Skellern. Peters & Lee (complete with their dull predictable repeatable relationship themes such as Welcome Home and Don't Stay Away Too Long) and Glen Medeiros.

Glen had no great range of singles but with Nothing's Gonna Change My Love For You where he sits resplendent on the cover in white T shirt, tight fitting jeans, brown leather jacket and complete with smooth greasy tan looking every inch the Kebab shop proprietor (small or ladge? Schalad? Wid onions?) he makes regular appearances. Little more than a second- rate George Michael.

10. Band Aid. It served its cause but the song itself now sits rightfully amongst the duffers.

9. Gilbert O Sullivan. Numerous offerings appear on the Mam label. One is worth having. Alone Again Naturally. Naturally I would leave it at that.

8. Brotherhood of Man. Off the back of their ' Kiss Saving' Eurovision exploits this band spawned a few further chart hits. They appear regularly in charity shop circles. They even did an album covering 20 Number One Hits at the height of their 'fame'. An indication of how shallow they were. Unfortunately the mould had been set further down the line for Bucks Fizz.

7. Jive Bunny. The epitome of mindless, throwaway 1980s bollocks. True to type this bunny reproduced numerous crass dance disco mega mixes. If ever one bunny fully justified doctoring at birth it was Jive.

6. Dawn. Largely due to' Tie A Yellow Ribbon' but also a healthy sprinkling of 'Knock Three Times' which actually stayed in the number one position one week longer than Ribbon.

Middle aged mums largely responsible once again for their popularity in the 1970s. Dawn actually released 26 singles but strangely enough post 'Ribbon' songs such as 'Who's In The Strawberry Patch With Sally' failed to garner much commercial success!

5.Barbara Dixon. Complete with eighties perm. Middle of the road, bland, turgid lady rock. Elaine Pagesque.

4. Leo Sayer. A raft of throwaway hits which obviously most mothers did judging by the number and variety filling the flea pit shop shelves. You can acquire his whole singles output for little more than a fiver.

3. David Soul. This cool dude had numerous top 10 hits and some were pretty damn catchy. The B side of Don't Give Up On Us being my favourite- Black Bean Soup.

He made two albums for the Private Stock label in 1977 and tellingly the latter was entitled Playing To An Audience of One. Strangely prophetic.

2. Modern Romance. Remarkably born out of the ashes of New Wave Band The Buzzards this group features heavily in the racks of discarded 45s and seemingly always complete with picture covers. Best years of our lives?

1. Alvin Stardust. Sorry Alvin but you are everywhere in both the 45 and 33RPM racks. Usually the later Magnet offerings such as Pretend/Buddy Holly/Won't Run Away rather than the classics Coo Ca Choo or Red Dress.

If you suddenly come to the realisation that Alvin is your man a tenner will comfortably cover his entire recorded output from 1973 thanks to these well intentioned albeit damp retail outlets.

Aside: Who the fuck was Kevin Kitchen? A double for the Paper Lace drummer? To his credit his charity shop appearances are fleeting.

The Record Label Dilema.

The frustrating thing about the charity shop hunt are the numerous occasions you spot a label which falsely raises your expectations . A label you know is associated with much sought after Glam/Punk or Mod bands thereby initiating unrealistic hopes. 99% of the time you are left hugely disappointed . Examples include:

CBS . The Clash, The Only Ones? So often Johnny Cash ,Chicago or Bob Monkhouse.

Stiff. The Damned/Elvis Costello? So often Tracy Ullman.

Polydor. The Jam/The Chords/Slade/Siouxsie? Frustratingly Jon And Vangellis, Captain Beeky or Our Kid.

Virgin. The Pistols, The Skids, The Motors, XTC, Magazine or The Members? Depressingly more often than not Mike Oldfield or Julie Covington.

Aside 2. What possessed Manhattan Transfer and Captain and Tennille to suddenly become The Manhattan Transfer and The Captain And Tennille? A misguided belief in their own self- importance? The records were still shit.

Just occasionally, however, you strike it lucky and all those wasted hours pale into insignificance when you uncover a gem as I did in Oxfam with Chuck Wagon's (of Dickies fame) Sole solo single on purple vinyl for 25p.

I know these shops are serving a great cause but irrespective of the pandemic they have always been places where both hand and body disinfection is essential on both entry and exit.

Q4. Football

In the 1974 World Cup Finals in West Germany (birth of the bland stanchion) Scotland played Zaire in the group stage.

What was the score and name the scorer/scorers?

V

The Grammar School Years 1976/78

Into The Future / Framlingham Calling

The gulf between Primary and Grammar was similar to that between a Blue Riband and a Yorkie. Passing the eleven plus was the first barrier. The catchment area was the next. Strictly speaking we were out of area for the much sought after Grammar School.

Somehow Geoffrey had negotiated a deal with the council whereby, providing the respective parents could arrange for the children to be ferried to and from the school bus stop in nearby Crowfield, we would be allowed to attend. This procedure (a two mile journey each way) continued for the next five years.

The Grammar School was run by Headmistress Miss L and Deputy Head Mistress Miss C. Both ruled with rods of iron and as they say on ITV3 before the screening of 1970s 'comedy classics' such as 'Bless This Bigot' or "Bigot About The House' practices,(rather than comedy), of 'a bygone era' were plentiful.

School assembly was held on a daily basis in rooms 10 and 11 and Miss L would stand on the small timber parapet often in bright red button up jacket and address the school visually in the vein of X Ray Spex's Polystyrene but sadly lacking the cry of ' oh bondage up yours'.

Many a fart was dispensed in the confines of Rooms 10/11 and the hard timber floor guaranteed a sharp rippling effect. This would lead to mass giggling before the culprit (usually me) was frog marched to the Headmistress's office.

Much of what was deemed merely disciplinarian would not be permitted now.

Examples

- The school rebel (it didn't have many) Stu who refused to cut his straggly hair was made to wear a lanyard stating 'Beware I kick. I am a donkey'.

- Another disobedient pupil was tasked with cutting the Almond Tree lawn with nail scissors.

- The academic grading system. The school was heavily into the issue of homework and the subsequent grading of pupils on a monthly basis. All homework was marked out of 10.

These figures were then amalgamated and on a monthly basis the whole school would congregate for Assembly fittingly on the hard timber floor of Framlingham Assembly Halls for mutual degradation in the form of oral pupil comparison. Pure humiliation for some.

For the natural geniuses of the school (those for whom learning came naturally and 9 out of 10 was deemed a major disappointment) this was great but for the vast majority it represented a monthly put down of the highest order. What on earth they were trying to achieve through this practice was beyond me.

I managed to attain a score in the low 70s pretty consistently (Mr Average) but this was definitely aided and abetted by the regular telephone calls to Bill and Andy P (both academics) particularly in respect of Maths homework .

This was a subject which I found unfathomable and having a teacher in Mr L (a broad Yorkshireman who taught at the speed of a Dickies track played at 78RPM) didn't help my cause. SOH, CAH, TOA, algebra, Pythagoras, obtuse angles,? As the John Foxxless Ultravox said 'this means (absolutely) nothing to me'.

The school trip option in the third year again was somewhat demeaning. The choice was either go to Holland for a week (Staying at the Waikiki Hotel) with travel courtesy of Townsend Thoresen from Felixstowe or a week at Sizewell in YHA accommodation sited in uncomfortably close proximity to Sizewell B Nuclear Power Station!

Possibly another unnecessary revelation of the haves and have nots?

Those of us that went to Holland were given effectively a ridiculously free reign once we were there. We were eleven, at best twelve years old but were allowed free unaccompanied access to the town and beach as well as congregating on our 'tour bus' one evening (with driver nowhere to be seen) to listen to the England V Wales Home International on the radio, albeit for a dismall nil- nil draw.

PE/Sports (Grammar School)

Around this time two new teachers joined the ranks Pete W and Pete D. Pete D was heavily into football (unfortunately a Spurs fan) but he was not a games teacher. History was his main remit.

In addition to being a geography teacher Pete W was unfortunately a Welshman and doubled as a games teacher which was particularly unfortunate as he was totally obsessed with Rugby Union. We were not.

Our football team was pretty good beating numerous schools into the bargain but all he wanted to do was concentrate on bloody Rugga.

As a collective year we were not the most intimidating from a physical perspective. Our best result in Rugga terms was a 7-3 defeat to a posh college up the road and yours truly playing Fly Half at the time kicked our points. The other results were utter thrashings.

I soon decided that the game was not for me and during games lessons I adopted an avoid the ball policy when rugga games were forced upon us.

The skill was to suss which way the ball was going and then drift subtly in the opposite direction. One or two of us adopted this but we were soon singled out as wimps by Pete W.

To show how obsessed he was with Rugga when I received my end of term Geography exam paper back I was astounded to see that in an answer on land reclamation I had been deducted a mark for saying the land had been reclaimed for use as a football pitch. Red mark through it and Rugby written underneath! Typical Pete W. Which leads nicely on to The Rugga Rant.

In England it remains predominantly played by over privileged public school boys (Richard Wrigglesworth anyone? Presumably not a pillar of state education) and historically covered in the media largely by those with double barrelled names such as Nigel Starmer-Smith and Mark Durden-Smith.

It is largely followed by middle class management types (attired in Barbour Jackets, beige slacks and obligatory brown shoes) who claim to follow Rugby but mysteriously only ever materialise in February for The Six Nations. No club allegiance. Real rugby fans?

Added to this in February you will always spot the middle-aged Scot in a kilt boarding a train somewhere in the Home Counties on Calcutta Cup day just waiting for a member of the general public to quiz him about his attire and passion for Scotland.

'Countries' as insignificant of The Cooke Islands play in the World Cup Finals as there is no process of qualification. Who next? Sark? (or maybe they could be incorporated into the six nations to make it The Seven Nations and elongate this in-bred public school bollocks even more).

Actually the thought of Sark possibly turning over the upper class, pampered, over-privileged posh boy Lillywhites is very attractive and after minimal reflection at least their introduction might give Italy the chance of actually winning a match.

There is an on-going obsession with hemispheres. Why?

No other sport mentions the hemisphere topic but it turns up in all rugby discussions. Thankfully 'Southern hemisphere' nations are apparently far more talented than Northern. This is proved in the next point.

We are so shit at Rugby that we have to club together all four home (Northern hemisphere) nations under the pseudonym of the British AND IRISH Lions to take on the likes, individually, of South Africa, New Zealand or Australia. How embarrassing is that?

Year 2000, Five Nations becomes Six. A new millennium so the Rugga boys decided it would be a good time to welcome Italy to the Northern Hemisphere party. The point?

Not only does this serve to further elongate this turgid over-rated drivel but it should be pointed out that Italy have won a mere twelve matches in that 20 year period. Added to this coaches of teams who have lost to them, often after fielding a 'second' 15, have tended to be relieved of their role soon after. A pointless inclusion at all levels.

What is the difference between the British (and Irish) Lions and The Barbarians? Something to do with Club socks apparently!

England and Scotland are boringly consistent. Both reach The Calcutta Cup final on an annual basis.

It's so predictable. There is no opportunity to change your formation. As a result if you have the best players you usually win. As such are the managers really necessary once the team has been selected? On the basis of this 'Iddie Jawns' the jovial, 'loveable' Aussie mock rogue should surely stand down. He now has!

On reflection long may he reign given the performance in the UK based 'World Cup' in 2015 when he managed to ensure that England failed to reach the knock out stages. Apparently no'Northern Hemisphere' team qualified. Bliss.

More nonsense. If an English player plays for a club side outside of the UK then he can't represent England. Great idea guys given the above.

The BBC are so infatuated with this upper-class minority sport (plus Rock Climbing, Tennis, Athletics, Cycling) when the vast majority of us have no interest in it whatsoever.

Radio 5 live effectively use the weeks in February to try to brain wash the listeners into thinking Rugby (and the 6 Nations) matters. Last week they were discussing the impact of having colour blindness on watching the upcoming Wales v Ireland 6 Nations encounter!

Why do the BBC employ some old aged, croaky voiced upper-class toff who sounds like he's been on the Port and Stilton all afternoon to advertise up-coming Six Nations encounters with phrases such as the rattling of sabres and all that pretentious bollocks?

The BBC has an over- exaggerated level of political correctness, in terms of sex, race and disability particularly in Sport. It has got to a ridiculous level and does them no favours.

I am finishing this book as The Ladies Football Euros is getting extensive coverage from the BBC which is fair enough but the presentation is nothing short of embarrassing. The main culprit is of course Alex Scott.

The other night she was the main presenter and her classics have included 'what a amazing half that was' 'England gave a tremendous preformance' 'this German side are roofless' (obviously severely underpaid) and 'England will now play the winners of Neverlands (presumably a Michael Jackson representative 11) and Swindon'!! She may be doey eyed (and this obviously appeals to the moronic male masses) but she hardly has a command of the English language and would never have been touched by the BBC in the old days.

Surprisingly the BBC have overlooked the fact that the teams on the archaic show that is University Challenge have been allowed to get away with regularly having teams parading three male (fashion averse) student squares and only one token female freak.

This, however, is an exception to the general rule. BBC should surely stand for the British Box-Ticking Company.

They recently were recruiting for football commentators. I was sorely tempted to apply. It then dawned on me that as I was not female, of ethnic origin or disabled my chances would be severely limited.

This is the company that sends a disabled man in his wheelchair up the Pennines to show couples around houses in Escape To The Country. At the end there he is beaming in the garden with the couple but the cameras fortuitously fail to show the poor old production team lying face down in the vegetable patch following seven days of logistical madness!

The Rugga fraternity are obviously so envious of football.

Austin Healey can't hide his hatred of footy and the Radio commentating 'legend' Ian Robertson during commentary of some Rugga game at Old Trafford once stated 'why do they waste arenas such as this on football'. Jerk.

Why is winning the 6 Nations not valued unless you complete 'the grand slam'?

What about Martin Johnson's narrow minded type cast comments when some Rugga boys were sent home from an overseas tour due to drunkenness and lechery. ' It's Rugby Boys on tour. What do you expect'? Mmmmm the word dick comes to mind.

Don't get me wrong Football has its faults (and many of them).

Although I still love it (less so since the distortion produced by the stupid money in the game) in broad terms four fifths of the fans who watch are pretty thick. I know that's a sweeping statement and probably not politically correct but it's true.

When the TV cameras scan across the crowd (particularly at places like Birmingham City, Leeds and Wolves) it is very difficult to spot anyone with more than a solitary Woodwork O level.

What about racism and irresponsible use of 'sawshall media' in the football fraternity? The two go hand in hand and the media surely should step up to the mark and declare it will never be eradicated because of the high proportion of thick morons who unfortunately follow the sport in conjunction with 'Saw-shall' media.

Our school year team was exceptional at cricket and football. We were crap at Rugby because quite honestly we didn't care. As for cricket we were certainly extremely good at the Grammar School and to a large extent this continued with the High School.

One exception of note sticks in the memory when we played an away match at Leiston High School. We won the toss and stuck them in skittling them out for 37. A tremendous bowling performance from our four strike bowlers and great fielding to boot. Job done surely.

After one dismissal their number 7 'Batsman' came out and stood at the crease. Our PE teacher umpire enquired 'do you want a guard?' to which he replied ' oh yes I'd better go and get one' and followed this up by scurrying off the pitch to get a box! They were that clueless.

We should have stuffed them given their complete non-understanding of the game but incredibly we were all out for a miserly 17 thereby facilitating a rare phenomenon, a supplementary school 'beer' match. Of course, we stuffed them, but it was too late. We had blown it. On reflection how can you skittle a team for 37 and not only get beaten but hammered? We managed it.

The Games teachers were rightfully furious and completely blanked us on the mini bus journey all the way back to Framlingham.

Contrast that with the time we took on the private College up the road, our local derby. These were the fee paying over privileged public school boys . They lived and breathed Rugby and Cricket.

Whilst we would have got absolutely spanked All Blacks Vs Italy style at Rugga, in Cricket we were pretty talented and fancied our chances .On this occasion we beat them (and I drew blood with a rising delivery off a length)!It resulted in a major Cricket Team announcement of Kerry Packer's Allstars proportions to open up the next day's School Assembly. We were viewed by all , albeit temporarily ,as Gods.

As noted live sport on TV was limited. School Summer holidays provided the chance to watch extended live cricket in the form of the Test matches and this was eagerly anticipated by both me and Sid.

In 1975 the third test between England and Australia was played at Headingly. We were enthralled and with the match delicately poised the final day was eagerly awaited by all in the sporting world.

The same can not be said of the criminal fraternity and unfortunately the supporters of one George Davis had other ideas and had broken into the Headingly ground the night before dug holes in the pitch, deposited oil at one end and daubed George Davis is innocent slogans all around the boundary.

I had no idea who this Davis fellow was, what he stood for or the significance of his wrong-doings. I cared not as to his possible innocence all I knew was that I was mightily miffed and had to resort to physical Cricket participation on the rec. George Davis was innocent in the eyes of Sham 69 but in my mind he was guilty. Guilty of robbing this besotted cricket fan of his day's entertainment.

Surely they could have just shuffled along to the next square and continued? Apparently that's not Cricket.

Punk awakenings. The Sounds Of The Suburbs

Punk was happening on a commercial scale during this period.

Regular outings on TOTP for the likes of Buzzcocks, The Jam, The Stranglers, XTC, The Vibrators (just the once), The Members and all being lapped up by yours truly .Visits to the legendary Parrott Records in Ipswich swiftly followed.

More later.

The Cransford Fete. I Don't Care.

The school's female boarding fraternity were housed at a manor house called Cransford Hall not surprisingly in Cransford.

Each year a fete was held in early May at the Hall to raise much needed funds for the school. It was a very important event in the Grammar School calender. All pupils had to produce something along the lines of homemade sweets, jewellery etc to sell at the fete and attendance was obligatory.

On one particular occasion the fete clashed with live coverage of the England-Scotland Home International footy match. Yes one of the few live TV offerings. I handed my form teacher Miss M my homemade Honeycomb Toffee offering on the Friday before, (a solid block of treacalised matter in a plastic container) together with a declaration that I would not be attending.

Her reaction was one of astonishment. This turned to utter despair when the England Scotland international reasoning was declared. She was one of those people who just didn't get Sport, however, as live TV matches were such a rarity I was happy to absorb her wrath and stand my ground.

Strangely enough this also ties in neatly with a very similar ill feted parental 'treat scenario' a few years prior to this. A visit to Windsor Safari Park on Saturday May 24th 1975. A kind gesture from the parents you may think.

Surely this was the perfect day for the offspring who had declared their liking for all things wildlife related with the pilfering of those card sets but unfortunately the parents had failed to view their decision objectively given the date of the Home International between England and Scotland. It was live on TV and to rub mountains of salt into our already gaping wounds England beat the Scots 5-1.

Never had the Windsor Safari Park staff witnessed two more disillusioned looking kids on a safari tour. The attendants there could have been forgiven for presuming we were blind given the total lack of facial appreciation.

Summer 1978 Diabetes Arrives

I have to be honest I was ridiculously thin when I was thirteen. Because it was a gradual loss of weight I think it went largely unnoticed by my parents.

On Friday 16th June 1978 there was a school trip to Lords for the second day of the test match series against Pakistan.

Naturally we armed ourselves with our top of the range cassette players and a selection of tapes for the journey (Jam, 999, Clash, The Dickies spring to mind) noting the famous punk venue The Army And Navy Pub as we travelled through the pit that was / is Chelmsford.

It was a cracking day with mighty Beefy Botham crowning it with a century although the school took the ridiculous decision to leave the ground when he was on 97 to avoid the crowds! Doh!

I spent the whole day glugging coke, fizzy drinks and water. Bill filled up the 2 litre bottle in his swag bag every time he went to the toilet (with water not his piss) and I proceeded to down it as soon as he returned to his seat.

Something was clearly not right.

I continued drinking all the way home resulting in numerous unplanned service station stops to relieve the bladder much to the anger of the others on board the coach. Finally I was dropped off by the grocers shop in the village and I remember struggling to walk the 300 yards or so up the hill to our house.

When I got in I physically collapsed.

Cue parental panic and calls to the doctor who got me into the hospital pronto. I was diagnosed as a type 1 diabetic. Franny fainted on the spot.

A week in hospital followed being trained about how to inject, and balance carbohydrate intake against insulin plus the intake of horrendous hospital food such as Cod Mornay.

At the time I remember being reasonably chuffed as the diagnosis had clashed with my Summer exams and I missed the lot (no resultant Grades Pressure to be endured on that front for once).

In addition I was aware that the bass player from XTC Colin Moulding was diabetic (I'll ignore Gary Mabbutt) so surely it wasn't that bad. It didn't stop him playing bass for one of the top New Wave acts did it! For once in my life I was making a positive out of a negative.

The School Disco (in Moscow).

This was a bi-monthly event.

It was held on a Friday night 7.00pm to 11.00pm in St Michael's Rooms (the headquarters for the metal detector team in the TV series The Detectorists) which doubled as our exam room in darker times (O levels).

The guys providing the discos had, to the girls at least, a magnetic dodgem attendant status and despite being run by a combination of plasterers, farm labourers and electricians their fairground worker aura resonated and was lapped up by the female fraternity.

The main protagonists were:

Zodiac.

A mainstay for the Grammar School.

Always played a 'healthy' mix of mainstream American rock, Kids from Fame, Meatloaf, (Hi Ho Silver Lining was a cert) and smoochy numbers at the end. Cringingly parents were allocated door duties and were on hand to ensure there were no shenanigans and to usher out the kids at the end of the night.

The Jeff Beck penned High Ho garbage caused mass rustic hysteria on the dance floor complete with arms raised aloft and a heady mix of patchouli and body odour.

On the one occasion Geoffrey had door duties this had a serious limiting impact on both my cool dance floor moves and romantic advances but from a positive perspective it did avert the need for a 15 mile cycle home at 11.00pm (see below).

Spectrum.

Very similar in offerings to Zodiac with an equally bland 'DJ'.

I once slipped Paranoid by THE DICKIES to the DJ and requested he gave it a spin which he did. All the heavy metal boys did their hip wiggle belt dance blissfully unaware that this was the sped up punky Dickies version and not Sabbath. How we laughed.

Talking of The Dickies credit where credit is due. What other band could get away with releasing a single (Eve Of Destruction) where the combined running time for both the A and B sides is a mere three minutes five seconds! A real PuNk ethos.

Chase.

The guy in charge of this was different class. He was the uncle of my mate Colin L and he clearly liked his music. As a result he had a good range on his playlist and many a time he would play a track like Fame (I waan live forever) and follow up with a track such as Nasty Nasty by 999 or Automatic Lover by The Vibrators! You had to admire his courage.

He had a great range of tracks and seemed genuinely overjoyed when requests for punk songs came in and could break up the monotony of the disco tunes. Chase was ahead of its time in that respect and we loved them for it.

The grammar school was run on a very tight budget. Things were borrowed and we even used The Town's football and Cricket pitches which were a good ten minute walk from the school.

Luckily there were no rugby pitches up there so in the early years at least we were able to avoid this intolerable pursuit for a while but our days were numbered.

This changed when the school acquired a patch of land to the rear of the modern school. In their wisdom the school 'developed' these into two rugby pitches and participation was compulsory. I think one Pete W had a heavy influence over this decision.

Aside: With regards to the upkeep and maintenance of the buildings and grounds of the grammar school site this was conducted by a local company by the name of - F.Ingram Smith this was plastered across their vans. Pure Carry On

St Michaels Rooms

As noted above the scene of numerous Zodiac/Spectrum School Discos and worrying Exam sittings. Here I chanted the infamous Magazine lyric 'Maybe it's right to be nervous now' as we nervously waited outside.

Q5. Sweets of the 1970s.

Rowntrees enhanced their Tot range in the 1970 to four different types. Can you name them and what types of sweets were they?

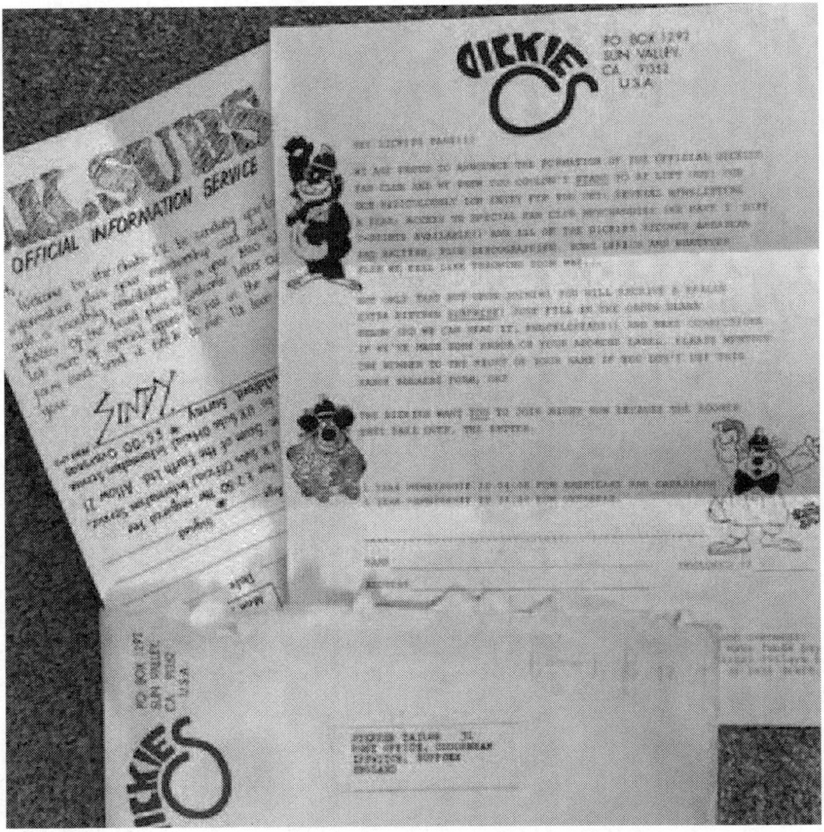

Letters from The Subs & The Dickies

VI

The Jam Fan Club
Standards?
I was Member 176 . I still have the card and all the letters including Jam stamped' envelopes.

£2 per annum plus 6 stamped addressed envelopes secured a bi-monthly newsletter (photo copy) including promotional badges, T shirt / poster offers, tour dates, the odd flexi but sadly absolutely no preferential ticket arrangements.

Photocopied letters were apparently stapled together and inserted into envelopes in the Weller's Coal shed back garden 'office' by Paul's sister Nikki at Balmoral Drive, Woking.

A real family affair as Paul's dad John allegedly sourced the A4 paper from the Polydor offices in Stratford place and utilised their photocopier on the quiet.

I classed this as my official connection to the band and their home base in Woking. The bi-monthly newsletters, as a result, were eagerly awaited.

The feeling of anticipation when you could see that the latest badge was lurking within the envelope and the joy of letters from Paul, Bruce and Rick complete with spelling mistakes and shocking grammar (the mis-use of the apostrophe being the biggest culprit) did not go unseen especially by the parents.

Tour dates, personal profiles, promotional photographs, the odd free promotional poster (In The City) even Tour programmes. I was in my element and as a result the merch seeds were sown.

I was mocked mercilessly by Bill for my allegiance but where else would I have found out in the 1978 band profiles that Weller's hobbies were 'song writing and sleeping' Foxton's favourite colour was 'Bottle Green' and that he disliked 'foreign foods' (apparently not averse to the odd curry now though) or that Rick's favourite album and single 'vary from week to week', that his hobby was 'indoor games'. His likes were similarly 'indoor games' and his dislike was guess what… 'outdoor games'. All put their 'SIGNITURES' at the bottom!

Gripping stuff. On reflection Bill possibly had a point.

My first purchase was a poster of the rear image from the This Is The Modern World album showing Paul alongside a classic leaping Brucey with Rick's shadowed drumming in the background.

The poster was duly bought (for 50p) together with further exclusive badges and Tube Station T shirt. A postal order (remember them?) was dispatched. All good so far.

The ensuing anticipation was gripping with each daily postal delivery eagerly awaited. Then after about 3 weeks a somewhat battered tube shaped package arrived in the post.

I could not deny that the poster was slightly damaged (crease and pucker marks) due to the lack of carboard protection but I was more than happy and I proudly added the poster to the walls of the developing Jam shrine in my bedroom. The T shirt and badges were sublime.

Franny was not so pleased.

Not content with merely criticising the items she sent a full-blown letter of complaint to the Wellers at Balmoral Drive. I thought that would be the end of it. Sadly not.

One Saturday morning Sid was helping out in the post office when the phone rang. He answered it and then casually turned to Franny saying ' Mum, it's Paul Weller's dad on the phone'!

I was in the adjoining room. I couldn't believe what I had just heard. I was struck cold by a combination of shock, intrigue and fear and broke out into an ice cold sweat.

A short conversation ensued. Franny was complaining about the battered nature of the poster. When she put the phone down she looked a bit shocked and exclaimed 'what a rude individual'.

I was intrigued as to what had been said. It had been a very short interaction and apart from her bristling demeaner she was clearly perplexed. He had apparently defended the packaging and said ' Sorry but we're not the f*****g Queen'.

If anything epitomised how out of touch my parents were with the 'current' music scene this was it! He had obviously said 'Queen' not ' The Queen' but Franny was not aware of this band and not surprisingly hadn't seen Weller senior's link. I duly explained but it all went above her head.

Whatever the merits and in spite of John Weller's animated explanation in Franny's mind he was uncouth and extremely rude. It didn't help my burgeoning interest in The Jam Fan Club at least as far as my parents were concerned. Future merch purchases were strictly vetted.

Either way John Weller was clearly not one for budging and no offer of compensation was forthcoming. I didn't care. I now knew that not only did Paul have my address but also my phone number and would no doubt soon be contacting me to smooth things over.

Another example of parental detachment from the music scene came in the early 1980s when I was talking for some reason about China Crisis (probably slagging off their latest chart offering). Geoffrey overheard and equated this with economic problems in the Far East!

Whilst on this subject (and I know, technically speaking this is post 1983) as Geoffrey climbed the career path at Volvo his work took him regularly to Sweden. On one occasion he returned home and told us that apparently someone famous was on his flight, a 'Feargal Sharkey'.

This immediately alerted Sid as he was a big Undertones fan. It must have been after his first solo 'Smash' otherwise none of the cabin staff would have recognised him so probably 1985.

We were pretty impressed but Geoffrey had absolutely no idea who this 'Sharkey chap' was.

In the Summer of the following year (1986) me and Juliet had booked a holiday in Malta.

We were standing at Gatwick Airport chatting about how we had never seen anyone famous on our limited travels and I reminded her of the Geoffrey / Feargal incident from the previous year and we chuckled once again about his lack of recognition.

We continued to kill time and I decided to nip to the Duty Free for some Scotch and there by the limited edition Johnny Walker Black label was no other than one FEARGAL SHARKEY!!! I was absolutely staggered. I swear that I had not seen him prior to our discussions.

What the hell were the chances of that happening? Juliet naturally was non plussed .

I was blown away. Not only this but he was also on the same flight as us to St Pauls Bay in Malta and we saw him a couple of times with his girlfriend in the beach/bar areas.

Weird, very weird.

The Jam obsession begins.

The first Jam badge, a large Modern World single image. was bought from The Sunday Street Market on Piccadilly , London in 1978, (opposite The RAF Club our accommodation link with the West End) and adjacent to Green Park.

The market was quite diverse (ranging from pottery to photo frames to punk based framed montages) and the badges were mounted on display panels attached to the park fencing. 40p secured me a badge the size of a side plate. Not very mod at all.

My first Jam single was also The Modern World. Naturally I adorned the cover with my name in blue biro to ensure it would not go walkies at a party. Crazy logic. Who takes records to another person's party (pretty insulting) and even if they did how would a name on a cover offer any form of protection?

Okay writing your own name is loosely excusable what is unacceptable is when you acquire a disc from a second-hand record shop or record fair and the previous owner has endorsed the cover with their credentials. I recently acquired Slade Alive from a record fayre and the cover was plastered with Rikki's numerous pledges of love for Josie. Intense cover grafting was conducted to obtain a level of acceptability.

Forget third parties I am equally guilty having endorsed front and inner sleeves plus the label itself on my first album purchase The Jam's This Is The Modern World (bought first purely on the basis of the impressive Brucie jump on rear cover0. It was followed swiftly by In The City.

Both were immediately proof vetted from a swearing perspective to note which tracks were not to be played in parental earshot.

I admit I was caught out with the title track with the 'two fucks' completely taking me by surprise. I was fully expecting a damn rather than the spitting of 'two fucks'. Paul clearly could not be trusted. Luckily no parents in proximity when first aired.

Back to those bi-monthly Jam newsletters which whilst a bit tame were eagerly awaited nonetheless. I certainly wasn't as sad as my mate Roots. A major Damned fan he bought 10 copies of Sensible's Happy Talk in 1982 in a vain attempt to 'keep it at number one'!

Avid listening to John Peel was essential at the time as he aired the punky new releases first. As the release dates approached I would be there radio cassette recorder in hand waiting in nervous anticipation to suss the new material out before the necessary early purchase to guarantee the picture sleeve. Lessons had been duly learnt.

My radio cassette recorder was very useful in obtaining early rudimentary copies of these first airings and would suffice until such time that I could get to Parrot Records (see later).

In terms of missing picture sleeves I was guilty with regards to the following.
Stranglehold UK Subs,
Holidays In The Sun Sex Pistols,
Something Better Change The Stranglers,
Silent Night The Dickies
David Watts The Jam.(initially no picture sleeve but on rare French white label. I blame Selfridges where, unfathomably, I bought it)

For the record the picture sleeve on the last one was hunted down and subsequently obtained.

Fan Club mail outs were bi monthly and literally photo copies and poor quality all round. These were crucial fan club links and included profiles with 'signitures'. Rick obviously put a lot of thought into his! Proof reading clearly not a priority for The Jam Club..

Before long I got wind of Carnaby Street. About three times a year our family would meet Brian and his family (RAF friends of Geoffrey and Franny) in London for a weekend .

We stayed at the RAF Club on Piccadilly and would be dragged to a West End Show (Elvis on one occasion which didn't sit well with me and Sid with our Punk leanings).

It was on one of these occasions that I entered Carnaby Street for the first time and was exposed to the delights of Sherry's, Melandi, Mod World and of course Shelly's.

Why The Jam didn't insist on commission from Shelly's is beyond me as about 80% of all Jam fans had a pair of Shelly's, whether it be Gibsons, Bowlers or Badgers/Stage shoes.

I bought four pairs of Gibsons (black and white, white and black, green and white and pure white). All three eyelet with perforated aprons. I also had pure black and pure white Bowling shoes. I never bought the Badgers as to me they just looked like a jumped up trainer.

These were supplemented with a grey boating blazer (3 button) complete with vertical blue and white stripes and a pair of sky blue Brucey Hipsters (tight fitting clinging stretch fabric trousers).

From a parental perspective my change in image was a pleasant change. I looked neat and tidy for once which sat well with the parents.

Due to my over-protective nature I took steps to add steel blakeys to the heels of my Shelly Gibsons. To the uninitiated general public the shoes were already a pretty poncey affair and this modification didn't butch them up in any way merely adding a distinctive click. Overnight I morphed from Paul Weller into Lionel Blair.

Another anal faux pas on my part was the application of polish/whitener to the perforated white upper apron of the Shelly's Gibson shoe , This effectively filled all the little inlets and killed the look of the shoe.

Once the error of my ways became apparent I spent the next couple of hours needle in hand meticulously clearing each individual inlet. About 250 per shoe.

An error never repeated.

Charts 2 and 3. (INDEPENDENT JAM CHARTS)

Pure self-indulgence on my part but this band deserves a couple of charts all to themselves.

The Jam had a six year career producing six classic studio albums and eighteen consecutive top forty hits (excluding imports) with four of those making the top spot.

Weller rightly split them up at the top of their game and that is why they are still revered to this day.

Chart 2. The Top 6 Albums by THE JAM

6. In The City. Essentially early Jam live captured on 33rpm. R & B based. In retrospect (to me) nothing special apart from title track, Art School, Away From The Numbers.

5. The Gift. Final album and veering towards soul. Still some good tracks in Happy Together, Running On The Spot, Malice, Ghosts and Carnation but the writing was on the wall. Still miles way ahead of anything else released in 1982. Brucey's Circus deserves a mention too.

4. Sound Affects. Weller's favourite. Simplistic, varied and heavily Beatles influenced (which is why it is not higher on my list). Great play on the BBC Sound Effects cover re the design. Great tracks including Pretty Green, House Ablaze, That's Entertainment. Weller ahead of his time.

3. This Is The Modern World. I may be biased as this was my first album purchase. A progression in musical terms from the debut In The City and includes classics such as the title track, Life From a Window and Brucey's under-rated Don't Tell Them You're Sane.'

2. All Mod Cons. The one that effectively broke the band. Exceptional song writing and a great range of sound (from English Rose to 'A' Bomb In Wardour Street'). Changes week to week for me in terms of personal favourite. Also contained the imperious Tube Station.

1. Setting Sons. For many the ultimate Jam album as it shows the band at their most powerful best. Part concept it includes delicate tracks such as Thick As Thieves alongside classic such as Eton Rifles. Pity about Heatwave the only filler. Couldn't Strange Town have nipped in here?

The preferences, particularly with the regards to the top two albums, are effectively inter-changeable on an almost week to week basis (just like a real chart) such is the quality of the albums concerned and many would argue that the significance of All Mod Cons as a game changer for the band justifies a position of number one. (or Sound Affects ranking above Modern World!) It was make or break for the band at this stage following Weller's temporary writing block.

The inter-changeability is a reflection of the quality of the musicianship and variance of song writing. No other UK band could touch The Jam at the time (although The Clash came close) and they effectively swept the board re the music paper polls at the end of 1979 and 1980.

Although The Clash ran them close, and some would say XTC had a similar breadth of quality, there was something truly special about The Jam and this remains relevant to this day.

Chart 3. The Top Ten Jam Singles (UK Issue)

10. Absolute Beginners. New horn- based sound and arguably the best video.

9.David Watts/'A' Bomb. Good combination of obscure cover version and cutting original.

8.Going Underground. Great video. Shook up the nation at the time.

7. All Around The World. The Jam at their punkiest.

6. The Modern World. Storming angry track. Weller classic.

5. The Bitterest Pill. A change from the usual (if The Jam had a usual).

4. A Town Called Malice. Pure commercial pop with cutting bleak lyrics.

3. Strange Town. Highlighted isolation. Great B side too in Butterfly Collector.

2. Tube Station. What more can be said. A brilliant concept single if there is such a thing.

1. The Eton Rifles. Tirade against the public school boys. Cameron declared his love for it! A representation of things to come for the band and a first tentative toe into the top 10.

Despite my awakening to Punk/Mod I have to admit to some unforgivable record purchases at this time: I was guilty of the following.

When A Child Is born. Johnny Mathis. Why? To appease the parents? Absolutely no excuse. Bought Christmas 1976. Arguably pre Punk (my excuse) and unbelievably I followed this up with:

Mull Of Kintyre. Wings. Another Christmas Number 1 in 1977. I was truly messed up. Two Christmas number ones and Punk had definitely broken by then. Definitely no excuses.

Money Money Money. Abba a great band, (Eagle, When I kissed the teacher, Ring Ring etc) but this single was bland and unimaginative. Added to that it didn't even get to number one!

Figaro. Brotherhood of Man (utter crap). The template for Bucks Fizz in the eighties. Smashed in a display of anarchic showmanship at Coddenham Youth Club. Another Number 1 though!

Rocking All Over The World Status Quo. I blame the Suffolk influence. Three chord repetitive shite. No evidence of any mental health issues around this time. I am surprised.

Fact no picture sleeves were obtained for any of the above as all bought when firmly established in the chart. Not an issue. The same rules didn't apply to crap of this order.

Sound of confusion/This Is Pop?
Why I was buying this bollocks at the same time that I was buying the likes of Pretty Vacant (and foolishly daubing my name in green felt pen on the back cover) I have no idea.

There was no rhyme or reason.

Records loved and lost plus those fortuitously gained.

Purple Hearts Beat That!
Seminal first album release on Fiction Records. I was mightily disappointed with it but there was no excuse for selling at a ludicrous trade price to Andy's Records Ipswich. See E bay value now!

Mods May Day 1979.
A live mod revival compilation album on the Bridge House label featuring Secret Affair, Squire, Beggar , The Mods and Small Hours recorded at The Bridge House Pub Canning town .

Say what you like but this self-funded release became as iconic for Mod as the live At The Roxy albums were for Punk and was the first insight into many of the above bands. Why I sold it (again to Andy's) I will never know.

I also made the mistake of thinking that Secret Affair's single Let Your Heart Dance (with fake crowd noise/clapping on the intro) was the same track that would appear on Mods May Day. It was not and the quality of the Mods May Day version was far inferior.

Not suspecting this I sold my Secret Affair single in advance of acquiring Mods May Day and then was mightily distressed to discover the relatively low quality recording I had acquired on the live album (which as I said above I later sold on) bared no resemblance to the polished over-produced/dubbed single release.

Original albums command a healthy price on E bay and I know. I've had to re-buy on E Bay

Dream acquisition - Magazine. Shot by Both Sides.
Acquired in exchange for What A Waste by Ian Drury. Result. It set me off on the intriguing developing path that was MAGAZINE. An affinity I have retained to this day.

Tomorrow's Girls UK Subs. Blue vinyl.
Sold to Roots once I acquired Another Kind Of Blues (again on blue vinyl) as the single was on the album. Strange logic. What about the B sides for God's sake and of course its bluezyness?

With Punk bands B sides were an opportunity to really experiment and many bands provided B Sides which were as strong as the A.

Classic examples were The Stranglers who paired Something Better Change with the equally brilliant Straighten Out and The Jam with Absolute Beginners and Tales From The Riverbank.

The classic singles and albums of Punk had vibrant graphics on both the sleeves and the labels; and a number of the bands I followed released limited amounts of their singles on coloured vinyl. Prime examples were The Dickies and UK SUBS but The Members and The Tubes were also guilty.
A high proportion of companies (both independent and major) used the record label in addition to the picture sleeve to further enhance/portray the band's image.

Again this was a new concept and completely in contrast to the crusty old, stuck in the past rock bands and their respective labels.

Many Punk bands had striking labels especially in the early days. They wanted to be seen to be different. United Artists were possibly the biggest exponent of this.

Not only did they produce bright striking colour clashing picture covers (album and singles alike) but the labels often had official band logos emblazoned across the record label itself.

The Stranglers, Buzzcocks and 999 (singles and albums) are prime examples of United Artist's emphasis on the importance of image on sleeves and labels.

Buzzcocks Ever Fallen In Love single, Love Bites album, 999's first two album covers, singles such as Emergency and Me And My Desire and associated ticketed label designs are clear illustrations of this.

Pure inspirational brilliance.

Aside. As mentioned above name labelling your records is unforgiveable and unfathomable. In the early days I was guilty. I 've mentioned this already regarding the This Is The Modern World albumwith outer cover, inner sleeve and record label inscribed with Step. To be fair at least I added a Jam M style reverse tail loop on the base of the P in Step to give the labelling a degree of authenticity! Still inexcusable.

The Punk/New Wave labels were effectively further marketing ploys with strong emphasis on band logos.

Q6. Music.

Paul Weller once quipped that the band played one venue so often that they should take up residence above it.

Name the venue.

Q7: Music

Gary Tibbs played bass for which three prominent Glam/Punk/New Romantic bands?

VII

Ipswich
Strange Town
Where do you start?
This is the town where the hot dog vendors are forbidden to cook onions !

Coddenham was linked to Ipswich on a twice per week basis by Bicker's limited bus service (Tuesday and Saturday from memory). The first bus left at about 10.00am and the second lunchtime. The final bus collected from Towen at about 5.30pm.

The route included numerous village stops where a wide range of rustics (some complete with bailer twine belts) would board the bus and chat excitedly in their broad Saarfolk accents as they were 'off to towen', the capital of Suffolk. Everyone appeared to know the business of everyone else.

Ipswich was a 'shopping empire' built around a retail crossroads. This ran from the Co Op at one end (scene of countless pressurised bowl haircuts) to Peachy Sports which marked the beginning of the dodgy end of towen at the other. This road was bisected by one which had Sainsbury's at one end (with Mick McNeil sports in very close proximity) and Ipswich Library at the other.

At the intersection of the Crossroads was/is The White Horse Hotel which also catered for live music in the mid/late 1970s, early 1980s.The Cleaners FromVenus played there and 'Cleaner' Giles Smith in his excellent book Lost In Music states that Nick Kershaw also graced the boards before he lost his c and become the iconic Nik.

The Bickers Service dropped off in the towen at two points. The library where the more affluent, educated middle aged departed, and The Blue Coat Boy Pub (opposite the public loos) where the rustic reprobate riff raff made good their exit, ourselves included.

The majority of the shops (as with all towns) were the everyday shoe shops, department stores (Ipswich's Show Store being the now sadly departed Debenhams sited opposite the Towen Hall) plus newsagents, electrical outlets (of course with record departments) , bookshops etc of negligeable note.

One or two shops stood out, but not too many. Broadly classed as 'dour' or 'exciting'.

Grimwades. The official school outfitters. this was bland/faceless personified.

Sited opposite Debenhams this place was as grey as the dull school gabardine trousers they procured .Torturous in the extreme.

I remember as a nervous eleven year old being hauled along to this place for the obligatory school trouser to be fitted, the cumbersome heavy duty fur based navy blazer to be measured up and the school badge/crest acquired. In latter times apparently it had a café. There was no such facility in the late 1970s, at least I never saw it or the parents never let on.

Accessories such as stiff collared white shirts, plain white PE T shirts (no stripes or emblems permitted) and shoes etc could be acquired from a slightly cheaper outlet Coes. Another similarly monotone store. Necessary evils for the burgeoning Grammar School new boy.

Jean Jeanie- EXCITING

A shop of legendary status amongst the youth of these parts in the 1970s/80s.It was sited towards the Peachy Sports end of the 'crossroads' and it stood on a prominent corner site. As the name suggests it sold one thing, denim 'jeyans'.

All sorts of makes (including independents) were on offer. In the mid1970s and for some time after, the pavement sweeping high waist banded flares were the order of the day usually adorned with side pockets and some made purely of squared denim patches. Pure Ipswich.

The unofficial ruling (at least for men) was that the flare had to completely cover your shoe. The trendy thing was to ensure that the material just grazed the floor as you walked which induced that rough, frayed look. All a bit hippyesque.

By 1978/79, due to Punk, the more switched on amongst us were veering towards tight drainpipes and Jean Jeanie moved with the times and were now offering all sorts of colours and styles in the jean department plus a variety of denim trucker jackets. Flares were retained for the uninitiated countrified rocker rustics. 'but I like Quo boiy and Meatluff'.

The top brand (from a punk perspective) in terms of colours and fit were Rebs. A more tight- fitting Adam Ant style jean could not be found. There were jean retail rivals but nothing could de-throne Ipswich's Queen Of Denim-Jean Jeanie.

Top Shop. Exciting.

Not the one you know from recent times this was an independent shoe shop and the scene for the purchase of my first two tone Gibson style Jam Shoes. Sid thoughtfully crossed through the price and halved it with the word Sale on the box to placate the parents. It worked.

The first outing for the shoes was the private Ipswich Hospital (a strange debut) where Franny was recovering from an op. They set her recovery back 10 days. Distraught.

The Badge Shop -The Doll's Hospital. EXCITING, VERY EXCITING. Not many will remember this place. It was essentially Ipswich's version of London's iconic Punk T shirt and Badge outlet Fans, which was located on Charing Cross Road in London. Ipswich's offering was found in The Butter Market on the righthand side just before the impressive Grade 1 listed Ancient House Bookshop (dour) on the left.

The Badge shop was about the size of two adjacent toilet cubicles. It was only big enough to sell badges (and a few Mod patches in 79) which were on display (optician style) on boards along the walls and on limited revolving displays in the centre.

From memory it was run by a European chap (possibly Greek). His turnover of badges was impressive and he centred largely on Punk (latterly Mod Revival).

I was in my element in this place and many a purchase was made to supplement my constant supply from The Jam Fan Club and those from Fans and (via the NME) Better Badges.

On one occasion in 1979 I bought a large target for the back of my Mod Parka. I showed this to Bill. A bad decision. He criticised the unimaginative type casting of my choice.

More to the point Geoffrey had already decided that the concept of wearing a target on my parka with associated badges was 'derogatory to the RAF'!

I had to return it and exchange for a good old The Jam spray logo patch.

Easy you may think as both were the same price but my mate Bill had to be built into the equation. He decided to complicate the proceedings by putting a small drop of blood on the white ring of the target patch. Idiot.

This was spotted (not surprisingly) by the aforementioned shop proprietor and he said he would have to sell at a reduced price because of the 'damage'. He refunded half my money (50p) as a result increasing the outlay required for The Jam patch. Tough times.

I never forgave Bill for his part in this prolonged extensively negotiated transaction.

East End Bargains - Exciting (I think).

This shop was sited (not surprisingly) in the Eastern part of towen and although I have classed as exciting this is a bit of an assumption as I never actually crossed the shop doorway!.

It was a retailer of secondhand musical instruments and always had an alluring array of electric guitars hanging in the window which I would regularly gaze at longingly (prior to my acquisition of the mighty Jedson Telecaster). For that reason it has to be included.

Mick McNeil Sports. EXCITING

Think traditional sports shops. Think of this place.

Mick McNeil Sports was sited on Taaaack't (Tacket) Street. It was predominantly a football based sports shop and was run by the former Middlesbrough, England and latterly Towen player Mick McNeil.

This was the shop where I bought:

1979 Arsenal Away Shirt (Yellow/Blue trimUmbro)

1982/83 Arsenal Away Shirt (Green/Blue Umbro)

1983/84 Arsenal away Shirt (Shaded yellow Umbro)

1977 England kit. Yes I was a full kit wanker. (White shirt, blue shorts and white socks with red/blue trimmings. Admiral) * Latterly sold to fund the purchase of. . . . A 1978 Scotland Home Shirt.(Dark blue with white Umbro diamond sleeve trim. I was muddled).

The thing I remember most about Mick McNeil's was the smell of the place especially the footy shirts .The England shirt I sniffed feverishly for days on end once I had acquired it! It was heavenly.

Rovian Sports EXCITING

This again was a traditional sports out-fitters with none of the leisurewear / fitness dominated stuff that flood sports shops today.

They concentrated largely on Cricket which was possibly not the best business move given the seasonality of the sport concerned. I have to be honest and admit that there was also quite a leaning towards Rugga too which implied that it probably served many of the private schools in the area.

In addition to the Scotland shirt bought in 1978 (£3.75) my first Slazenger Cricket bat complete with wide diagonal green band on the upper bat face was bought here.

My hero Alan Knott used one. I subsequently discovered that it had no semblance of a sweet spot which was a serious misgiving bearing in mind my limited batting skills. I needed all the help I could get. I rarely found that illusive 'sweet spot' and subsequently blamed this for my limited run contributions.

The overlord of Coddenham Cricket Club JP succinctly stated that it's only use was for firewood. He wasn't wrong.

This lot started it. From Glam...

Classics of the time

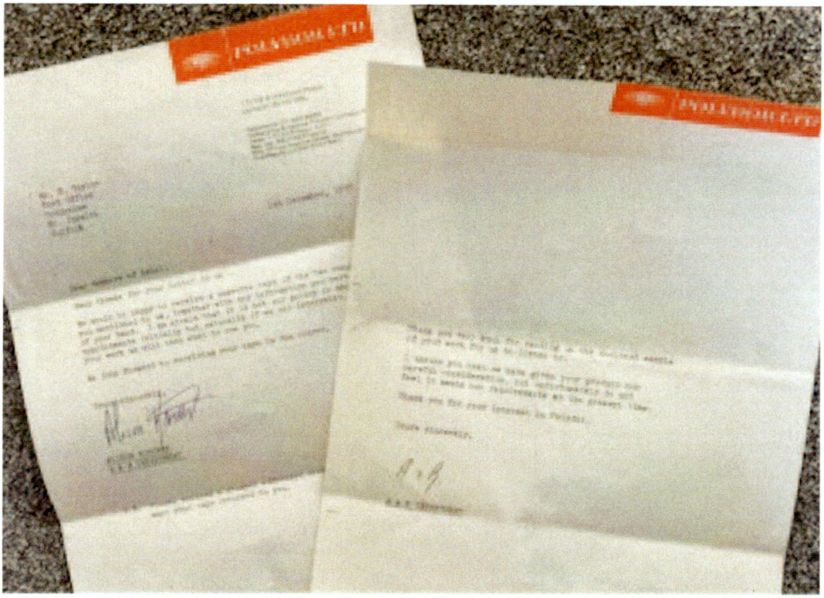

Hope and despair

Geoffry plus moody post punk teenager

The coolest shop in town

Iconic T-shirts

The cause of the rift with John Weller

Actually they both only did 30MPH, but which was the 'chick puller'!

Limited editions (apart from the Dickies)

This music mattered

The JAM
The JAM
The JAM
THE JAM
THE JAM
THE JAM
THE JAM
THE JAM
THE JAM

... To The Jam

Pads and gloves followed. We could never get our hands on the recently released St Peters mitten style glove which was 'sweeping the nation' due to use by England captain Tony 'looks pretty adjacent' Greig. We had to settle for the common or garden sausage finger style. We never lowered ourselves to the standard school issue green rubber spikes.

Our cricket obsession in the Summer was born out of the fact that test match cricket was shown live on the BBC (in the days when the BBC had proper sports coverage rather than the minority sport dog ends that they show today) and in particular the antics of the commentary team.

The interaction between Peter West, John Arlott and Ritchie Benaud remains the stuff of legend in particular Mr Benaud's prose. It was upbeat, witty and unique.

Example: 1981 'Morning Peter, morning everybody. Welcome to Headingly for what should be great day's cricket.' 'It's pretty hot out there.' 'That's gone into the confectionary stall and out again' (Botham 6) and of course the famous 'Bawled 'im' .

For football David Coleman was the equivalent of Ritchie. 'Stokes, one nil'. The two were untouchable (although not flawless) in their respective commentary fields. Coleman repeatedly referred to Brian Talbot as Tablet in the debacle that was the 1978 FA Cup Final!

*Football Shirts:

Worth mentioning that the 1975 England shirt (the one with that great smell) effectively marked the start of a craze in respect of shirt designs for all the domestic clubs that continues to this day. Not surprisingly Paul Flint was the first to acquire an England kit and I have to admit this inspired me to get one.

I kept mine for a year and then sold it to a person a couple of years below me at school (as noted above) using a fraction of the proceeds to fund the Scotland shirt as I preferred the colour and diamond sleeve piping design. It didn't smell as good though. Obviously the England Scotland rivalry bypassed me!

Leicester company Admiral were essentially the catalyst for the football shirt craze but soon the other main sports companies Umbro, Adidas, Bukta (no Nike leisure company in those days) joined in. What it amounted to in the early days was the company's logo symbol stitched down the side of the shirt sleeves and shorts with Umbro having a boarded row of diamonds and adidas the classic three stripes. Admiral had their medal style design.

95% of the clubs in the top two divisions had these flashy style kits. Unfortunately for me one of the 5% that didn't was Arsenal. I was not pleased, I wanted one.

There was Tottenham with white shirt and a lovely dark blue Admiral stripe down each arm (and indeed the shorts), Chelsea had white diamonds down their arms, so did Wolves (although theirs was the stingy design that lacked the stripes around the diamonds leaving just a thin strip of diamonds and it looked crap), Even Brighton had the Bukta stripes and Ipswich were in on the act with Adidas. Man City strangely had diamond piping on the arms but not the shorts.

Strangely in 1978 Liverpool had the strip of diamonds down the sleeves of their tracksuits but not on the sleeves of their shirts. Very weird. This made Man City's shirt/short aberration almost acceptable.

Arsenal's shirt design (red shirt white sleeves) did not lend itself well to sleeve adaptation so it was understandable but the away shirt was plain yellow with blue trim. Surely that could have accommodated a couple of blue armstripes of enclosed diamonds? Unfortunately not.

It would be the mid 1980s before Arsenal caught up and thereafter both the home and away shirts would be changed alternately on a seasonal basis.

Be careful what you wish for. (Icicle Works).

I digress (again) back to The Towen shops. I have saved the best to last. Step forward....

Parrot Records EXCITING. . . THE ULTIMATE

This quite rightly was (and still is) revered by all who encountered it as a legendary music retailer. The West Runton Pavilion of record stores. It was not for the chart crowd.

Sited in Quyerns (Queens) Street this shop was two along from Rovian Sports and next to The Music Centre (which is still there and where I acquired the Magazine single Give Me Everything) this moderate sized mid terrace shop was the epicentre for all musical genres.

Usually manned by three surly sales 'assistants' who were young, trendy (for Ipswich) rude and cutting edge. They didn't hold back in taking the piss especially with the limited chart offerings hiding on the shelves. These guys coolly flip inspected the vinyl. They were vinyl technicians.

Many a housewife or unsuspecting chart inspired teenager would come in and ask for the latest offerings from the likes of Shakin' Stevens, ELO or (extremely) Dire Straits, and be met with cynical sarcastic abuse and an invitation to seek out other more appropriate retail outlets such as WH Smith/John Menzies or one of the bland electrical retailers with record departments.

On three occasions however I too fell foul of the sales assistant mockery.

In 1978 I went into get the latest single by Buzzcocks (Ever Fallen In Love from memory). I had seen it advertised in the music press as coming in a 'picture bag'.

The disc was duly bought and the assistant put the record, with full colour sleeve, into a Parrott Records bag. He passed it over the counter to me after taking my 70p. I waited. He ignored me for a bit and by now I was getting in the way at the counter. He raised his eyebrows and enquired 'anything else boiy?'

'Where's my picture bag?' I tentatively mumbled. He looked at his fellow assistants took the Parrott bag off me and produced the record from within. 'There' he snapped, the picture sleeve is the bag'.

I was not up with this trendy record terminology and had completely misinterpreted the concept. I was fully expecting a full blown Buzzcocks carrier bag for my record! The guys behind the counter naturally and rightfully pissed themselves.

With cheeks burning a Ribena hue I hurriedly departed.

The second occasion was in the Summer of 1979 when to be fair I was ahead of the game. I went into Parrott to obtain the first single by Mod Revival maestro's Merton Parkas on the day of its release in order to obtain the limited edition Parkas patch.

I boldly approached the counter in my full mod regalia (Brucey hipsters, Black and white Shelly Gibsons, Mod T shirt and parka) and asked 'Do you have the new single by Merton Parkas, 'You Need Wheels'? The response was a disdainful look of bemusement and an enquiring .. 'You need what? Your head examining' ?

I repeated my request (less confidently on this occasion) foolishly adding that it came with a limited edition free sew on patch for the Parka. The hole was deepening.

'Never 'eard of it'.

End of conversation. Once again I scurried out of the shop suitably shaken with the sound of laughter ringing in my ears.

Undeterred one week later I returned. I had to get that disc with picture sleeve (bag) and the limited edition patch before it became a multi-million selling hit. Unluckily they remembered me. Luckily this time the record was in stock. The assistant tracked it down and as usual a brief look and spin of the disc was given to ensure it wasn't scratched. The patch tumbled out.'What the hell is this' he sneered. ' A little bit of decoration for mummy to sew on to your fishtail?'

Once again cue much behind counter merriment but at least I had what I dearly wanted.

For the record my expectations of Gold Disc status proved unfounded. The record stalled at number 40 and I subsequently lost the patch.

Third occasion, perhaps the least embarrassing. marginally.

In the early 1980s new wave outfit Cuddly Toys (why did I always like bands with silly names?) released a 12" single called Someone's Crying. They were very much a cult band. It came with another limited edition. This time a free 1" button badge. It was a good solid post punk track released just before the album Trials and Crosses. Parrot of course had just the one copy.

They smirked when I asked for it (presumably because of the name) and when he passed it over the free Cuddly Toys badge was not forthcoming. 'Excuse me' I stuttered' is there not a Cuddly Toys badge with this?'.

The assistant looked on the stock shelf and sure enough there was the badge. 'he muttered something along the lines of 'you'll look cool wearing this' with a mocking look on his face. In comparison with the previous two episodes this was bordering on polite and I scuttled gleefully out of the. I still have the badge.

The shop itself was relatively small with albums stored against the 3 walls and centrally located displays. Record stocks themselves were held in their inner sleeves on shelving behind the counter at the far end. Shop based outer covers were protected with the obligatory 12" clear plastic sleeves. Listening booths did not exist.

Most of the stock was of no interest to me but on the left-hand side about two metres from the counter itself was the section that I visited time and time again. Punk and New Wave L.Ps.

It was one, maybe two racks of covers (about 80 deep each) in alphabetical order. The hours I spent flicking through, plucking out interesting sleeves and eagerly reading through the information/track listing. Your time in the spot was limited as others wanted access to this section. I was drawn in by the covers many of which were striking and hinting of rebellion. They were intriguing. The ones that grabbed my eye at the time included:

The Damned (Damned Damned Damned) complete with shaving foam and coloured sunglasses.

The Jam (In The City) with its minimalist bleak largely black and white cover.

The Stranglers IV (Rattus) with the spooky imagery of the band within a manor house.

XTC (Go 2) with its self-explanatory 'This is a record cover' wording.

The Vibrators (Pure Mania) massive black V with Knox alongside and classic pure mania pink logo.

Magazine (Real Life) the intrigue of those spooky ghostly heads.

Elvis Costello This Year's Model. Classic simple image. Proper camera and tri-pod. No I Phone Elvis.?

Sex Pistols (Bollocks) ransom note logo and pink/yellow imagery. A classic image banned by *Woollies , WH Smith and my parents. Not by Parrot.

Ultravox! Auton like band shot. All glossy faces and starey eyes. The ultimate attention grabbing cover.

Also the likes of Buzzcocks (Love Bites) band in red and blue circles, white background, 999 (Separates) Brightly coloured attire. Similar to the first 999 album. Garish pinks, greens yellows and blues. .

UK Subs (Another Kind Of blues) weird submissive gimp mask connotation sleeve or is it actually just a deep sea diver and I am missing the point … and strangely enough a compilation called simply New Wave which attracted me as it featured a leathered jacketed yob with white T shirt lurching towards the camera gobbing beer! Very Punk. These covers alone lured me into parting with my hard earnt pocket money.

What was strange was that Parrott would only hold one copy of any album. You would take the sleeve to the counter and they would source the inner sleeve and record, (check the disc of course) and insert into the inner sleeve. This was because they were very much a specialist outfit and bought in to order. Clearly not a chart returns shop!

Strangely myself and Bill decided to buy the first two 999 albums (one each) on the same day. We had already acquired matching yellow 999 T shirts with green ticket logos from Fans in Charing Cross Road a few days before.

As noted above the 999 album covers were very similar as were the inner sleeves and it was only after we had got home and played our respective discs that we realised that the song titles on the record label for 999 didn't match those on the sleeve. Adding to the confusion Separates had no track listing on the outer or inner covers anyway. I had the Separates record and the 999 sleeve. He had the 999 record and Separates sleeve.

Was this another example of the Parrot staff having another cheeky joke at the customer's expense?

Over the years the shop changed and became Rex Records. Still good but not quite the same.

A genuine rival, Andy's Records appeared just around the corner and was a real threat to Parrot's air of invincibility. It was a cross between Parrott and John Menzies in that they catered for both Chart and indy. Additionally they diversified into second hand discs at first floor level.

Stupidly I sold them Beat That! by Purple Hearts and Mods May Day 1979. I know not why. Was cash short? What I do know is I received a paltry trade price for each only to find them selling both at three times the price a week later.

In 1982 Andy's in Mill Road, Cambridge was the scene of the greatest of all of my record shop embarrassments. I was there with Bill coolly flicking through the post punk when unannounced Geoffrey burst into the shop clutching an exposed banana in a brown paper bag exclaiming 'here you go Steve, just in case you go low' (a diabetic term).

There is absolutely no answer to an invasion of your perceived cult status at times like these. Bill pissed himself. I was left looking for a gaping gap in the floorboards (and possibly a song from under them) into which I could gently subside. Unfortunately it wasn't there.

Back to Ipswich, a town epitomised by a sleepy nature and at the time an enclosed local yokel community with the only visitors coming from the surrounding village network. The proof. Ipswich had no Indian restaurants in the late seventies/early eighties. In fact the first Indian restaurant to open in Ipswich was 'A Passage To India' in Fore Street. This was in 1991 some 30 years behind the likes of Birmingham, Coventry and London! They still have a blue plaque on their door to honour this.

Whilst the sleepy backward nature has changed in some respects it's fair to say not always for the better.

What with improved rail links (particularly with the East End of London) increased irresponsibility and extended use of all things 'sowshall meedia' crime has spiralled in recent times including gang and drug culture.

Whilst twattish chavs peddle their evil on the streets the council, in their wisdom continues to prioritise clamping down on normal folk merely looking for a portion of fried onions with their hot dogs.

Recently I walked back from a TV Smith (Adverts) gig at The Steam Boat Tavern in the Ipswich Dock area (about 2004). It was about a two mile walk and given my experiences of the town in the 1970s I thought nothing of it. To say the atmosphere was intimidating in some parts of the town is an understatement. In spite of the snow/ice I covered that distance like a performance enhanced David Bedford (one for the teenagers out there).

Aside Woolworths was a phenomenom. Not only did it have a pretty healthy record department complete with 49p bargain bin singles but also a range of stock which often toyed with the principle of copyright.

How could they get away with retailing a Winfield version of the three stripe football boot? At the time the Adidas Beckenbauer Super Boot was all the rage Woolies produced a very similar light green striped version at a fraction of the cost.

Similarly in Lasso they had an in-house Jeans brand that mimicked Levis and provided the masses with a viable cheap alternative lapped up by the rustics.

Pick and mix deserves a mention. Why was this concept ever acceptable without the perceived need for the use of gloves or shovels? The bare shit/piss stained hands of jammy faced brats caressing the confectionary was, if ever there was such a thing, a classic recipe for diarrhoea

Bold as brass those Winfield Boys.

Q8. True or false. Glam star Barry Blue's real name is Barry Brown?

1980. The Choice is Yours

VIII

The Grammar / Modern School Merger. 1978/1979

Nasty Nasty / Days of Change

This was a confusing time for me both academically and musically as by 1979 the Grammar school was merged with the Modern School and 'blossomed' into a High School.

Musically the Mod Revival had gained momentum in no large part due to the continuing success of The Jam and also Quadrophenia. Mod bands were springing up left right and centre and many were very talented (The Chords, Secret Affair, Purple Hearts, Squire, The Lambrettas). My single and album acquisitions reflected this but always alongside plenty of Punk/New Wave.

My dress sense also alternated. A move towards the tight Brucey hipsters, two tone Shelly Gibson Jam Shoes, Boating blazer and Mod T shirts. (see Jam Fan Club Chapter above).

On one occasion I was fully dressed up in the above and standing in WH Smith in Ipswich looking through a music mag when an Ipswich oik walked up to me crossword in hand and rudely barked 'oi minny mod. Selector single On My … '? Now The Selector were two tone not mod but was I going to correct this rustic oaf? I resorted to an abrupt ' Radio' and hurried off hiding my embarrassment.

As for the school merger. Initially the fifth year were left at the old Grammar School site. A year later we all convened at the old Modern School site and we were then officially a single site fully mis-functioning High School. The Modern/Grammar site divide was no more.

There followed an instant change of atmosphere. This spread and lead to the gradual decay of standards across the board, both staff and pupil alike. Forget skirts below the knee. A skirt vaguely flirting with the bottom of the arse cheeks was the most the school hierarchy could expect.

The writing was spread across the wall when the Grammar Head of English removed his son (Spindly) from a school environment he had been part of (and loved) for four years and placed him at the fee-paying College, sited less than a mile away, just short of his O level exams.

Teacher culture and diversity:
In the Grammar School days this amounted merely to a bit of unauthorised extra curricula 'teacher interaction 'between English and Art Teachers and a Combined Science and another English teacher' so to speak.

This was taken down a level or two following the merger with the Modern School largely courtesy of the two Boys Games Teachers (I will protect their identities and refer to them merely as X and Y). Suffice to say they took physical education to another depraved level.

Their attitude and actions were completely inappropriate.

One whilst married was (allegedly) in a relationship with a sixth former whilst the other was (allegedly) permanently on the prowl for girls from the fourth year upwards.

On one school skiing trip to Italy a female Games Teacher was allocated the task of guarding one girl's hotel room to ensure no unauthorised access was attempted by a certain Mr X.

To be honest my girlfriend probably didn't help the situation when one afternoon we decided to partake in some after school swimming in the outdoor pool. She didn't have any swimwear and so my classic (now very rare) green and blue Arsenal away shirt (1982) and knickers (hers not mine) was seen as the obvious Benny Hillesque style answer to the problem.

Needless to say this did not go unnoticed by Mr X who happened to be pool attending.

To be fair Mr X did act nobly on one occasion.

He was overseeing a mixed PE swimming lesson in the new Almond Tree lawn swimming pool at the former Grammar School site when a lad with learning difficulties allowed his dick to become dislodged out of the side of his Speedos.

He made no attempt to re-insert despite numerous requests, merely ignoring the predicament.

The girls were, naturally uncomfortable with a water bourn lazy lob protruding through the tight silken Speedos and thankfully Mr X took the necessary remedial action and poked it back in.

That was his only redeeming action of note. On reflection this could (under existing protocols) have landed him in hot water bearing in mind no stick was used to poke back the offending appendage.

Thuggery.
Up Against the Wall.
This was an unknown medium to the former Grammar fraternity.

The ex- Modern school thugs such as R.B., Yeti and Augie delighted in picking on the tougher elements of the former grammar school clientele.

I witnessed Steve A being mercilessly battered up against the wall of a portacabin classroom by a 'brave' group of these backward Suffolk neandertals for daring to like Elvis Costello and The Attractions rather than the faceless shite that they indulged in (Pink Floyd The Wall, Dire Straits etc etc). Undeterred we continued our musical journey and punk became increasingly influential.

I once saw Augie walking along a narrow path between classrooms and a keen academic chap complete with blazer, briefcase and tie was running up behind him desperate to get to his next lesson.

Augie glanced over his shoulder and just as the boy attempted to run past him he dropped his large black Adidas Sports holdall in front of the boy who went sprawling across the concrete path. A cruel calculated move albeit delivered to perfection.

*Interesting note re Pink Floyd/ The Wall. Floyd at the time (February 1979) arrived at the same London Studio where The Tom Robinson Band were recording. TRB were recording the single Bully For You and looking to resurrect their chart career. Allegedly members of Floyd walked in on the band as they were playing Bully For You. They liked the riff they heard.

A few weeks later Floyd released Another Brick In The Wall (complete with a multitude of double negatives to grab the attention of the uninitiated record buying public). To say the musical riffs and chorus sound remarkably similar to TRB's Bully For You is a major understatement. Make of that what you will.

For the record Bully For You stalled at number 68 in the chart. As for Another Brick In The Wall?

Not surprisingly Tom and Co remain rightfully miffed to this day.

Aside: Rock music is the only area where use of the double negative is a totally accepted medium. It is essentially part of rock folklore. How wrong would the likes of - I can't Get Any Satisfaction and The Modern World's I don't need anyone to tell me about the right and wrong, sound? The double negative is frequently purveyed in rock songs. It's never challenged being viewed almost as a rite of passage by those in the rock world.

As noted earlier I was dabbling in Fan Club matters and my annual subscription to all at Balmoral Drive in Woking was a given for the next two years. The rustic rocker dim-wits were not going to dissuade me.

Following the huge imapct of Going Underground and subsequent rock and pop award for single of the year I started to feel that The Jam were no longer 'my secret'. They were becoming overtly mainstream and hugely popular and for that illogical reason I relinquished my Jam Fan Club Membership at the end of 1980.

Around the same time I made tentative enquiries about Fan Clubs/Information Exchanges for less mainstream acts including The Dickies and UK Subs.

Both essentially second wave punk in terms of breaking onto the scene from 1979. I had got into The Dickies pre the commercial break through of Banana Splits having already acquired Give It Back,Silent Night and Paranoid in respective coloured vinyls and I had UK Subs records from Stranglehold onwards including Another Kind Of Blues their first album on deep blue vinyl.

I got a very Americanised reply from Los Angeles. California from The Dickies (complete with Banana Splits caricatures and Ipswitch noted on the envelope)! In fact it put me off a bit as it all seemed a bit Razamatazy.

The Subs letter was naturally a more localised downbeat affair with a letter from Sindy in Guildford and a PO Box address. Rather informal and not at all inspirational.

Neither option taken up.One too gimmicky the other too bland.

On a personal level the NME was bought on a weekly basis (trip to Ipswich necessary to acquire) and I trailed the ads within for Better Badges, Melandi, Modern Works and ACME Clothing for latest clothing, patches, badges and indeed records (including imports) etc.

Tuesday lunchtime. New chart day.
The uninitiated thought the chart countdown on a Sunday evening was the first reading. Wrong. This occurred on a Tuesday at about 12.40. Cue mass huddles around the tranny in the locker rooms. This was a time of great tension.

Where were the likes of The Jam, The Stranglers, The Clash, XTC? Why had David Watts only risen to number 25 in the chart despite three outings on Top of the Pops? Completely unfathomable.

- Britain's Number One!! Quite a way off for the Woking wonders at this stage but the snowball was steadily building.

Breaking news. School vinyl exposure!

The concept of playing your LP in a Music Lesson was muted as an idea by the teaching fraternity and it duly came to fruition. I snapped up the opportunity to expose the class (and Teacher Cruddster, an amalgam of Jeff Lynn and Gerry Rafferty) by default to three punk/new wave classics on three separate occasions.

I opened with V2 the second LP offering from The Vibrators on the Epic label (now viewed as one of the ultimate New Wave albums). Cruddster was unimpressed from the off with both the band name and vinyl offering.

In typically overindulged prog terms he dismissed it after the opening four tracks as three chord, three minute throw away rubbish. A relative compliment given his demeanour. And those tracks included the mighty Automatic Lover! I can still remember the distain etched across his face.

Undeterred two weeks later I produced my second offering- Dawn Of The Dickies, the second album from San Francisco's manic crazy Ramones inspired ensemble. Was I mad?

Bearing in mind Dickies tracks rarely lasted more than two minutes maximum the whole of side 1 was played. The girls in the class wanted to hear track one side 2… Nights in White Satin and The Cruddster grudgingly obliged. A bonus.

This speedy punked up version of the Moody Blues 'classic' met with derision from both The Cruddster and the girls in the class.

Needless to say he was as derogatory about The Dickies as he had been about The Vibrators but hey ho (let's go) I was pushing Punk music to the masses. In retrospect at least I hadn't risked The Dickies first album!

Amazingly no one else offered an album for dissection two weeks later. Could I risk another? You bet. How about The Jam Setting Sons?

I was confident that even The Cruddster would appreciate the musical ability of Paul, Bruce and Rick. They were consistently voted Guitarist, Bassist and Drummer of the year in the NME polls so what was the argument?

All Mod Cons was considered but the blatant swearing on Mr Clean early on side one made this implausible so Setting Sons it was. Surely this could not go wrong.

The problem was predicting how much of side 1 he would play? There was a dodgy lyric within Girl on the phone (track one side 1) which included the line ' my leg measurements and the size of my cock' but it was relatively garbled (so to speak) and I was confident he would not pick up on it. He didn't.

Tracks two and three Thick As Thieves and Private Hell were in anybody's opinion masterful Jam tracks. He would surely warm to this. If not the stylus would be duly relieved of its duties.

Unfortunately for me he appeared to be warming to it and track four was approaching, the imperious Little Boy Soldiers. I was beginning to think Cruddster was actually enjoying this offering? Contrary to previous form he was allowing this record to run and run.

I certainly had not anticipated this and a plan needed to be hatched and quickly The problem was that Little Boy Soldiers, one of the Jam's finest in my opinion, contained a whispered verse delivered by Mr Weller where he quotes (as clearly as The Members clear vinyl Sound of the Suburbs) ' the fuckin' lot but we don't feel bad'.As the track meandered on my mates looked at me gauging my stance. They knew what was coming.

I intimated that a correctly timed co-ordinated cough by all three of us was necessary to disguise the word but they either didn't understand or were revelling in my predicament. My poorly delivered isolated mis-timed cough failed to cut the mustard.

Cue jaw dropping across the class and a stare of Paddington proportions from The Cruddster.

Without delay he unceremoniously swept the stylus across the vinyl (Wasteland taking the brunt) in his haste to remove the offending disc and scornfully ordered me 'not to trouble anyone's ears with any further offerings'! As they say better to have tried and lost than not to have tried at all. Mission accomplished.

How else would those pupils (and a sad old crusty prog rocker) have heard album tracks from the likes of The Vibrators, The Dickies and The Jam? From a school perspective it was a brave, and in hindsight, ill-judged move. They (not surprisingly) were oblivious to the ethos of the burgeoning punk scene at the time. I'd like to think I opened their eyes and ears.

I suppose they were expecting more uptake from the girls in the class (bit of Dire Straits, bit of Abba, bit of David Soul) or possibly a bit of heavy metal from the uninitiated straight guys (Aerosmith, Meat Loaf, Def Leppard) or even a bit of turgid prog rock (Stackridge, Uriah Heep) that would have delighted The Crudster but what they got were three cutting edge New Wave/Mod classics. Unfortunately Cruddster's lack of appreciation culminating in that fateful Weller outburst effectively terminated the whole concept and I bear full responsibility for this.

Around this time our English teacher Mrs S had a son who had recently secured a show on the local radio station Radio Orwell. One day she came in and said that her son didn't have many requests for that evening's show and he needed some suggestions.

Unlike the majority of the class who put forward standard chart requests we opted for Because You're Frightened, the opening track from Magazine's excellent new album The Correct Use Of Soap. It was the only track selected that night with Tom stating that some of the pupils at Pills High felt that Magazine's output was seriously underrated....... my quote!

The girls in the class naturally felt unfairly overlooked. Why had a deaf ear been turned to their suggestions?

Tom clearly had a bit of class and was not turned on by the chart fodder and dirge rock of the time.

Whilst on the subject of The Correct Use Of Soap' there was a pretty average track on it called Philadelphia. This track had the line 'maybe it's right to be nervous now' which was repeated after each chorus.

At exam times when we were queuing up outside the St Michael's Rooms awaiting entry to take the exam I would be continually chanting 'Maybe it's right to be nervous now'.

Given my limited academic abilities, if anyone should have been apprehensive in this scenario it should have been me. I was not popular given the tense atmosphere and it incensed all around me!

When I bumped into Roots at a UK Subs gig at The Lewes Con Club in November 2018 some 38 years later this was one of the first things he reminded me of!

Happy days.

The Rough Book.

Now here was a concept of the time!

This was essentially a small A5 sized exercise book which was used in conjunction with your chosen subjects for jotting down notes and useful information presumably to help you with your homework.

In many respects it was a indication of standing. You were 'judged' by your rough book, or at least the cover of it. These books would always have pride of place on your desk in every lesson and as such depicted your allegiences.

In that respect they played an important role.

The 'squares' didn't view them this way and would use these in a sensible structured manner (in line with teacher guidance) for Home Work related info plus time tables, Pythagoras' theorems, and important French/ German translation materials etc etc. A perfectly formed The Jam spray logo across the cover wouldn't have entered their minds.

Others (me included) were far more concerned with what went on the cover rather than with what went into the book and hours were spent adorning with authentic Punk logos of the time. Mine featured The Jam, Cuddly Toys, Classix Nouveaux etc.

Undeniably I spent far more time attending to my Rough Book cover than the ramblings of the teachers which also undeniably contributed to some of my homework and exam performances. Results such as my Physics Multiple choice test in 1980 (a part of my mock O level exam) where I obtained a score of 7 out of 50 prompted the teacher to remark, in front of the class. that one of the characters in the PG Tips Tea adverts would have achieved a higher mark than me.

This was harsh and tough to take but my rough book cover was distinction material.

The guilty Rough Book from 1982. Note not only was Bill responsible for the excellent Robot's Dance sketch (which was cool) he also added the Haircut 100 logo as a joke. They were not a band I was remotely interested in. Indeed when they played Norwich in 1982 and my girlfriend was attending I nobly/selfishly/sensibly refused her request for attendance.

The Rebels

It had to happen. First muted in 1979, our Punk years, we had to create a band and live the dream. Naturally we had to be a three piece so step forward Colin L and Andy P.

I take full responsibility for the totally unoriginal name.

Rebels? Let's get this straight. We hardly resided in the squats of Brixton. It was smug middle- class backgrounds all round with everything on a plate for us. What did we have to rebel over? At worst forced wholemeal bread over the beloved Sunblest.

I wrote two tracks School Days and Rush Hour Traffic (the latter inspired by the Bruce Foxton 'classic' London Traffic Side One track 2 This is The Modern World).It was essentially me singing lead vocals backed by Colin L on Premier drums.

I had not acquired a guitar yet and Andy P had not acquired a bass at this stage. He was there purely for his clean good looks which bore a vague resemblance to John Taylor of Duran Duran who admittedly hadn't exploded onto the scene yet. We thought this would help garner us some female support. Andy had an unhealthy liking for Peter Frampton and the LP Frampton Comes Alive. It took some doing but we eventually knocked this firmly out of his system by goading him with our version of the album title- Frampton Drops Dead.

Audaciously T shirts were produced which read THE REBELS - Step, Andy, Colin. Even the white Ariel font on black shirt was mundane. To say the tracks were crude is being extremely generous. They were worse than that. Far worse.

To make matters worse, following an initial enquiry, I naively sent a rudimentary recording on a Scotch C60 cassette of the two tracks to Polydor. Why that label is anyone's guess!

Whilst the first letter back was encouraging 'we would be delighted to hear your compositions (they hadn't heard the product yet) the second was blunt, and rightfully to the point. It read along the lines of

Dear Steve (Step not deemed cool enough at this point)

Thank you for the submission of your tape. Unfortunately it is not the kind of thing we are looking for at this stage blah,blah,blah. Fully and totally justified. Who did we think we were?

In essence what they were saying was 'Stop wasting our time with this crap. Fuck off'. I was disappointed.

I wanted us to be on the same label as The Jam but the response was not unexpected. Other labels would beckon (surely)!

Following this set back we approached RAW Records, an independent company based in Cambridge who, worryingly without listening to the tape agreed to press up 500 copies for £200. No picture sleeves.

Surely we should have been suspicious of such a carefree, non-vetted attitude towards our works. Were they really interested in our career progression or just a quick buck?

With no option of picture sleeve my interest waned. Added to this could we really raise £200? The concept of cash pledging was years away and we didn't have enough friends for pledge support (a bit like me with this book). Both of the tracks submitted were utter crap, If ever a Double B Side was warranted this was surely it. A double B Side? We missed a trick there. We could have been the first. What an anarchic Punk concept.

Credit where credit's due. RAW were one of the up and coming independent labels of the time and lasted for many years (The Users were on the label) so at least it was a pretty cool company to approach from our perspective.

Ideas above our station was a huge understatement. Shockingly embarrassing on reflection but we were young. The seeds, however, had been sown and just over a year later the three of us together with Bill decided we should form a proper Band (to rival the Monty Python Boys prog rock outfit Avalon).

We were by now Post Punk. The name chosen reflected this. We emerged as Danzig. Bleak, very bleak.

The line up was:

Step T lead vocals and occasional Jedson (Telecaster copy) Guitar

Bill W Bass (Burns) and backing vocals. Principle songwriter.

Andy P lead guitar and backing vocals and pull the chicks looks

Colin L Premier Drums

Bill's Burns bass was pretty cool and was worn in a Simenonesque low slung style. Andy had a rudimentary guitar and myself the legendary Jedson Telecaster (Strummeresque) copy. Colin was the king pin with his Premier drum kit as he was already plying his trade in his dad's jazz ensemble. Note one consideration for a band name was 'Cheap Guitars and Premier Drums'. Whilst accurate it was deemed too punky as we were now on the Joy Division trail.

The Jedson acquisition. An explanation.

For weeks I was combing the pages of The East Anglian Daily Times as on a Thursday the second hand musical instruments section appeared. Naturally as a student I had limited finances and as usual there was the infuriating parental logic to deal with.

Three years before I remember the experience of trying to buy a second hand train set with Geoffrey. My square phase. Again it was sourced via The EADT (that's what the locals refer to it as) and we ended up in some dodgy house in Stowmarket with a guy trying to convince us that his unusual triple 000 gauge (we were after the standard 00 gauge) set was unique particularly as the engine was ' The Duchess Of Montrose'. I was not convinced and nor was Geoffrey.

Strangely enough watching an episode of The Antiques Trail tonight the experts visited The Brighton Toy and Railway Museum (opposite the famous Prince Albert Pub) and they were working on a model train in the workshop which was none other than the Duchess Of Montrose!

No purchase resulted and I ended up with a new standard Hornby 00 gauge weeks later. The inexplicably sad fad lasted about three months. Three months of my life I could never retrieve.

The Jedson.

Back to that Thursday when I spotted an ad that listed ' Fender Telecaster Copy plus combi amp £40'. I was on the phone in flash.

It was located in a village called Henly which was about three miles from

Coddenham. A date was pencilled in and myself and Geoffrey duly arrived. The vendor was about 18 years old with cascading permy brown hair. He demonstrated a few licks on the guitar and Geoffrey looked suitably bemused. What's wrong with a train set Steve?

At one point the guy said 'you can play chill out music like this' (bluesy strumming followed) 'or of course if you want to Quo it up a bit you can play this' (volume whacked up on the combi amp). Cue Geoffrey clutching his ears cartoon style and raising his eyes to the ceiling.

The Quo reference did cast an element of doubt into my mind (was this a first tentative move towards Prog Rock) but as Joe Strummer used a Fender Telecaster it was effectively as good as sold to me before I even got there. If it was good enough for Joe it was good enough for me.

Guitar lessons were hastily arranged in 'Stumaarkt', (Stowmarket) which was a small town near to where John Peel resided, in a room above a large Co Op Department Store.

The tutor looked like that guy out of Magpie Tommy Boyd. The lessons were a bit turgid. There were three of us pupils all strumming out nylon stringed acoustics. After a few weeks Tommy said we could suggest a song to play to the following week.

I brought my In The City Song Book with a view to playing the title track. Despite having a limited chord structure I couldn't manage it and instead all we got was Tommy's bluesy version. It remains to this day the worst rendition of the track that I have ever heard.

After a few weeks I gave up. The one positive coming from the lesson experience was the acquisition of both Slade In Flame and Slade Nobody's Fools LPs for £2.99 a piece courtesy of the Co Op department store below and the sale within their music section which was sited adjacent to the electrical items. Every cloud.

Danzig band rehearsals commenced one Saturday morning in the lounge of Bill's parent's end terrace house in Station Road Framlingham. Bill had written two good songs Bleak House and Danzig and we did a few obscure covers Novelty by Joy Division, Innocent Man by The Jam (A Brucie B side of News Of The World) and Subway Song by the Cure. Not wanting to miss on any future song writing royalties I contributed one vaguely plausible track Strong Words. In song writing terms I was definitely Foxton. Bill was Weller.

The rehearsals continued and we fine-tuned our act. A gig was arranged for the youth club based Shalom Centre which adjoined the High School.

It was deemed that my vocal range was not varied enough to cover Subway

Song or Novelty so we arranged for Bill's brother Ollie to be guest vocalist on those tracks. On Novelty I played a one string guitar solo which was rightfully mocked by the Avalon boys on the night of the gig.

For the gig we all dressed in army surplus gear. Bill was heavily influenced by Warsaw/Joy Division at the time and this was reflected in his original compositions. Our range of cover versions was on the other hand quite varied. No Smoke On the Water for us!

A reasonable crowd materialised and at the end of the set an encore was demanded! This had not been anticipated. We were ready to depart and not having any more songs repeated one of our originals. Even the Avalon boys seemed quite impressed (although not with my 'guitar solo).

Call it musical differences but the fact was that Ollie was the spitting image of Bono (he even starred in an early U2 single video), had a wide vocal range and a great stage presence all added up to one thing. My days were numbered.

Musical differences could not be blamed.

I opted out and immediately formed National Grid And The Pylons with Roots and Pete T (a Tubeway Army obsessive who wore black shirts with white ties). This amounted to one rehearsal at Earl Soham Village Hall. The next village along from Ed Sheeran's Framsden.

In OMD style it was me on rudimentary rhythm guitar Roots on bass and Pete T on basic Moog synthesiser. We produced one fairground style instrumental similar to Magazine's Great Beautician In The Sky but with no vocals and nowhere near as good.

It was our only attempt. We subsequently folded.

In The Monks terminology it was a case of Nice Name Shame About The Output.

To be fair without me Danzig went from strength to strength playing school discos and the alternative Flying Stilton Club, a youth club style arrangement run by The Reverend Peck in conjunction with the Avalon boys which took place on a monthly basis in Earl Soham Church Hall.

Although this arrived in the later sixth form years it's worth elaborating on at this point.

To be fair it was ahead of its time. It gave local school acts the chance to play live in front of a relatively big 5th year/6th form crowd. In true early 1980s fashion they had a bit of alternative comedy and of course the obligatory disco. Obviously no alcohol. The classic 0.1% Top Deck Shandy or Limeade And Lager were the best you would get.

Strangely enough the atmosphere was far more relaxed than the regimented school discos. This was because of rather than in spite of the fact that it was run by a Reverend.

Two of his sons were in the prog rock outfit Avalon (they were the alright ones) and let's just say anything went with regards to their social lives. Strangely one had gained God like status amongst his peers by boasting that he 'couldn't fit his prick inside the inner of a toilet roll'. He also had a beard at 15 years old which was a godsend for those in the rocker world.

The true prick in Avalon was one Clive B. A typical Prog Rock self-indulgent smart arsed Monty Python infused jerk and as boring as twats who give you the details of their dreams. He ticked all the boxes. The wrong ones.

He hated the Jam and on one occasion when looking at the back cover of The Jam's The Gift he declared 'I hate Weller, only he would be cool enough to write Roll the Credits on an album sleeve'. That was the nearest he got to a compliment. He was one who didn't like change and would never admit to the importance of Punk. We didn't expect him to.

On another occasion he really riled me when I changed my hair style from spiked centre parting to a bouffant plummy coloured Classix Nouveaux style side parting. I was standing in the school bus queue when he came up to me and said ' shame about the hair Step. With the old style you didn't half look like Bruce Foxton'.

He may have been winding me up, maybe not but my image was evolving and whilst Brucey was a great bass player a fashion ikon he was not. If he had said Paul Weller that would have been a different matter and very difficult to stomach.

At this point I need to reflect on the subject of hairstyles. Clearly my Dave Hill yob bob was not suitable in these aspiring Punk/Mod/New Romantic days. As luck would have it a new Salon opened about three miles from Coddenham. I give you Mark's.

Sid experimented first and opted for a punky spike cut which looked ridiculous on return having been pummelled by his full face helmet (which he wore on his Motorbecaine). A parent lift was my only option and worse than this the parent sat in with me.

In those days the done thing was to take a picture of your favourite music ikon and demand a cut that would transform you into rock star status. Foxton worked quite well for me as even Mark could handle a centre parting.

As noted above in the early 1980s the look changed and a picture of Classix Nouveaux guitarist Garry Steadman accompanied me to Mark's. More of a style challenge this one and difficult to clear with the parents but manage it I did. For a short period Mark was a legend.

In the 70s/early 80s there was a tribal allegiance to your chosen music genre and to be fair no matter what your chosen genre was you took pride in your image and dressed accordingly to impress your peers. Contrast this with today's lazy chav generation for whom three quarter length tracky bottoms worn with socks and sliders or jeans with the arse hanging below the knee are perceived as cool and cutting edge. I give up.

ASIDE 1:

Why do young British female 'fans' annually declare,(often on placards), their undying love for British tennis players such as Liam Brody (in 2015) following a first round Wimbledon win when the day before they weren't even aware of their existence?

Q9 Place the following bands with their town/city of origin.

The Vapors	The Icicle Works
Merton Parkas	Magazine
Skids	XTC

ASIDE 2:

Why does the simple task of inserting a duvet into a double duvet cover become a logistical challenge comparible to one of Ted Rodgers' Three, Two. One riddles after a couple of Stellas?

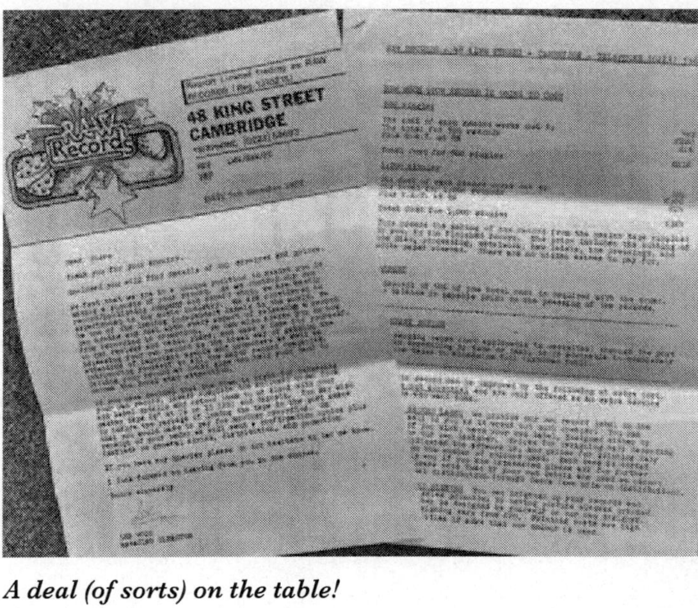
Records
48 KING STREET
CAMBRIDGE

A deal (of sorts) on the table!

My gig baptism

Jam Fan club goodies

IX

The Gigs Begin.

I'm In Love With a Rock 'n Roll World/ Time For Action.

Live football and music were extremely limited on the TV screens in the 1970s. As noted FA Cup Final, England V Scotland and the odd European Cup Final plus Top Of The Pops and The Old Grey Whistle Test were the main offerings. TOGWT at the time was introduced by 'whispering Bob Harris' Mr Prog Rock himself. Luckily it screened too late for most of us to be subjected to this bland brainwashing.

He would introduce the show in dulcet tones at about 11.00pm and a crusty bearded band would open up. At the end of the track Bob would swing round on his office style chair and whisper something along the lines of 'what a wonderful way to open the show there with that intriguing offering from Stackridge. How can we possibly follow that'?

Preferably with the detonation of a pre-laid ton of TNT planted discretely around the studio. It was dire, uninspiring, unimaginative, shit.

By default Top Of The Pops was the only accessible option for us from a band exposure point of view. This plus occasional performances by bands on Tiswas (The Jam suffered an unholy soaking in the cage with Weller still continuing to radiate cool even with hair lank with shaving foam) and occasionally Swap Shop (Icicle Works and Time UK amongst others).

Let's confirm at this point that The Jam were very much a Tiswas band rather than a Multi Coloured Swap Shop band. It was the classic Blue Peter / Magpie scenario.

Then there was Marc. A show introduced by fading glam star Marc Bolan. This premiered numerous punk bands including The Jam and The Damned. Sadly this was the last offering from Marc as he died in a car crash halfway through the airing of the series. The Jam performed All Around The World live on that show and it famously concluded with Rick somehow losing control of his drum sticks as the track came to a chaotic end leaving him looking totally bemused.

Who could forget Cheggars Plays Pop! Hosted by the cheesy Keith Chegwin (of Brown Sauce I Wanna Be a Winner fame) this show actually highlighted a number of good bands including Classix Nouveaux playing Because You're

Young, the follow up to the hit Is It A Dream. Despite this exposure it stalled just outside the chart at 41. The swaying 10 year old kids in the TV studio were clearly not convinced although the track was far better than its predecessor.

With the advent of the unruly Channel 4 in the early 1980s music on TV took a turn for the better with The Tube and live performances from cutting edge bands. The Jam opened the series with their final ever TV showing which added up to a hapless pre gig interview from Muriel Grey followed by a classic 30 minute performance from 'the best band in the f*****g world! Toy Dolls (an act local to the studio) were also on that night which was appropriate given that Olga was (and still is) a huge Jam fan.

Football : Up to now my physical attendance at live footy had been limited (by the parental police) to Ipswich reserve matches due to the perceived spectre of hooliganism and I clearly remember the game V the Chelsea stiffs where a Chelsea player with a hairstyle akin to flailing loose banana skins, ran the show. That was one Clive Walker who remained little more than a bit-part player doing little outside of Stamford Bridge and to add insult to injury is now sans skins..

By 1979 a degree of trust was being shown towards me by my parents and Big Boy Ipswich matches became a viable option. One problem – I hated Ipswich. They were so bloody good. Why did this hatred manifest itself in me?

The impact of the 1978 FA Cup final should obviously not be overlooked but I hated them well before then. They were a small- time country club followed by a bunch of delusional farm labourers who perceived London as being in a different universe. Credit where credit's due the away following were arguably the only people in the town who ventured out of Suffolk.

Looking back now this was extremely harsh and smacked of jealousy.

In Bobby Robson they had a manager clearly ahead of his time and the first to take the bold step to bring in foreign talent such as Muhren and Thysen long before the so called big boys plucked up the courage (and excessive cash) to do so.

For once Ipswich was leading the way. At least the club was. Eventually others would follow.

That said I detested them and as a result my initial outings to Portman Road involved standing in the away section in the notorious North Stand cheering on all the away teams (Spurs excepted) including the likes of Aston Villa, Liverpool (Saw Rush's debut?) Everton, Derby County (Franny Lee's last appearance when he netted two in a 6-2 away win) even Man Utd (how times have changed) and of course The Gooners, who never seemed to win there.

In 1983 I took my then girlfriend (now wife) to watch Arsenal's annual defeat to 'Towen'. As expected the Gooners lost 2-1.

The Charlie Nicholas consolation was not witnessed by me as I was beneath the North Stand terracing comforting Juliet who had managed to lose a shoe in the baying masses above. No appreciation for anything these girls and a Charlie Nic goal missed as a result.

Football coverage in those days essentially amounted to Match Of The Day on BBC1 (two match highlights) and the localised version on ITV on Sunday (Big Match for London, Star Soccer for Midlands, Match Of The Week for East Anglia etc). Strangely The Big Match screened on the Saturday.

Re runs are currently being shown on ITV4 (Big Match revisited) and the contrast with today's offerings are stark. The stanchion exposure however is fantastic. A blast from the past.

On one episode of Big Match revisited an interview was shown of two Man Utd players post match (Greenhoff and Pearson from memory). Resplendent in the engorged lapelled jackets , flapping collared shirts and kite sized tie knots. The players supped Skol from tins and chatted to the interviewer in the stadium's kitchen with the caretaker wiping the formica kitchen units down in full view of the camera. He was actually adjacent to the players in his overalls. Unbelievable.

On another occasion we were treated to Arsenal V Spurs from 1975. The first league game for two years for Arsenal's keeper Geoff Barnett (my last recollection of him for me being in the disastrous 1972 FA Cup Final defeat to Leeds- 'Clarke one nil' see below).

Geoff Barnett was the epitome of the ventriloquist Keith Harris. Orville was not on his arm in the Spurs game but he might as well have been such was the lack of agility in the performance of the man in this match and his on-going goalkeeping in general. In spite of this we still managed to win one nil . The commentators at the time were legendary (at least some of them).

Brian Moore was as confused then as he was in his latter years, Hugh Johns (Huge Ones the hilarious nickname at the time) was notoriously biased towards the Midlands clubs and Gerry Harrison was the genial East Anglian commentator covering the delights of Towen, Naaarwich, Luton, Colchester, Peterborough and Cambridge. Boy we were spoilt.

The stand out, however, was undoubtedly the BBC's David Coleman.

Minimalistic in approach he remains the greatest exponent of football commentary there has ever been. 'Porterfield , one nil'. Pure genius. The recent advent of all things politically correct and in particular female on the BBC is galling and Vicky Sparks is a prime example. A bit of Coleman research would not go amiss. Less is more.

The rise and rapid fall of 606.

Another example of how the BBC have ruined a great idea/show.

The man behind the original offering was the legendary Danny Baker and in its infancy it was a brilliant show due largely to the genial spontaneous natural wit and repartee of Danny. In the eyes of the BBC he took certain matters too far and after a few glorious years he was axed.

The replacement was no other than disgraced politician David Mellor. This was akin to a lord talking down to his serfs. Patronisation at its worst.

This however is nothing compared to the levels it has fallen to now with the dim- witted Robbie Savage partnering Mr Controversial Chris Sutton. It's so forced. Most people debate whether Shrewsbury is pronounced Shrew or Shrow? Not our Robbie. He calls them Shewsby.

THE FIRST GIG (barring Lenny Henry at The Spa Pavilion Felixstowe) - The day it all started.

The Clash + Kidz Next Door + Lew Lewis

Ipswich Gaumont 14th January 1980

At the end of 1979 The Clash released what has become widely regarded as one of the most respected albums of the 80s. Work that one out. I didn't buy it at the time. My mate Bill did and we swapped temporarily in 1979 to compare and contrast (as you do at school) this album with my favourite Jam album (also from 1979) Setting Sons.

Undoubtedly both are/were classics but The Clash's offering gave a varied adventurous breadth of music whereas the Jam's was , in comparison, more one dimensional (a bit harsh I know) and ultimately for many represented the classic Jam sound. Their experimental phase came with their next album Sound Affects in 1980.

At the end of 1979 and early 1980 The Clash embarked on their 16 Tons Tour in support of London Calling and joy of joy Ipswich Gaumont was pencilled in for January 14th 1980.

This was a major surprise given the raft of shite that frequently appeared at The Gaumont (Darts, Showaddywaddy, Baron Knights plus heavy metal of the likes of Quo/Rory Gallagher/Sabbath/Megadeth etc).

Amazingly permission was granted by my parents for attendance for myself, Bill and my brother. It was the night that kicked it all off!

It was a bitterly cold night. We arrived early. Mistake number one - being dropped off by my parents into a mass of Punks in the full neon glare of the Gaumont entrance steps. Why could they have not dropped us in a quiet seedy, side street and allowed us to casually saunter in. Not cool. We were full of anticipation.

What I was wearing I dread to think but the Ipswich Punks were out in force with their displays of Mohican haircuts cut off leather jackets etc and all ready to gob (still trendy?) on the bands. Good old Ipswich. Never at any stage were they cutting edge. Apparently they retail 'compooters' in Ipswich now.

Mistake number two. Seats in the circle (albeit to the front) which on reflection, for a relatively short 16 year old, probably wasn't a bad thing.

Aside. A lesson learnt.

In 2018 I was slow off the mark re Weller tickets for The Brighton Centre and eventually sourced from the Weller forum albeit in the upper tier. I had to buy two so looked to sell my spare outside the venue.

One dodgy character offered me a 'Pony'. I declined without hesitation. I had no intention of trading for a term of which I had no understanding but would obviously be weighted heavily in his favour. I later sold for face value to a normal punter. My conscience was clear.

I wanted to access the stalls so in the build up to the gig I took it upon myself to create a road crew style lanyard.

This creation served to potentially allow me to forego my distant seat in clouds for a place in the mosh pit at this Weller gig. An air of confidence is a necessity. I approached the steward on the door to the stalls and marched purposefully forward pointing casually to the swinging lanyard. I was welcomed in.

Unfortunately at The Brighton Centre this scenario has to be repeated regularly according to how many beers you want as every time you pop to the bar for a pint you have to leave the stalls area, I had to stick to the same doors/steward to ensure repeat entry. He merely acknowledged my perceived 'importance' as I came and went.

Back to January 1980 and the Ipswich Gaumont .

Support came from Lew Lewis followed by Kidz Next Door (Jimmy Pursey's brother on lead vocals and ICF Punk/Mod nutter Grant Fleming on bass). The latter were a mixture of New Wave/Mod. They were good but to be honest, being the first live band that I had ever witnessed The Grumble

Weeds would probably have won me over.

Then came THE CLASH playing a blistering set including classics from the first two albums (to the demand of the baying spitting Ipswich Punx) and a cross section from London Calling. I was in awe of them. Transfixed.

The stalls below were a mass of moshing bodies and sporadic violence broke out. To be honest I was actually quite relieved to be above all of this mahem. At one point Strummer picked on an Ipswich moron and made him look a total twat for his persistent gobbing. The Ipswich Punks were totally unaware that this was no longer Punk gig behavior.

After the gig we took steps to loiter around the stage door at the rear and after twenty minutes all of the band bar Topper (who probably had other priorities!) appeared for a chat and they seemed genuinely engaged and interested in our comments. Sadly I didn't have the foresight to get anything signed.

How we swung this with the parental pick up scenario I have no idea. These were the days long before mobile phones so we probably lied about what time the gig would end to allow for a bit of hero worship!

Either way this capped a memorable night which lives long in the memory.

Sadly the feeling was obviously not mutual as The Clash never saw fit to return to return to planet Bumpkin. Who can blame them.

On the same subject apart from The Manor Ballroom in 1977 THE JAM never played Ipswich again. In 1980 (14th Nov) they were pencilled in for The Ipswich Gaumont but it was cancelled, probably for the reasons noted above. So near yet so far for me.

For the record I should be eternally grateful that this was my first exposure to live music. Although my brother Sid was also in attendance his first gig had been a few months prior to this at The Corn Exchange Ipswich. He was exposed to the rock dinosaur Rory Gallagher! (Whispering Bob would have been proud of you Sid).

Further isolated gigs of note followed 1980/1983

Adam And The Ants + Gods Toys

12th December 1980 Ipswich Gaumont. Gods Toys were excellent effectively setting a standard that The Ants would always struggle to match. Soon after this show (I think after The Toys home town Coventry gig) and following despicable treatment from The Ants (no sound checks etc) they were dropped from the tour.

Gods Toys performance in Ipswich remains clear in my memory. Adam and The Ants had just broken commercially and as a result there were quite a lot of teeny girls in the crowd. I remember little about them other than the twin drummers and ex Vibrator Gary Tibbs on bass.

Classix Nouveaux + Cuddly Toys West Runton Pavilion Cromer
16th April 1982
Four weeks prior to this our school organised a day trip to London's West End (for what reason a I cannot remember). We ended up in Oxford Street and alighted at The Dominion Theatre, just past the Virgin Megastore at the crossing with Charing Cross Road. The posters in the window were for the Classix Nouveaux La Verite Tour with support from Cuddly Toys.

In 1980/81 I had become gripped by the Classix Nouveaux bug having acquired the Guilty single from Bridget L J's parents Newsagent shop in Framlingham for 50p!

I had acquired all their singles, debut album Night People and they had just broken big with the lacklustre single release Is It A Dream (Isn't This Shit a more accurate title) and the second album La Veritie had also been acquired.

Here I was in The Dominion Theatre with this tempting spectacle before me. A decision was made. The gig was on 17th April. Parental negotiation was clearly needed for a gig/location of this magnitude but I had to attend.

NO CHANCE!

This was never gonna happen but an alternative was offered. The night before they were playing as a warm up show the intimate venue The Pavilion way out in West Runton Naaaarfuk and my parents were up for running me and Bill out there and killing a few hours before returning home.

This was a very generous offer given the distances involved and the need for them to hang around the desolate village of Cromer for 4+ hours whilst we attended what was a venue of legendary status. Snap it up we did.

Unbeknown to us at the time bands of varying magnitudes were playing this small,remote, isolated venue purely for that reason (Pistols, Damned, Jam, XTC, Clash, Adverts etc).

It was so unspectacular and remote the critical music press were disinclined to attend.

It was hence used by many bands as a warm up venue prior to the playing of the more high profile venues such as The Dominion, The Rainbow or The Hammersmith Palais.

So on the night of 16th April 1982 whilst my parents killed four hours in a restaurant in Cromer we enjoyed the rural delights of Classix Nouveaux at West Runton Pavilion.

Support was from Cuddly Toys. Albeit the Mk 2 version of this band they still stood out as a very competent outfit with lead singer Sean Purcell goading the still punk based crowd who were looking for tracks from Guillotine Theatre rather than the follow up Trials & Crosses which had seen the band move more towards a commercial new romantic style sound. They were excellent. Then came Classix Nouveaux.

What a stage presence the bald glowering Sal Solo had and the band were fine tuned in their musical artistry which was a kind of synth guitar sound backed by BP Hurding on octagonal electronic drums. The small dark venue augmented the atmosphere.

For the first time gig merch was acquired in the form of a Classix Nouveaux T shirt and associated badges. I have never looked back in this respect. Strangely I didn't buy any Cuddly Toys stuff (possibly due to limited finances) but this followed soon after in the form of both album releases and the hunting down of previous singles. The merch affliction remains uncured.

GIGS THAT DIDN'T HAPPEN 1

Soon after this 999 and The Vibrators were to share the bill for two consecutive nights at The Electric Ballroom in Camden Town. The perfect gig at a classic London venue.

Amazingly parental allowance was granted for me to go with Bill and stay with his friend Francis The Punk in Clapham, by the Common .

We were to attend the 999/Vibrators gig on the Saturday night having travelled up that morning.

999 had recently released The Biggest Prize In Sport LP (following on from 999 and Separates) and The Vibrators had already provided us with Pure Mania and the classic New Wave LP V2. Guilty was the latest LP offering.

I was picked up by Bill's parents with Bill sporting his newly acquired white bondage trousers with black zips which he paraded in front of my parents to their utter disdain.

No such gear for me.

I had spent the previous month feverishly sewing a variety of zips onto some old drain pipe cords , the ones that my mum had applied her home made Slade and Sweet felt patches to the front pockets back in the mid 70s.

Mine were authentic punk in the true sense of the word in that they were recycled, old and vaguely drainpipe but they were embarrassing nonetheless.

Bill spun me a story that Francis's family were from Bulgaria.

His dad's name was Brian (true) but he stressed that it was rude to not address a Bulgarian without use of both first and second names.

His surname apparently was Lifeof.

Naturally being completely oblivious to Monty Python 'wit' I didn't twig and a look of utter bewilderment and confusion crossed his face when I boldly ventured 'Nice to meet you Brian Lifeof'. Cue Francis and Bill pissing themselves uncontrollably on the front door steps. Luckily the dad saw the funny side and followed suit.

Unfortunately Francis was suffering from a full blown sheets of snot style cold and it was evident he would be in no state to attend the gig.

We being timid country boys did not have the front to go it alone down to The Electric Ballroom in Camden (no punk ethos shown here then) and as a result we didn't attend . I still bitterly regret our lack of adventure.

I was left mightily impressed by Francis when the following day he vaulted over the Clapham Underground ticket barriers to the applause of two American tourists to avoid the fare.

He was undeniably punk and could obviously shake off a cold.

Although great credit has to go to my parents in respect of The Clash and Classix gigs noted above nothing could have prepared me for the ultimate gig snub.

This was the one gig that I simply had to attend.

GIGS THAT DIDN'T HAPPEN II

The Jam Beat Surrender Tour

Thursday December 2nd 1982.

Wembley Arena.

Forget 999 and The Vibrators that was nothing in comparison to this no show.

In October 1982 the announcement was made in the music press that THE JAM were to split in December.

I was on the school football tour to Devon at the time and this was the shock news that confronted me in the NME that I purchased for the long journey home. Fellow members of the team were merciless in their ridiculing.

When I arrived back at school people were approaching me in the common room to see if I needed counselling and asking how I would cope!

I hadn't even managed to see them live!

A plan (ill thought) was hatched and naturally endorsed by Bill.

A five day stint at Wembley Arena was included on the Beat Surrender Tour. This was the closest they would get to Ipswich (of course) so I wrote off to good old Harvey Goldsmith (without prior consultation with the parents) and successfully obtained a pair of £5 tickets for Thursday 2nd December. Once the tickets arrived the subject was broached with the parents.

Minor details such as how we would get there, how would we get across London to the outlands of Wembley and more importantly how would we get back to Liverpool St Station before the last milk train to Ipswich had not been considered but were deemed by myself and Bill as not insurmountable. Unfortunately, for my parents they were.

What I had failed to allow for was the perceived importance of a MOCK History A level which I was due to sit the next day. The parents were not going to budge on this one. This would have been reasonably understandable for the real thing but for a mock? For fuck's sake!

Needless to say I had to return the tickets and I never got to see - ' The greatest band in the whole f*****g World'. I was devastated.

What made it even worse was that Barry M (aka Stoat and one of the Monty python loving, progressive rock bores in the year above) had a ticket and attended. He came up to me jauntily the next day looked me in the eye and said ' I absolutely detest The Jam and all that they stand for but I have to admit that was the most mind blowing gig I have ever attended'.

I could, and indeed should, have decked him but I'm not like that.

At this point I shamefully have to admit that I never forgave my father for denying me the opportunity to see The Jam. Sadly he died last year after a long battle with dementia. I am still finding it very hard to forgive him!

I continued to follow the fortunes of Bruce and Rick after the demise of The Jam (and naturally Weller / The Style Council) but the best band in the UK were officially no more.

Bruce released four singles and an album up to 1984 plus one for his new label Harvest in 1986. Rick's Time UK three singles.

Paul Weller: A Man of Great Promise

Tired of the limitations of a three piece band and even more tired of the mindless Jam Army who gave short shrift to support acts, and continually caused violence at the gigs Weller took the brave decision to call time on the band in October 1982 and the last gig was played on December 11th in Brighton.

At the time Weller could have released a fart on vinyl and The Jam hoards would have snapped up the 7" single and followed it up with the purchase of the 12" extended mega mix. Quite rightly he had had enough.

Just looking at some of the titles on the last album The Gift really should have left no-one surprised when he announced the split. Running On The Spot shows how he felt about The Jam and its following as did Ghosts, The Gift and Happy Together.

They could all be broadly aimed at the knuckle headed Jam Army, their disrespect of support acts and lack of musical awareness/adventure. Essentially they got what they deserved and unfortunately buggered it up for the rest of us.

He was sick of the dim football crowd style mentality of crowds at Jam gigs. He had the courage of his convictions and went down a more soulful path with The Style Council (to the horror of many a Jam fan) and then a completely varied path with his subsequent solo projects.

Initial Style Council singles included the first Speak Like A Child (positively jaunty in comparison to The Jam), and classics followed in the shape of Long Hot Summer. Shout To The Top, My Ever Changing Moods, Promised Land etc. With Long Hot Summer he outraged many a Jam fan when the video showed him lovingly cavorting with Mick Talbot on the Banks of The River Cam.

He knew how to wind people up and delighted in doing so. Still does.

He has remained at the top of his game for over forty years and continues to evolve. To have written a song of the calibre of Tube Station when only 20 years of age is remarkable. He has gone from strength to strength and full credit to him. Arrogant bastard though!

I am saying this with my rational head on now. This was not the case at the time!

GIGS THAT DIDN'T HAPPEN III

The Icicle Works circa 1983

The Tin Can Club Digbeth Birmingham

My girlfriend was on a visit to see me at Cov Poly at the time and I decided I would treat her!

Thirty minute train journey from Cov to Birmingham (following 20 minute walk to station through some of Cov's more dodgy areas).Short walk from Birmingham New Street Station to The Tin Can Club (sited above The Sunset Strip Joint). Classy. Girlfriend not warming to this.

Due to the nature of the venue the band were not due to come on until 10.30pm. I hadn't accounted for this and with three hours to kill until last train back to Cov at 11.00pm discretion was the better part of valour on my part and the decision was taken to abort and get back to Cov , the city of love, to enjoy that pleasant stroll back from Cov Station to my digs.

I was not popular and rightly so. Bloody idiot.

Gigs that unfortunately did happen:

Echo And The Bunnymen Porcupine Tour (apparently). 29th January 1983
Ipswich Gaumont

Dragged along to this by Bill to see a bunch of dour Scousers with a typically Scouse droll sense of humour. Not my cuppa and no gig recollections. Not a patch on The Icicle Works.

Notable only for meeting John Peel during the interval when he destroyed my mate Roots's positive perception of The Damned's The Black Album which Peel slated for being borderline progressive!

Roots claims this was actually at a Siouxsie And The Banshees gig and as The Black Album was released in 1980 he is probably correct. I have no recollection of ever seeing The Banshees which is troubling such is my love of McGeogh's guitar artistry.

On the subject of Peel he was not my favourite DJ. The man whose tastes matched mine was Mike Read. He was my double in terms of the bands he promoted (often on the breakfast show) namely The Jam, 999, The Icicle Works, The Lambrettas, The Members and The Vapors. Credit to the man and he still follows them today.

U2 War Tour (I think) October album release time 15th March 1983
Ipswich Gaumont

Let's be transparently clear here. I did not want to be there. Even in those early days (with two highly acclaimed albums behind them) Bonio on stage was the archetypal pompous, overindulgent self-righteous git (albeit with a competent band behind him) that we continue to know and loathe today. Once again Bill was to blame.

I have absolutely no recollection of the gig other than of that pompous God Like figure Bonio. He remains, in my opinion, a tosser of immense proportions. U2 cite The Clash as their inspiration but I saw no similarity between the act I saw on 15th March 1983 and that ground breaking act seen at the same venue on 14th January 1980.

One was down to earth and clearly grateful to be in the position they were, the other was already showing signs of outward pretentiousness and set to become a bland new wave stadium band version of Coldplay. I could see what would materialise. Stadium/arena music for the masses lapped up by middle aged music festival loving wannabees. I was correct.

I was more into bands like The Saints at the time. This was a love that I shared with my mate Roots who lived opposite the school. Many a lunchtime would be spent at his house necking a 'cuppa cawfee ' and taking in a few discs.

Often The Saints would be our choice and Kym Bradshaw's flares on the cover of the album I'm Stranded was always the source of a good chuckle given the band's punk context. We would study the NME whilst talking music and footy.

Classic Saints. Paralytic was played endlessly in March 1980 when heavy snow denied me access to school.

Aside. In music terms clearly Man City are your Joy Division. Man United are very much your Simply Red. Enough said.

Q10. In 1978 Coventry City had the infamous Admiral Brown/Yellow Banana split away shirt but which Home International Team had a home shirt of similar design (although different colours)?

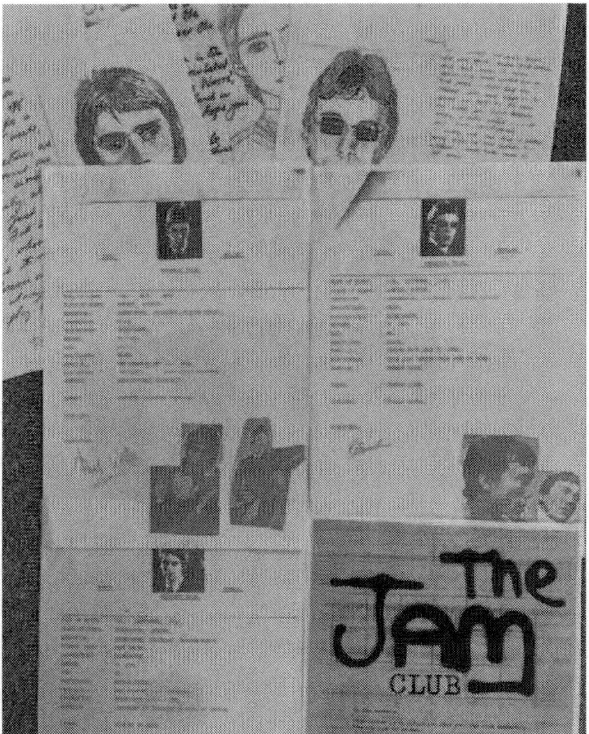

Those insightful band profiles

X

The Sixth Form Years 1981/1983.

The sway to partial New Romanticism/Post Punk.

Guilty/Madman/Never Again

This was another musically confusing period for me. Sade was merely a poor man's DC Lee in my biased Weller clouded opinion. Although I was moving towards Post Punk New Romanticism I retained my likings for Glam, Punk, New Wave, and Mod Revival.

From a personal perspective The Icicle Works, whilst not Post Punk were far too good to ignore so I didn't.

At this time even the UK Subs appeared to be dipping their toes in image-wise, thankfully not from a musical perspective. The album Diminished Responsibility remained pure rather than post Punk, but you could have been fooled by the album artwork.

The Jam Split in December 1982 and, as noted above it was very difficult to take at the time. The biggest band in England at the time and of course 'the best f*****g band in the world'.

This effectively triggered my interest in the Post Punk/New Romantic genre.

This is perhaps a bit of a sweeping statement as my new interests were limited to Classix Nouveaux and Cuddly Toys who had started as Punk band Raped and changed their name to Cuddly Toys in 1979.They were essentially a Roxy/Bowie influenced glam punk band in the early days and their first Album Guillotine Theatre proves this in terms of attire worn on the cover and the music itself.

By 1982 and the album Trials And Crosses they were viewed to be in the New Romantic mould and the album warranted commercial success. Sadly this was not the case.

As for myself a change of image was deemed essential. I was a true part time punk. I dipped into Punk, Mod and New Romantic simultaneously such was my love of all these music genres.

First to go was my spiky feather cut Foxton hairstyle to be replaced with an authentic over-enhanced droopy side parting with fringe pulled over one eye in the style of Classix Nouveaux 's Mik Sweeny/ Gary Steadman, not Phil Oakey.

Initially this was coloured on a very short term semi-permanent basis with a black spray on dye applied via an aerosol. This looked ok although one student's parent did comment that she had seen my girlfriend hanging around with 'her Indian boyfriend'. I knew I had a tan but this was pushing it a bit!

The dye was in place when we played an away football match at Leiston High School. This was to have consequences. It pissed it down with rain throughout the match and I became aware that many on the pitch plus respective coaches were pissing themselves laughing. (as the flames grew higher) giving me unexpected time and space to weave my magic on the pitch.

Once back in the changing room the reason became apparent.

I glanced in the mirror and what looked back was the face of a pit miner from Orgreave Colliery. The black dye had run in the rain leaving black streaks all over my face and eyes. It was arguably Goth but the piss taking on the journey back to Fram was relentless.

Even when dry the dye would flake off particularly at night when you went to sleep giving rise to a crispy coated blackened pillow case by the morning. As a result the decision was made to find a more permanent user friendly application and to be a little more adventurous in terms of shade. Step forward Spicy Plumb. This gave me the almost radiant Classix look as depicted on the cover of La Verite (at least it did in my biased opinion).

Then came the clothes. Pleated/gathered trousers were all the rage with the New Romantics and I acquired a couple of pairs. One pair pin stripe black and the other a deep plumb (to match my flowing locks).

These were matched up with heavy duty white denim Wham style sleeveless shirts with collars always turned up or sleeveless T shirts. I hacked the sleeves off my gorgeous Classix Nouveaux Night People shirt to fit the look. Even my beloved Bruce Foxton T shirt got the sleeve amputation treatment even though his solo output was not in the New Romantic mould. More evidence of my confusion at the time.

White Foxtonesque pumps or black/grey suede winkle pickers completed the look. A gold chain looped from a badge into my shirt breast pocket. All very Classix.

It was a bit of a dilemma as I was still heavily into Mod and Punk. All these genres retained an enduring, tribal appeal.The Mod Revival gear and the Punk T shirts etc as a result were not ditched. They remained in place ready for use as and when required. A Part time Punk personified.

Events:

- 20th April 1983 A Winter's Tale. Shakespeare. Theatre Royal Norwich.
- 20th April 1983 Norwich City Vs Arsenal . League Division One. Carrow Road. A stroke of luck, a serious dilemma?

We were studying A Winter's Tale as part of our A level English. The school had arranged for a party of about twenty of us (plus two/three teachers) to attend a showing in Norwich at The Theatre Royal on the night of Wednesday 20th April and a bus duly left the school in Framlingham at about 5.00pm.

I should add at this point that in addition to the English teacher came a History/Sports teacher (and Tottenham fan) by the name of Pete D! Why he wanted to attend God only knows. It says a lot about the limited options in Framlingham on a wet weekday night.

The Gods (at this stage) were clearly smiling on me as on the very same night Norwich City were playing The Gooners and paying on the gate for this top level match was a valid option!

Unfortunately the Gods were to have the last laugh.

From memory we endured half of the first scene of Winter's Tale and then discreetly myself, Jools, Roots and Keith F snuck out of the theatre and wended our way to Carrow Road.

We handed over £2 and there we were on the terraces of the away end with all the Gooners. Unfortunately from this point onwards the Gods generosity waned.

My hero Graham Rixy Rix tore his hamstring early on and was hauled off before half time (replaced by John Hollins) , ex Towen player Keith Bertschen netted one of the Naarwich goals and The Gooners were dispatched 3-1.

My 'mates' taunted me by singing 'Rixy's pulled his hammy, Rixy's pulled his hammy' for the rest of the evening. How immature.

We re-appeared post- match at the Theatre Royal in time for the last scene.

I was greeted with the site of my girlfriend Juliet snuggled up to the sixth form Gary Davies lookalike hunk Guy (which was alarming) but as she succinctly pointed out 'you shouldn't have sodded off to the football'. Fair point.

Teacher Pete D (Spurs fan remember) merely glanced up and muttered 'did they win'? He had obviously sussed us all along. How he smirked when I told him the result!

On reflection his 'serves you right' summarisation probably hit the mark.

I think they call it poetic justice (well a certain David Pleat did at Anfield in 1989 but that's another story).

25th May 1982 Wembley Stadium England 2 Holland 0 (Rixy's finest hour ,well 45 minutes).

A school trip for a night match at Wembley. A brave school decision.

The coach journey in those days took us through Chelmsford and past that well known Punk Venue The Army And Navy which was noted as we went round the one way system.

A dismal goalless first half had the crowd moaning. I was yelling for the introduction of Graham Rix (of course) and in the 46th minute my wish came true as he came on for Alan Devonshire.

The impact was immediate. A goal followed two minutes later from Tony Woodcock and another (following an immaculate 17 yard pass from Rixy) came courtesy of Paul Mariner. All players with Arsenal connections.

He quite literally ran the show and 69000 happy fans filed out at the end of the game. My post- match Rixy talk of course was unbounded. I talked Rixy for the next 3 hours on the coach journey home boring the tits off one and all but they couldn't argue. That one night he was a genius. Despite many appearances it was effectively his only shining moment in an England shirt.

We all agreed that night that night that Rixy was truly better than Hoddle (Devonshire actually).

The School Football Team Tour. Devon October 1982

PE teachers Mr X and Mr Y arranged a football tour in, of all, places Devon.

A journey of some 330+ miles from Framlingham to the first stop Ilfracombe. A mere five hours forty five minutes for twelve of us crammed in the School mini bus.Who sanctioned this one? Certainly no one with any semblance of Health & Safety / Risk Assessment considerations. This was the early 1980s. Such things didn't matter. Needless to say we arrived safely.

Match One Ilfracombe College v T Pills High School

A 3-1 defeat.

Following the game it transpired that Ilfracombe had fielded a semi-professional ringer (a former pupil who was currently playing for Barnstaple Town). He re-joined purely for this match. and was rather good. arguably the difference between the teams. From memory he netted a couple.

X and Y were furious with this perceived cheating. It was no reflection of the school's actual current team.

Match Two Bideford School v T Pills High School

We drew 1-1. Good solid, professional team performance and a professional score too.

Match Three Barnstaple College v T Pills High School.
We won 3-1. A great all round team performance and a great culmination in football terms as we had grown in confidence match on match.

The evenings were strange affairs but not surprising given that Messrs X and Y were our guardians!

The first night in Ifracombe found us initially feasting at The Dolphin Fish & Chip Restaurant. From there X and Y responsibly took us to a harbour front pub (possibly The Boat House).

This had an elevated mezzanine floor with pool table and we spent all night there drinking and playing pool. As a group made up of a combination of upper and lower sixth formers this was quite an achievement given the ages concerned and level of alcohol consumption!

X and Y spent the night in the bar below chatting up the local chicks before DRIVING us back to the youth hostel! As the 999 punksters put it (X And Y were the best of friends, best of friends).

That night in the dorm I was knocking out farts left right and centre (probably due to the alcohol) and the legendary line was uttered by Mr X ' 'will you shut the fuck up? You'll start a hunt in a minute!' How we chuckled.

Whilst on the subject of farts I remember at school we had to sit in alphabetical order for exams and there was a set of female twins (obviously with the same surname) who were 'after me'. They effectively drew lots or tossed a coin to establish who would have to suffer sitting behind me (and my arse) for the period of the exam. On more than one occasion they complained formally to the invigilator about the off-putting aromas!

Back to the tour.
I remember little about the second night other than we were at the same hostel and went to the same pub.

For the final night X & Y hatched a plan.

Clearly tired of the local totty in Ilfracombe they decided it would be a good idea to up sticks and travel over to Barnstaple where Mr Y's parents lived.

They were away on holiday at the time and it was decided that rather than kipping in the relative luxury of a YHA dorm it would be a far more sensible to stay in close proximity to the location of the final match and indeed a new set of hostelries.

The accommodation was tight. Twelve 17/18 year olds crashed out in the lounge on a combination of settees, chairs, rugs etc. X & Y naturally utilised the bedrooms.

A night was spent in the pubs of Barnstable where once again we were effectively left to or own devices whilst X & Y checked out the local talent. Nothing new there. We were within walking distance from the town centre and so I can only imagine the amount of alcohol consumed by team and teachers alike. How we got back is still a gap in my memory.

The same cannot be said for the torturous journey back to Saaarrrfolk the next day. This remains firmly etched in my memory. It was the day I sauntered into a John Menzies (remember them?) in a service station en route to Bumpkinland where I picked up an NME and was met with the horrifying news that THE JAM WERE SPLITTING!

It was the longest most mind numbing journey home I have ever encountered. I was shell shocked. The mocking from my team mates was incessant. Bastards. Counselling was not an option in the eighties.

Independent Mobility You Need Wheels (Desperately)

My mate Colin L (the drummer) was obsessed with Barry Sheene the world champion motorcyclist. More importantly he was obsessed with Suzuki, Sheene 's bike of choice.

When we were 16 years old the alluring option of a 50cc moped/bike appeared. We both acquired a Suzuki. The similarity ends there.

Colin acquired the flashy Suzuki X1 which looked like a motorbike but due to new speed limitations on 50cc machines it was limited to 30mph. It looked the part.

Due to my burgeoning Mod interests at the time I was interested in acquiring the Vespa 50 Special (and carried a small picture of one around in my maths book).

Sourcing a second hand one was virtually impossible (finances would not extend to new).

Suffice to say intense parental caution/concern re the dangers of being ' on the road' meant the parents took the decision to select a 'suitable' machine for me. Unfortunately this was to be the Suzuki FZ50. (Google it)

I'm not one to criticise unduly but in terms of style, speed and performance this came lower in ratings than the Honda Dax in the classic Top Trumps Card game of the time. In fact it didn't even warrant a place in the pack. I should say at this point that compared to Sid's first moped the FZ was a dream. He had a ' step through' Motobecane. The kind of machine a postman nearing pension age would use to get to and from the sorting office.

Geoffrey being the cautious type would always insist on familiarisation prior to freedom of use. As a result we both had to endure 'circuits' on our respective machines.

This amounted to riding around a predetermined route with report back to base after each circuit. On one occasion Sid returned with his machine sounding like a Norton 750. Confused looks all round. Undeterred he conducted another circuit this time returning with a hefty piece of metalware under his arm. The silencer.

To be fair Sid did latterly acquire a stylish Kwaka but he certainly earnt the right following months of unrivalled ridicule courtesy of the full face helmet/ Motobecane combination.

Colin's X1 was a classic 70s chick pulling machine. My FZ 50 by contrast was a grannified runaround fit for shopping duties

Effectively the FZ amounted to half a Vespa (unfortunately the shitty bottom half) but for all its faults (and there were many) it could virtually match the X1 for 'speed' given the enforced limitations in place for 50cc machines. There were no gears but to be honest what was the point in changing gear four times to reach the heady heights of 30 MPH?

Amazingly in 1979 a Motorcycle News Road Tester described the FZ50 as "the most attractive moped I've seen and must take the run-about class into a new area of perfection" with "sporty alloy spoked wheels". Really? Was he deluded?

He must have been suffering from some form of learning impediment and obviously neither he nor his carer had ever given it a test run. Certainly not in the rain. (see below).

If you were in luck you could, (if riding down a one in four incline with a strong prevailing wind at your back), rinse 30 MPH out of it. To make matters worse like my brother before me I rode this embarrassment wearing a full-face helmet (largely to hide my identity rather than protect my head)! In image terms it was an unmitigated disaster.When potato picking at Easton (about 4 miles from Framlingham) during the Summer Holidays of 1980 I was trying to impress a potential girlfriend. Juliet S.

There she was spud plucking in a tight fitting yellow Starsky & Hutch T Shirt (not a great look). I was in relatively cool attire, punk T shirt, jeans and cheap plastic sunglasses in The Dickies/Captain Sensible mould. How could I fail?

The question was could I be her Dave Starsky? Not a hope. A sky blue and white FZ50 was no red Ford Gran Torino complete with white stripe.

One morning whilst picking in close proximity to her kneeling romantically in the wet rotting potatoes she looked me in the eye and bluntly asked:

'Where is your moped?........Silence....... I knew she knew.

She followed up with the cutting

Why do you park it in the next village'? ....Silence. She had a point.

She was correct I had ridden on to the next village to park it under a porch at the end of a church path because I was so ashamed of the step through monstrosity that was the FZ50. This didn't aid my romantic advances in any way. My mode of transport clearly was a hindrance. Any perceived 'cool persona' was shattered. It was about as cool as drinking own brand supermarket lager at a party.

On top of this on the day concerned there were high winds and it pissed it down with rain that afternoon. When I returned to my steed and turned the key it failed to start. It didn't even offer a timid splutter.

Roots had already cycled off back to Fram. I had no other option than to start the walk, some four miles (plus one mile courtesy of parking in the next village) back to Fram, in the pouring rain.

On the plus side at least my hair dye was no longer spray on! Luckily Roots returned with his parents in a rescue party car with trailer to save me after about 3 miles of toil.

When we arrived back at Roots's pad he exclaimed in his put on Saaarfolk accent 'you've got a soggy spaaarky boiy'. I nodded sagely but not being technically minded I would never have come to this conclusion. He soon had it back in working order thanks to kitchen rolls and a hairdryer. In summary style and panache were never words associated with the FZ50.

Social Life Sixth Form Style

Party In Paris

The sixth form years were characterised by social events such as discos, live local gigs, lunchtime sojourns at the house of Roots and Head of Sixth Form evening drinks sessions.

Quite frankly this was yet again an amazingly outgoing relaxed attitude being shown by the teaching fraternity (who says Suffolk is backward). Many of us were not anywhere near 18 years of age but they we were effectively propagating alcohol at midweek (school night) soirees.

These were very relaxed affairs where the academic guards were down and you could talk on a one to one basis with the teachers about sport, music whatever you wanted to the backing of your punk tunes.

By this time the forces of shame had led me into ditching the FZ50 (together with full face helmet) and I had acquired a silver racing bike ('with crumm (chrome) fawks (forks) boiy') from Roots. Image-wise I was more than happy to sacrifice that 50cc engine for pedal power.

Usually we managed to arrange for parental lifts to and from these 'parties' but sometimes conditions meant this was n't an option. One such occasion occurred when the snow fell heavily all day both settling and drifting.

The promised lift with Sarah G's dad was not going to happen and my parents had a company function to attend that night (how they got there I have no idea) not that they would have driven such a long distance in those conditions either.

I had to attend as I had just started seeing Juliet (miraculously she was still on-board in spite of the FZ debacles) and a scrawled note of explanation was dutifully left for the parents. I remember it as a bitterly cold night and treacherous conditions. Not ideal for the manoeuvering of a narrow gauge tyre racing bike 16 miles each way in the dark on deeply packed snow.

For the ride I wore a sweat top, shorts plus classic Captain Sensible beret. (I carried my party gear in a plastic bag hooked to the handlebars which played further havoc with my balance). The sixteen mile journey there starting at 6.00pm was manageable and quite an Enid Blyton style innocent adventure. I arrived at Roots's pad and changed into my killer gear.

Andy P lent myself and Juliet the keys to his cool Mini Cooper (his journey was a mere two miles) which was parked outside so we could 'get to know each other'.This was fine for 15 minutes until we realised we were locked in. That Mini Cooper wasn't cool. It was bloody freezing.

The return journey at midnight (another 16 miles) following numerous beers was one of It'a A Knockout proportions. The snow had largely turned to ice which negated use of the front brake. I arrived back slightly battered and bruised after one or two slide offs at about 2.30am which was not bad for a sloshed teenager in those conditions. The house lights were still on.

I had a lot of explaining to do. Surprisingly they were quite amenable and appeared to just be relieved that I had got back safely.

The Driving Test

Car Trouble/Fast Cars/The Motors/You Need Wheels.

Pressure was building from 'my new chick' to get the driving test passed so that we could 'do things together'. After about twenty largely floundering lessons with The Healy School Of Motoring a date for my test was in place.

Hardly a confidence inducing institution my instructor Mark was nonchalant in the extreme and when I stalled on a roundabout in one of my first outings he merely muttered ' nice place to stop mate'!

The test seemed to be going relatively well (even the dreaded reverse around the corner) when suddenly I misjudged/ignored an approaching cross roads and I ploughed across without stopping. Upon realising my error I knew I had failed and asked whether it was worth continuing. Behind his startled ghostly white exterior he muttered 'yes' as it would be 'good experience'. Piss taker.

I was devastated .Not so much as Juliet. It was back to the Chrumm fawrks for the next few weeks. Another ten lessons followed (Healey's profits must have quadrupled that year) and I sailed through test two.I was now upwardly mobile. The pressure was off.

Unfortunately more disdain/embarrassment was to follow. I couldn't seem to shake it off.

The first car I accessed was my grandad's old Riley Elf (once he had passed away).

An automatic.

This was effectively a mini chassis/body with a classic front grill. Quite Mod really but unfortunately my mate Andy P outclassed me having the real thing in The Mini Cooper. I was a novice. Back in those days you had to use a choke to start the car in cold weather. I was unaware of the implications of leaving the choke 'out' once the engine had warmed up.

One day I decided to use it to go to school. It was cold and the choke was needed to start it. Once mobile it soon occurred to me that the car was literally driving itself. All I needed to do was steer and brake manically as and when required.

The force was immense. I remember desperately forcing my foot down on the break pad at junctions etc to stop the car from veering forward and sweating profusely into the bargain even though the temperature outside was less than zero. Eac time I took my foot off the break pedal the car shot off again.

By the time I reached my school destination, following my Mr Bean style antics I was physically exhausted.

When I explained the scenario my logical mates pissed themselves pointing out to me the need for the choke to be reinstated once the engine was warm thereby avoiding the flooding of the engine with fuel. This had quite literally propelled me to school. No such dramas on the return journey.

What a fuckwit. One for the memory bank.

School Lunchtimes. (stick with it).
As noted above the 5 minutes (and you're almost dead) walk to Roots's abode was often chosen. Cups of Cawfee (coffee) and listening to The Saints being the order of the day but on occasion a group of us would go to The Railway pub in the centre of Framlingham. Age dictates that this must have been from late 1982. One such visit was in the Summer of 1983.

I had driven to school that day in my mum's Volvo 343 complete with sun roof hatch and had given Sarah G from my village a lift. It was a blisteringly hot day and the chance to cool off with a chilled beer at lunchtime was irresistible and a few of us decided to gather at The Railway pub.

I mention beer but unfortunately there was another far more tempting option for a hot Summer's day, Cider. The cider in question was a legendary local brand called James White. It was so strong that the pub would only serve it in halves. I must have necked a couple as the lessons that afternoon flew past in a blur. Rough Book untouched the journey home dawned.

I located Sarah G and sensibly decided to go the quiet way home. This ,however, involved numerous narrow track bendy country roads. It was still burning hot so the biscuit tin lid hand operated peel back square in the roof of the car purporting as a 'sun roof' was opened up. The music was on and (at least in my mind) I was Mr Cool, The Cappuccino Kid. Mistake number one.

Within 5 minutes of take-off I miscalculated a bend near Roots' house and veered across a narrow ditch into a Barley field before looping around and rejoining the road. With the 'sun roof 'open' we harvested a sizeable proportion of Barley grains / kernels (I am no farmer) with it flying in through the sunroof opening and covering both myself and my passenger. Amazingly she didn't bat an eyelid merely brushing the kernals from her top. I apologised profusely. No worries she said!

Upon my return to Coddenham I engaged in an extended clear up process with Barley based foliage and grains being extracted from the radiator grill and brushed off the upholstery.

Never has truer word been uttered when my dad next used the car with his comment being the classic 'my god Stephen it looks like you've been through a hedge backwards'. I had but at least It wasn't in reverse.

Happy times.
York 1982:
My parents decided a break in York was needed and generously invited Bill along too. York was a great city and in Red Rhino had one of the trendiest independent punk music/T shirt shops so my aim was true. To acquire music and merch.
I settled on a 7" single by Cuddly Toys (Astral Joe) and 12" by Goat (the band formed by Cuddly Toys lead singer Sean Purcell following the demise of the Toys). In addition I purchased a beautiful Night People Classix Nouveaux T shirt.

The following day Classix were live on TV from the Futurama Festival. Bill however was not keen and suggested a day out in nearby Leeds with the possibility of a visit to a Blue Cinema thrown in. Stupidly I succumbed.

It was the classic scenario. Dimly lit flea pit, numerous seedy old men dotted around and probably insufficient Fire Exits/Extinguishers! The film (Insatiable starring Marilyn Chambers) was shit and I had sacrificed Classix. On a par with the U2 debacle of a concert which again Bill was instrumental in encouraging me to attend. I was not happy.

School Squares/Stiffs. Straight jeans were made for these guys.
(Wake Up) To The Twentieth Century
I mentioned back in the Grammar school chapter the concept of school grading and the shame/embarrassment that this heaped on many of us. Naturally for the many who were habitually humiliated they were of course a few who shone.

I have nothing against those who worked hard to achieve their results (within reason) as at least they were justified in the 'glory' that they strove so hard for. I cannot say the same about the naturally gifted. The ones who didn't have to try. The ones who were mightily miffed with an average grade of 90+% during those humiliating times.

Those people were frustratingly aloof. They had no concept of the problems this continual assessment caused for the rest of us and the struggles we endured in obtaining an average 70% grade. Many were not normal.

By the time of the sixth form there were a few in that bracket who came to the realisation that perhaps there was actually more to life than pure academia and made a last ditch attempt to enter the world of the hip and trendy. Our sacred territory.

Andrew B was one such lad. He made it to Cambridge Uni, which, arguably was a cut above Cov Poly. In terms of Physics, Chemistry, Maths, Advanced

Maths, Biology etc he was untouchable. He was naturally gifted. He was shit at PE.

He couldn't really address his lack of sporting prowess short of grabbing a Rugby ball occasionally and running down the flanks in an attempt to be a winger , (which contrasted starkly to my avoid the ball attitude) he did feel he could muscle in on the music scene.

As a result of this he attended many of the midweek parties and took quite a liking to Bill who it has to be said was of a similar standing re academia but was also into his music and footy.

At this point in time post punk was the genre and Bill was heavily into Joy Division, Bauhaus etc. (Danzig had been built on these solid foundations).

Andrew B took to sitting with Bill in the Common room attempting to talk music. He borrowed a couple of albums from Bill as his confidence grew but whilst polite Bill was obviously a little uncomfortable with this attention and attempted to keep his distance.

Whilst Andrew B is probably now a world-renowned Nuclear Physicist I can categorically state that he will have never seen The UK SUBS.

Another who tried to jump aboard the music bandwagon was Richard M. He was averagely bright (relatively speaking) but a bit square. Once again in the sixth form he decided there was more to life than lessons and unfortunately for me he decided The Jam were the band for him.

To emphasise how late to the party he was his first Jam single purchase was Absolute Beginners in 1981! What pissed me off was that he (in addition to my girlfriend) got the limited edition picture/lyric insert and I didn't and he hadn't even bought it until it was entrenched in the Top Ten. There is no justice in life.

He pissed a few people off and on one occasion in the fifth year when we were waiting to enter the Science lab a scuffle broke out between David B and him when David called him Richturd MyArse (a play on his name). David let loose with a couple of head punches and then, after a few more blows, he relented as there was a clinking sound. He thought he had knocked a couple of Richard's teeth out. The blows resumed once it was established that the tinkling noise was not that of teeth falling to floor rather lab coat buttons !

Pete T was another harmless square and certainly not guilty on the academic front. Again he jumped on the music bandwagon a bit late on in the sixth form, bought himself a rudimentary Moog synthesiser and vertically wall mounted Amstrad music centre into the bargain.He was later to surface briefly as ' a pylon' in National Grid And The Pylons.

He was guilty of that 1980s Cliff Richard endorsed black shirt and white tie combo (often worn to the school discos) as he was heavily into Tubeway Army. Enough said.

With regards to the academics arguably they should have been happy with their lot and left the rest of us to the music/ footy scene. Very few could pull off all three facets.

Bill came close although his sporting ability was limited to borderline school football team (sub at best). His skill at Subbuteo, however, cannot be ignored. He had the full stadia with floodlights, managers, substitutes and about ten different interchangeable teams.

Contrast this with my second- rate equivalent- Big League. This was the one where each player had one moveable leg on a spring which you pulled back and let go to kick the ball. Naturally leg breaks were the common injury. No hamstrings for the fellas. Such was the frequency of the leg break that in time you would be forced to reconfigure the game to a 5 a side basis.

Andy P was bright, good at most sports (Cricket excepted) and had pretty good musical taste although he had a tendency to stray into Rock. Frampton Comes Alive had to be hammered out of him. Frampton Drops Dead was our frequent taunt.

Perverse credit to him in that he flunked his A levels, at least by his standards. Polytechnic was not an option for consideration and he re-took at a school in Cambridge which ensured his rightful passage to university, albeit a year late.

I was good at most sports (bar Rugga for obvious reasons) also heavily into music but didn't really trouble the academic masters. I was at best Europa League standard in that department.

The likes of Andrew B had no hope on the sporting front and struggled unsuccessfully to break into the music scene with the rest of us. People like him had no chance of looking or indeed acting the part.

In life you are dealt your hand and by and large you should stick with it and the perceived cool social/sporting stuff and cutting edge music should be left to those who are comfortable with it.

Aside 1/2. Does anyone trust a 48 hour deodorant?
Does anyone answer the dentist's standard 'How often do you floss' question honestly ?
Q11. Which advert in the 1970 had the famous scene where the mother says 'course you can Malcom'?

XI

Sent to Coventry 1983
Pure Mania/ Violent City/ Trouble/ Destroy/ Hateful –
The lot. City of culture?
My academic limitations ensured that a place at Oxford or Cambridge was pure fantasy. Being filmed by the BBC joyously opening my results envelope was never likely or desired (why do they always show the cocky Head Girls of this world rather than the honest grafters). I was destined for low grade A level passes at best and this was duly reflected when my results came in.

I passed English Literature and History with D grades. OK it was a Double D but unlike the lager of the time it was hardly special. However I am surely borderline unique with regards to my other subject 'pass' . . . . . Politics.

I must be one of the few people in the country to have acquired a Politics O level.

Not an O level option at the time and only recently introduced as an A level in 1983 whilst in reality it amounted to a formal recognition of a failure to acquire a rudimentary Grade E A level pass it did not warrant an out and out fail. I was awarded an O. A deliberate ploy on my part to acquire a truly unique O level? I think not.

With this limited certification of my academia by default Polytechnic (the working man's University), was the only option.

At the time the University Of Reality, Life and Fun rather than that of perceived geekism. Interviews duly followed at Cambridge and Trent.

Strangely Coventry offered on the basis of application form only. Presumably this was based on the realisation that anyone visiting the city prior to successful application would leave via the nearest ring road junction never to return.

Some quite rightly describe Cov as either a dump surrounded by a ring road or a ring road with a dump in the middle. Both are true.

And so it was at a time when Frankie was welcoming all and sundry to the 'Pleasure Dome' in order to 'Relax' I was , by default, sentenced to three years in Coventry.

Although recently awarded a 'City Of Culture' status let's be honest these cultural awards tend to be granted to bleak deprived cities in an attempt to falsely regenerate. Coventry was a shit hole in the early 1980s (as portrayed on numerous occasions by The Specials) and I see no evidence that it has changed having recently been deemed the most crime ridden city in the country.

However, with a music history of Gods Toys and Two Tone plus a first division footy team it really was a no brainer for me and of course the subjects matched up perfectly. Funnily enough my brother Sid, (much more intelligent than me) secured a place at Salford University two years before. Strange that bearing in mind he supported Man City which was certainly a labour of love in the late seventies. The course was again naturally perfect for him!

Back to Cov our first night in year two, (the first away from the security of Halls of residence), in our £7 per week mid terraced hovel in Hamilton Road just around the corner from the Sex Shop at the Highfield Road end of the city, our washing was nicked from the line after dark ('your washing gets nicked when the lights go out' Weller was indeed a prophet) and one of my mates was mugged for a bag of chips. It was bleak.

Football was a good relaxation and took place in Whitefriars 'indoor' arena. Effectively this was akin to playing in an industrial sized cold storage unit. It was devoid of heating but for the minimalistic lukewarm showers which generated a little isolated warm steam.

You played a short match and then stood in an open viewing pen area adjacent to the arena and awaited your next game.

At the end you took a rudimentary mildly warm shower and then returned to the freezing open pen to change. On one occasion by the time I had dried and got my gear on my hair became crisp to the touch. It had actually begun to freeze!

Apparently football legend Alan Smudger Smith played in this place (he has a languages degree acquired from The Lanch). He denied all knowledge when quizzed on this subject by my Gooner buddy Graham when he was interviewed for Graham's great book 12-nil to the Arsenal (and a goal in extra time).

Over the Poly period we Gooners on my course took in a few live local footy matches of note:

Aston Villa 2 Arsenal 6 29/10/83- The one I missed.
This one still hurts enormously.
Early in my time at Coventry a few of the Arsenal boys on my course decided to go to this one and asked me to join them. It was at the time when I was

travelling regularly to Brighton to see Juliet. Finances as a result were tight. I declined.

This was only the historic night that Tony Woodcock bagged five of the six Arsenal goals. A match of legendary status for all Gooners putting up with unrivalled crap during this period. I should have been there. No excuses.

My mates still regularly remind me of this some thirty eight years later.

I vowed not to miss the next match for the Gooners at Villa Park which came mid-week in March 1985. Naturally I attended and witnessed the dullest nil nil draw of all time.

Coventry 1 Arsenal 4 31/3/84

The Gooners won despite playing the last twenty minutes with midfielder Stewart Robson in goal following a bad injury which side-lined keeper Pat Jennings. In front of an amassed away end Robson was faultless. Pitch invasions and utter jubilation at the final whistle.

Leicester City 1 Arsenal 4 31/10/84

Generously Arsenal gave Leicester the lead after thirty three seconds through a Viv Anderson own goal the Gooners responded to thump the Foxes.

On entering the stadium we were frisked and the Policeman found my skin blemish cover stick in my back pocket. When I declared what it was he let out a cry of 'backs to the wall guys' to his fellow policemen. Classic eighties. Not a good start.

After the fourth Gooner goal many Leicester fans left the ground early and started lobbing bricks and concrete into to open elevated seating area where many Gooners were sitting leading to a minor pitch invasion. Cue mass trouble after the match behind the stands.I always thought Leicester was a family club!

Aston Villa 1 Arsenal 1 Milk Cup Quarter Final 22/1/86

The night when we thought a 1-1 draw was credible only for (from memory) Paul Mariner to be played in central defence in the return and Villa turning us over 2-1

The night did not start well. We disembarked at Whitton Station and made our way through dark threatening streets to the ground where my mate got a burger. The vendor literally hacked two thick slices off a white loaf and stuffed the burger and onions in. Brutal.

The game went well (Charlie scored) but Rixy missed the chance to win it when through on the keeper. Post-match we sought a pub to watch the highlights and I ripped the arse out of my prized pin stripe jeans crossing the elevated centre section of a road. Abandoning the idea and returned to Whitton station with my programme carefully wedged across my boxers.

There were still plenty of Villa miscreants around. We boarded an away train and stood pressed up close to the window. A huge thug of a Villa fan walked across the platform to our window and spat the thickest greenest gob of all gobs at us.

It smacked the window and hung in suspended animation two inches from our faces. Despite travelling for about thirty minutes on a high speed express train to Coventry with speeds topping 70 MPH the gob, whilst wobbling a touch, remained in situ. It would not be moved.

On reflection the Aston area of Birmingham actually made Cov seem relatively civil.

Cov Nightlife

To say there was a strange array of pubs in Coventry is a serious understatement.

Many in the city centre were effectively chav pits with the clientele getting bevvied up in anticipation of the late night club scene and late-night scrapping outside The Parson's Nose chippy. One or two had their plus points. Water's Wine Bar for instance which was sited opposite the Lady Godiva statue in the city centre.

It was a wine bar but only in name. There were no bland style lagers such as the 'classic' Coventry Tennent's Pilsner. This was the place that brought you draught Pils. The type advertised by Griff Rhys Jones in classic Eddie The Eagle style bottle bottomglasses. The stuff you could normally only find in a bottle. With the strength rivalling that of James White Cider it was lethal. This could be our lucky day!

On one occasion when Juliet was down we went as a group to Waters. I ended up prostrate on the pavement in the shadow of Lady Godiva honking up on the pavement.

The rest of the party carried on merrily in Waters until closing time when they hauled me off the pavement and back to my seventh floor room in The Prior Hall Tower where I continued to spew horizontally into a bucket on the floor while my girlfriend was next door being chatted up by my mate Martyn. A perceived justification for that Winter's Tale/ Carrow Road incident back in the day.

My room adjoined Martyn's on the seventh floor of our Halls of residence

Priory Hall. On one occasion an ill- released burp on my part led to Martyn banding on my door. Steve was that you? I was alarmed surely it wasn't that loud. Apparently the wall mounted electric fan heater had acted as an amplifier and filtered the burp sound crystally clear into Martyn's room.

A plan was hatched. The next time Juliet was down I notified Martyn a time when we would both be in my room. Martyn then proceeded to whisper Juliet's name spookily into the fan heater in his room. She freaked.

He kept it up for about 5 minutes and Juliet was yelling at me 'can't you hear it? My name is being whispered'. I played dumb for as long as I could until eventually there was a bang on the door and Martyn fell in pissing himself.

Further pubs included the Silver Sword and The Golden Cross.

The Sword was close to our halls in the basement of a concrete monolith and pretty Chavvy. The Bar Man in the Cross was gay and fancied Martyn so appearances became increasingly limited as his advances were unsubtle and a bit unnerving for Martyn.

Another city centre pub we visited briefly was The Tally Ho. This was a cavernous place close to the Parsons Nose chippy. Despite being full of chavs getting Tennent's Pilsners down their necks before venturing to Tamangos Night (Fight) Club, we still went there for one reason....The Video Juke Box.

It was a concept doomed to failure from the start. OK so MTV had just burst onto the scene and no band worth their salt in the eighties would release a record without a lavish video but these Video Juke boxes turned the respective boozers into lifeless morgues.

The Tally Ho naturally attracted the Cov Chavs often dressed in mauve and many resplendent with their newly acquired Duran inspired floppy blonde fringes through which they gazed at the TV sized video screens.

They consumed unlimited Pilsner pints which stood them in good stead for the late night scrapping in Tamangos Night Club (depicted in Fight Club by the Specials) and the taxi queue outside The Parson's Nose chippy in the early hours.

I will not go into huge detail about Cov but suffice to say in terms of music and gig culture it was a significant step up from Ipswich.

The Poly people there were switched on and I managed to associate with the Economics crew as they were more cultured certainly from a music perspective.

My course, Modern Studies (more like Modern Stiffies) were more concerned with debating the pros and cons of past dictators, communism and socio- economic affairs. Hardly cracking pub talk. Luckily many were Gooners which made it loosely bearable.

There was a good range of night clubs some (Busters) having great alternative nights. As noted above Cov was heavily chav orientated within the city centre and the majority of the clubs catered for them. Tamangos was a classic case in point. This was a prime example of the hate filled disco inferno so brilliantly portrayed the The Specials track Nite Club. Naturally a Tenants fuelled night in Tamangos could only lead to one thing. Post club scrapping outside the legendary Parson's Nose chippy.

Gigs at the Poly either took place in the Main Hall or the intimate Down Stairs Bar. Although I mentioned that Poly students were more streetwise/down to earth than their Uni counterparts this did not dilute their exaggerated air of self- importance and a year into my course the Students Union took the decision to rename the Main Hall and The Downstairs Bar. The Main Hall became The Biko Bar and The Down Stairs Bar, wait for it….The Mandela Bar.

Why? Did they seriously think this momentous decision would have any impact in lessening the restrictions on Nelson? It was pure unwarranted student arrogance. Utterly pointless. To us they rightfully remained the Main Hall and The DSB. Bloody students.

The DSB was a great venue , really atmospheric lending itself brilliantly to bands such as The Icicle Works, The Armoury Show, Spear Of Destiny and UK Subs.

I attended these (and many others)with gig mate Shauny Boy. The man who taught me how to yell 'Bollocks' in a burp. The perfect word for this crude action and one that has been religiously repeated through 80% of my burps in the 40 years since. 'ats right, 'ats correct' as he would say.

The bigger more commercial bands played the main hall (likes of Boomtown Rats). Not only was this the hall where I eventually sat my finals but it was also the hall that featured in The Specials video for Rat Race with Messrs Hall, Golding and Dammers walking sternly between the stressed out disillusioned students.

Up the road we had Warwick University with its venue The Warwick Arts Centre.

Both Killing Joke and Bruce Foxton were captured there (Foxton also the following night at Birmingham Odeon).

You have to question the business logic for Brucey playing two gigs in the Birmingham area on consecutive nights.

To say it was over optimistic is an understatement. Here he was with one hit single and a couple of less successful follow ups plus patchy debut album to his name and he was attempting to fill two relatively large venues within five miles of each other on consecutive nights. Sensible business planning? I think not.

There were no more than 40 in attendance at The Arts Centre and The Odeon the following night was stalls only and only about two thirds full. Put the attendances together and you would have had a decent Odeon turnout. This would have bolstered Bruce's self-esteem rather than deepen his obvious insecurity at the time.

Killing Joke were also captured at Edgbaston's Tower Ballroom, a bleak area. A vast cavernous venue from memory with plastic palm trees. Unfortunately it wasn't a Saturday night. I stood at the back with Shauny in my Red leather biker jacket complete with Cuddly Toys oriental style logo emblazoned across the bottom of it!

One act I refused to see in Cov at the time was The Style Council who played The Coventry Apollo Theatre. Why? Paul Weller?

The simple fact was that around this time the Style Council were busy allying themselves to organisations such as Red Wedge and CND. This gig was in aid of the latter. On principle I decided I would not attend.

Not being a sandal wearer. being partial to a burger or two and seeing the value of nuclear weapons from a defence perspective I was not cut out to stand with 2000+ misguided idealists for two hours. Not even Weller could alter this.

Okay had it been The Jam reforming for this cause my principles would have been severely tested and no doubt broken (a bit like Alan Davies ditching his CND rally in London halfway through as Arsenal were at home to Everton). It's a question of priorities. Sacrifice duly made. I still stand by my decision.

During this time remarkably my relationship with my girlfriend from school continued even though she was at Brighton Poly. Communication was limited to letters initially and cheap rate (after 6pm/weekend) telephone calls.

One day, in a moment of madness, she decided on a day return from Brighton to Cov (6 hours travel for about 3 hours together). I was staggered when she walked into my halls of residence unannounced at about 11.00am having set off from Brighton at 5.00am.Roy 'dedication' Castle would have been mightily impressed.

These visits naturally soon evolved into weekends and extended weekends and what it confirmed to me above all was that in comparison to Brighton Cov was a complete and utter shit hole. City of culture my arse. Needless to say Brucey's gig at Brighton Top Rank was incorporated into a Brighton visit in May 1984!

As noted above the night life in Cov was good but involved the hazardous ordeal of getting to and from the pubs and gigs concerned safely. The best pub in terms of atmosphere and music was right in the town centre and sited adjacent to HMV in the precinct. It was The Dog And Trumpet.

Relatively cheap drinks and a small dance floor in front of the bar where all the alternatives could skank around (square shouldered hen-pecking style) to the likes of White Wedding, Glittering Prize, Love And Pride etc. They also interspersed this crap with some decent tunes. King being a Cov band were pretty popular.

After the sessions an obligatory visit to to The Parson's Nose was a scary necessity for the reasons noted above. In this field Martyn excelled showing a mad addiction.

He would accompany me through the 'streets of Fear' (as The Coventry Telegraph once put it) to the hovel that was The Parsons Nose for his Chicken And Mushroom Pie and Chips. We would walk back to the halls by the cathedral and often he would decide he needed another portion and would turn on his heels and return to the battlefield that was the taxi rank outside Parson's all on his own. Nutter or what?

I won't go into details about the conquests that Martyn, Paul, Neil, Aide and his Rhodesian buddy Tirry accomplished at the chav hole that was Tamango's but let's just say one of Tirry's conquests resembled Michelle McManus complete with a solid eyebrow which ran the width of her forehead! They were not choosy the boys once The Pilsners had taken their toll.

Cov also first alerted me to the concept of the record fair (actually it was probably initiated on one of my trips to Brighton as they held massive events in The Brighton Centre).

This was paradise to me.

The chance to spend three or four hours flicking through record sleeves looking for that illusive Punk/Mod Revival disc and bartering with the dealer when you found one. More than the odd gem could be uncovered (Cuddly Toys Guillotine Theatre 12" Japanese import being a classic example) and many of my esteemed collection were acquired from these fairs.

Once when I was back visiting my parents in Cambridge I attended a Cambridge Record Fair.

I was flicking through the discs and got the impression that the stall holder was taking an unnaturally intense interest in me. Not wanting to show that I had noticed I ignored him but as I ventured into the Paul Weller/Jam section a cry of 'Woodrow' (one of my nicknames from school) was yelled. It was none other than old 'Chrumm Fawrks Boiy' Roots.'I thought it was you' he said ' I was just waiting for you to venture into the jam section before I collared you'.

Post Covid these fairs thankfully have commenced again. They have been sorely missed.

In spite of the efforts of The Specials in the early eighties Cov was still full of racial tension. It was bleak.One week a young Pakistani was killed on the Streets of Cov and a few days later two of my mates (Graham and Nick) were going from Cov to Wembley courtesy of Harry Shaw's coach company to see England play.

The bus had loads of Cov Townies on board and as it passed the spot where the young man died the thick racist Cov chavs sang disgusting mocking songs about the incident. Both of my Gooner mates said they felt sick to the bone and would have got off if they could. This was before these Chavs had even touched the Tennents. Morons.

Terry Hall and Co certainly had their work cut out in Cov trying to initiate racial harmony. You could certainly equate with the bleakness of their lyrics.

One of my biggest regrets from my time in Coventry was my lack of Curry participation despite Cov being second only to Birmingham in terms of Cuzza Houses. I did not partake in a single Curry in the three years I was there and for that I blame Ipswich.

As noted above the first Cuzza House didn't open in Ipswich until 1991 so I had no experience of this wonderous cultural delicacy (other than Franny's somewhat rudimentary Sharwoods offerings) before venturing to Cov in 1983.

I more than made up for this in the years that followed but at the time when my mates went out for their regular weekly Cov Cuzzas I would be back at the student digs listening to Foxton's solo album on the Dansette with my boring ham, egg and chips. Plank.

What an uninitiated Suffolk peasant. Nothing short of criminal. An insult to Cov, the whole Cuzza community and the world of Nagas and Vindaloos. My heartfelt apologies to all.

My final Cov incident relates to a monumental decision..... to have my ear pierced.

A 'sleeper' was inserted and after the advised 4 week settling in period this was replaced with a dangling anchor to match the anchor image which could be found on the cheek of Sean Purcell the lead singer of Cuddly Toys.

All was fine until I returned home. Geoffrey quite literally blew a gasket.

This was not what men in the RAF did. I was not welcomed at home and forced to remove it.

Fine I thought. I could merely insert and take out and he would never know. This was ok until one day I returned from Juliet's house and walked boldly into the lounge forgetting the anchor was still dangling. He exploded with unbridled rage and accusations of going against my word. I had never seen Geoffrey more agitated since the time we managed to get him to sample a pickled onion flavour Monster Munch which albut resulted in calls for a stomach pump.

Yes Cov was strange but I grew up in those three years. It was an invaluable life experience.

Q12A. True or false episodes of the late 1970s CI 5 detective series The Professionals always end up with a shoot out in a derelict South London warehouse?

Q12B. True or false prior to their classic gold Capri Messrs Bodie & Doyle used a Ford Escort?

That rough book. Not a hint of academia!

XII

Essentially Homework: If you are not a music obsessive I would skip.
Alternative Chart Busters
There's nothing like a good categorisation. So, I have compiled a few charts for your deliberation/consideration/total blanking.

These represent my preferences and are not based on sales or anything as specific as that.

The only ruling I had followed was to limit each chart to only one band entry (i.e no room for All Mod Cons and Setting Sons re favourite album).

Compile your own. It's not as easy as you might think.

Take a look, disagree and then make your own judgements.

Chart A Top Ten Punk/New Wave Singles 1977/79
10. The Members. Sound Of The Suburbs. Captured the times perfectly in two minutes 45 secs.
9. Buzzcocks What Do I Get? One of many faultless 45s.
8. The Stranglers Somthin' Better Change/Straighten Out. Pure Punk. Both sides.
7. Magazine. Shot By Both Sides. Punchy and addictive. Even better was to come.
6. The Saints. This Perfect Day. Rasping follow up to I'm Stranded.
5. XTC. This Is Pop. And it was. Raucous and catchy.
4. The Vibrators. Baby Baby. A mellow offering from this under-rated band.
3. 999 Nasty Nasty. Violent intimidating music. Smash Pow!
2. The Jam The Eton Rifles. Ultimate Jam before they broke really big.
1. The Clash White Man (In Hammersmith Palais). A faultless classy offering showing even at this early stage the accomplished diversity of this band.

In true Top Of The Pops terms here are a few which are 'Bubbling Under': UK Subs Stranglehold, The Adverts Gary Gilmour's Eyes, Sex Pistols Pretty Vacant, Ramones Sheena Is (one of 71 single releases by the band!).

Chart B Top Ten Punk/New Wave Albums 1977/79

10. Ramones Rocket To Russia. My first Ramones LP. Full of pop gems.

9. The Stranglers No More Heroes. Even better than Rattus. No hint of Pub Rock. Pure Punk.

8. The Saints Prehistoric Sounds. An evolution from Punk (Stranded) to blues.

7. The Members At The Chelsea Nightclub. Anthemic and lyrically spot on.

6. XTC White Music. Consistently good but far better to follow in the mid 80s (Skylarking)

5. 999 The Biggest Prize in Sport. Commercial classic and a step up from Separates.

4. The Vibrators V2. For many (not Cruddster) The Ultimate New Wave LP. Great cover and riffs.

3. The Clash The Clash. Brash and in your face. Sit up & take notice. We did.

2. Magazine Real Life. Prog PuNK at its finest. Even Bob Harris would come close to triumphantly swinging that Whistle Test office chair for this one.

1. The Jam Setting Sons. The ultimate 'Jam Sound' album. A band at their peak. A quarter concept with a wealth of catchy riffs and tunes. Lyrical genius. Heatwave the one filler.

Bubbling under: The Adverts Crossing The Red Sea, The Dickies Incredible Shrinking Dickies, UK Subs Brand New Age, TRB Power In The Darkness, The Undertones.

The Difficult Second Album Concept:

From memory I think this concept arose out of the Prog Rock fraternity. It was the kind of issue that would have had Whispering Bob musing furtively, stroking his structured bearded chin and intensifying his eyebrows when he gave serious consideration to the likes of Stackridge's second album Friendliness.

Was this a more progressive forward thinking product than their self- titled opening release? (clearly I have done my homework).

He would then give his prognosis.

All a bit hippified for me but you do have to ask yourself-

Did any punk acts fall foul of it? In my mind a fair few might have done.

The Clash Give Em Enough Rope. Not guilty.

A bit of an obvious one I know but it did still have a number of Strong tracks in Stay Free, Safe European Home, Drug Stabbing Time and the singles but to be fair whilst side 1 was good side 2 was at best patchy. The Americanised production from Sandy Pearlman was largely the cause of media criticism at the time but on reflection the album itself remained of a high quality. Harshly knocked at the time

Tom Robinson Band TRB 2 Guilty.
This very much falls into the category of difficult second album. The band had splintered, the hits had dried up and this was at best patchy. Still sounds weak today which rather proves it wasn't up to scratch. Nowhere near the level of Power In The Darkness.

Secret Affair Behind Closed Doors. In the late seventies/early eighties Secret Affair produced three albums all of impeccable quality. For me this band could do no wrong . Unfortunately the record buying public failed to keep pace.
Categorically NOT GUILTY.

Buzzcocks Love Bites. Not guilty.
Again at the time this was panned by the press. It came off the back of commercially successful singles in Ever Fallen In Love and Promises but it was seen as rather safe in comparison with the spikey debut Another Music In A Different Kitchen. I do not agree.

The Jam This Is The Modern World Not guilty.
I can't fathom the criticism this album received. For me this album showed a natural progression from City which was merely an R & B reflection of the live output at the time.

This Is The Modern World had classics in the title track, I Need You, Life From A Window and Standards. The song writing was more structured and even Brucey contributed positively with Don't Tell Them Your Sane (let's leave London Traffic aside).

Rick also got his famous 'Eggs, Eggs, Eggs intro in before Tonight At Noon (another classic) and the inner sleeve artwork was intriguing.

Unfairly slated by the media in my opinion (although I may be biased as this was my first album purchase). Weller slating it didn't help either.

The Adverts Cast Of Thousands Guilty.
Another obvious one. The first album Crossing The Red Sea was rightly critically acclaimed and is still viewed as a Punk classic.

Unfortunately the same cannot be said of the follow up which suffered from weak production, patchy song writing and terrible cover artwork. What were they thinking of? Worth a fair bit on E bay due to the limited number of units sold back in the day. Improves slightly over time.

The Lambrettas Ambience Guilty.

Yes even the Mod Revivalists had their guilty bands and this was the most obvious.

Their first album Beat Boys In The Jet Age was arguably one of the most complete mod revival albums but by the release of the second the revival had pretty well run its path and this offering was pretty directionless. It was an attempt to move on but only a couple of tracks of note.

Many bands of the time produced second albums which clearly surpassed the debuts.

The Vibrators V2

In Pure Mania they had produced a stunning debut but many see V2 as THE perfect New Wave Album. Only Troops Of Tomorrow is ditchable (although many love it). All the other tracks are stormers.

Ironic that the opening track on V2 is called Pure Mania the title of their first album. Pure punk logic. The hum of that fighter plane and the explosion as the intro is wonderful.

UK Subs Brand New Age

A step up from the slightly limited Blues and contains the classic Emotional Blackmail which still always forms part of the Subs live set today. Released on wonderful bendy clear vinyl too.

Artwork probably not as eye catching as the Blues album. It was declaring 1980 as being a Brand New Age!

Elvis Costello This Year's Model.

My Aim was good but this album took him to another level. Very few weak tracks and what a cover. No I phone camera for our Elvis. The Brand New Age of 1980 hadn't arrived yet!

Magazine Secondhand Daylight

A difficult one this as the first album was ground breaking from a Punk perspective.

The follow up I think is best described as explorative. It was borderline prog. Not the same urgency of the first but a more structured approach showing a real development in musicianship. It was above all beautifully bleak.

You could argue that it is very difficult to place judgement on Magazine albums in contrast with one another such was their individuality.

Plenty of Punk and Mod bands arguably could be deemed consistent in their first two deliveries and examples include

The Vapors New Clear Days and Magnets. Both utter classics. Slightly favour Magnets.

999 Self titled first album 999 and Separates. Inseparable and covers so similar. Their colourful clothing phase.

Secret Affair Glory Boys and Behind Closed Doors.As noted above all three of the albums (and indeed their last released in 2011) are masterpieces.

The Saints I'm Stranded and Eternally Yours.

For me the second is a more complete (if less abrasive) offering.

Ultimate sin I cut out one of the inner sleeve Eternally Yours Pink Hearts to declare my undying love for my girlfriend. Unforgivable irrational record abuse.

Killing Joke Killing Joke and What's This For. Both tribal. Both bleak. Both intimidating.

In my opinion when bands refined their sound they had more chance of equalling or bettering the first release. Mere repetition could lead to a predictable product. It was a difficult balance as often bands would be criticised by the press if they altered from their original path!

A more Punky debate is the one where a single B side is arguably better than the A. Again there are many examples.

The Jam. Absolute Beginners. Surely Tales From The Riverbank was superior. Weller still plays it to this day.

The Clash. Clash City Rockers as opposed to Jail Guitar Doors? Debatable.

The Stranglers Something Better Change. Better than Straighten Out? OK a double A.

Buzzcocks Happy Nowadays or Why Can't I Touch It? The latter for me any day.

Buzzcocks I Don't Mind or Autonomy?

XTC Grass or Dear God? Surely no question here. The latter effectively broke the band in America and was later released as a single in its own right.

Often it was the song writing rivalry within a band which determined which tracks were A sides and this would appear to be the case with XTC where Partridge and Moulding appeared to take it in turns in respect of A and B sides.

The same can possibly be said of the Buzzcocks who had the Shelley/Diggle rivalry.

Chart C Top Ten Post Punk Singles 1979/83

10. Classix Nouveaux Forever And A Day Rip roaring catchy 45 as usual. One of many released by the band. Is It A Dreamis not a reflection of their true talents. Do not be fooled.

9. (Rick Buckler's) Time UK. Playground of Privilege. Storming track. Should have been a monster but limited exposure (Saturday Superstore only). Effectively killed it.

8. The Vapors. Prisoners. The most commercially catchy debut single ever.

7. The Saints . Paralytic Tonight Dublin Tomorrow. Every one of the five tracks on this 12" is a classic.

6. The Armoury Show. We Can Be Brave Again. Chanting anthem. A short-lived underrated post punk super group that was half Skids half Magazine.

5. Cuddly Toys. It's A Shame. Cements the move from glam punk to New Romantic/ Post Punk. Commercial and catchy.

4. XTC Senses Working Overtime. Pure pop wizardry. Plenty more would follow.

3.The Clash London Calling. Great track. The album which followed showed a varied range of styles accomplished with ease.

2. Magazine Rhythm Of Cruelty. A progressive move from the Shot By Both Sides 45 which was punk. This was a skilled bleak tune.

1. Doll By Doll. Main Travelled Roads. Just listen to it. Utter brilliance. Fact: Lead singer Jackie Leven was taken to court on the basis that this record copied elements of Twelve of Never by Donny Osmond!

-Chart D Top 10 Post Punk Albums 1979-82

10. The Vapors Magnets A progressive darker follow up to New Clear Days. Superior.

9. Ultravox Ha Ha Ha Proper Ultravox (pre Midge). Foxx imperious.

8. Tubeway Army Replicas Ground breaking and interesting (for a while).

7. Cuddly Toys Trials And Crosses. Accomplished post punk album. It should have been a commercial success but once again minimal exposure/promotion killed it.

6. Classix Nouveaux. Secret. Aptly their least known LP. Quality from both a lyrical and musical perspective. Marked the end for the band as it didn't sell. A real shame.

5. XTC. English Settlement. Masterful double. A shape of things to come.

4. Doll By Doll. Doll by Doll. Another commercial failure but an utter masterpiece.

3. The Armoury Show. Waiting For The Floods. See comment above.

2. The Clash London Calling. A vibrant mix of styles. Masterfully produced.

1. Magazine. Secondhand Daylight. Dark, bleak, explorative and brilliant.

Chart E Top 5 Mod Revival Singles 1979/80

5. Merton Parkas Plastic Smile. A talented and criminally underrated band. Great song. Naff name didn't help but better than The Scooters!.

4. Purple Hearts Jimmy. In truth one of the few good tracks on their album Beat That! (which was, in all honesty a bit dirgy). Great single. Failed to chart.

3. The Lambrettas. Page 3 (Another Day Another Girl). Chart days long behind them by this stage and ironically 'screwed' by The Sun over the original title. Great song.

2. The Chords Maybe Tomorrow. Toss up between this and British Way Of Life. This just shades it. Aggressive Buzzcock/Jamesque stuff. Bang Bang You're Dead!!!

1. Secret Affair. My World. Still makes the hairs on the back of my neck stand up every time I hear it. Superb on all levels. Apparent distribution problems prevented it reaching the top 10.

Chart F. Top 5 Mod Revival Albums 1979/80

5. Merton Parkas. Face In The Crowd. A varied fun album. Once again ignore the name and enjoy the music.

4. Squire. Get Smart. Some cracking tunes from Anthony Meynall and Company. Underrated Mod revival band still going strong.

3. The Lambrettas. Beat Boys In The Jet Age. Track on track this is clever witty, musically crafted stuff. Great album.

2. Secret Affair. Behind Closed Doors. The second of three great offerings from the band between 1979 and 1982. This seals it with tracks such as My World and Seen That Movie too absolute gems.

1. The Chords So Far Away. An album to rival any album. Full of punchy tunes, inspiring vocals and luscious licks. Only one weak track on it. Remains a vibrant classic

The Mod Revival got tough unappreciative coverage from the music press at the time (Garry Bushel excepted). This was partly self-induced as the names chosen by some of the bands lent themselves to derision (The Vespas for instance). It was unwarranted.

Chart G The Top Ten Band Logos

10. Magazine Arrowed/Oval Soap Album logo

9. Sex Pistols Classic ransom note design (Vacant/Bollocks covers). Captured the tone.

8. The Stranglers. Handwriting style red logo on all the early white UA labels.

7. The Chords Arrow design. So mod.

6. The Vibrators Logo on first album. A logo retained to this day and rarely varied.

5. The Jam Classic In The City spray design. Very punk. Looks even better on the fan club membership card (dark blue spray on light blue tiles).

4. The Clash First album spray design. Very punky as per Jam above.

3. XTC Drums and Wires face design. Very clever. Very effective. Very colourful.

2. Cuddly Toys. Classic Japanese pink and green logo seen on Madman and first album Guillotine Theatre. One of a kind and lapped up by their Japanese following. Stunning.

1. 999. The ultimate. A Raffle ticket design which was usually pink or green in the early days. Always with i.d. number AS5802 at the top (exception the single Found Out Too Late when it was HS2725). Finger print enhanced top left corner. So good it has been used consistently by the band over their 43+ year career. Perfect for T shirts and badges.

Chart H Top 20 Gigs Attended 1980 –

20. The Style Council Brighton Centre 1984 Council Meeting. Met Paul and Mick after. Programme duly signed. First Weller/TSC exposure live. A circle wing seat didn't help.

19.Fossil Fools (XTC Tribute) February 2020 London Water Rats. Originals no longer available. Fantastic act, appreciative crowd (including Adrian Durham from Talk Sport). Last gig before Covid lockdown for me (chickened out of Ian McNabb in early March 2020).

18. Gods Toys (Adam And The Ants) Ipswich Gaumont 12th December 1980. The Toys were brilliant. A fan won over. We're All Gods Toys. Ants best forgotten (bar ex Vibrator Gary Tibbs on bass). Adam merely a commercial chart showman by that stage.

17. The Undertones Cambridge Junction 2019. Great gig/venue even sans Feargal. All the classics played. Met Mr Bradley after the show. Actually surpassed by their show in Brighton March 2022.

16.Bruce Foxton Brighton Top Rank Suite Brighton 1984. Second last gig of his Summer Tour. Smithers aired for the first time. Described by Sounds as Big Countryesque! All sorts of horns and saxes from M'ssrs Thistlewaite and Lorimer backing up Brucey and the band. Saw him three times on this tour .

15. UK Subs The Engine Rooms Brighton Dec 2010. A strange one this in all respects. I attended with my gig mate Chris. Beers before at The Windmill and then down to The Engine Rooms. Charlie eating his chicken drum sticks out of foil on the merch stand prior to going on stage. Proper punk and a proper punk venue.

Dry when we went in and full blown blizzard with 3" of snow settled when we emerged. Two mile slide home.

14.Jackie Leven The Greys (numerous). Saw him about 15 times before he sadly passed away in November 2011. Every performance a winner from this former Doll By Doll front man and raconteur. Brilliantly talented guitarists and lyricist who could tell a good tale.

13. From The Jam Concorde 2 December 2009. Setting Sons 30th Anniversary Tour. Classic jam played by Bruce, Rick and Russel Hastings. Do not dismiss this band. Check them out. Setting Sons album in full plus all the singles and classic album cuts. If you closed your eyes you thought it was the real thing and two thirds of it was. Recent compositions excellent too.

Still going strong (unfortunately minus Rick) with new material recorded at Paul Weller's studio with him guesting on a few tracks. It's as good as it's going to get.

12. The Dickies The Powerhaus Islington. 30th September 1990.Manic performance and members of The Vibrators amongst other punk celebs in the crowd.

11.The Vapors + Chords UK. 229 Club London 10th November 2017. Two cracking bands two storming sets. Venue great size but beers ridiculously expensive (£6 a pint even then) Vintage 1979 unfortunately beer prices way off those in 1979.

10.Buzzcocks Brighton Coalition Club circa Summer 2002. Great venue and band on blistering form. Wore my Magazine Give Me Everything shirt that night and Diggle clocked it!

9. Paul Weller Movement. Zap Club Brighton circa 1990. Small intimate venue and Weller back to his rocking best. John W naturally in attendance.

8. The Icicle Works Down Stairs Bar Coventry Poly 1983. The original band at their ultimate piss taking best.

7. The Saints + The Vibrators. The Marquee Club London consecutive nights 28/29th October 1989. Dream gig weekend at same venue so classed as one gig. Great venue in Charing Cross Road.

6. The Chords Another Thing Coming Reformation Tour 2010. The Garage London. Full original line up. A friction free night of classic , timeless mod anthems.

5. Secret Affair The Scala June 18th 2003. Full original line up. Great venue. I remember this one well. I spotted in the Evening Standard that Secret Affair were to play the Scala. I didn't even know they had reformed. Ticket booked. No questions.

As I left the train to go up to street level I remember graciously helping a lady who was struggling with her suitcase (one of those ones on wheels) so I dragged it up the stairs for her and covered the shins of my pristine white Levis jeans with black marks in the process. A noble moment ruining the cool attire of the night.

I went out to suss the venue at about 4.00pm and as a I did a taxi pulled up and a person who looked like 'Del Boy' got out and entered the Scala. I later realised it was Ian Page!

Great gig. Brought it all back with those momentous tunes.

4. 999 The Engine Rooms Brighton 2007. Great basement venue. Great gig. Allegedly broke all the fire regulations and no longer there (possibly as a result) but the scene of many a good punk gig.

3.Classix Nouveaux/Cuddly Toys. West Runton Pavilion April 1982.

Legendary venue and two great bands. Thanks mum and dad for taking us and killing 4+ hours in Cromer on a dark Wednesday night! I became a Cuddly Toys fan from there on.

2. The Clash Ipswich Gaumont January 14th 1980.

First gig. Blown away and met band afterwards. Second place only because we were in the circle. The one that started it all off.

1. Magazine. Kentish Town Forum 2009.

I will never forget the anticipation of the crowd and the thud of the bass as opening track the Light Pours Out Of Me commenced .Twenty five plus years dissolved away as Howie made his entrance in pink jacket and dark shorts. Full line up minus McGeogh of course.

Magazine were scintillating that night. To quote Brian Moore a momentous occasion.

Chart I Top 5 Punk/New Wave Instrumentals'

Instrumentals were not a big thing in the Punk/New Wave era and were avoided entirely by the vast majority of bands (probably as the concept carried a slight proggyness) but one or two dipped their toes in and the results should be admired, not sneered at.

5. The Jam . Circus. A jaunty Brucey composition found on the final LP The Gift (and often used over the PA when From The Jam are about to take to the stage) this little ditty was very nearly covered by Bananarama who wanted to add lyrics and release as a single!

4. Buzzcocks. Walking Distance. Tucked away on the second LP Love Bites this possesses an infuriating catchy guitar riff. A real gem of a track.

3. The Dickies. Rondo (The Midget's Revenge). Yes your eyes are not deceiving you. San Francisco's finest produced a magical vocal-less track on their manic first LP The Incredible Shrinking Dickies and incredibly it was actually 3+ minutes long (the longest track on the album by a country mile). Still played live by the band today it's a melodic beauty.

2. Classix Nouveaux . 627. This was actually the B side of the magnificent Never Again (These Times Erased) and it's a storming track.Try it on Alexa. You will be hooked by the end.

1. Magazine. The Thin Air. Haunting and beautifully crafted (I am sounding

like whispering Bob) and written by the supremely talented John McGeoch. A classic track from asuperb album'.

Festivals. Heartland of middle aged saddos and precocious wannabies.
Why attend what is essentially a social event where you have no firm interest in any of the acts, the acoustics are likely to be sub-standard given the open air context and you are surrounded by a combination of students and middle class middle aged Coldplay loving desperados trying to prove they still have it even though many didn't have it in the first place.

Added to this there's a good chance that even if there are a couple of acts you are remotely interested in you will probably miss one due to a clash of timings. Whilst Leeds/Reading have a degree of credibility the one that really bugs me is Glastonbury. Tickets sell out well in advance and before any of the acts are confirmed. Does this not prove my point?

All the attendees (many a Monty Python fan) want to do is brag about how muddy they got. It's so old hat and BORING. Not rebellious in any way. Although smoking is no longer cool Vaping is. Kipping down overnight in a tent full of 'vaping students' doesn't bare thinking about. Comparable to lock down in a Tooty Frootie factory (one for the teenagers).

Give me a small sweaty venue with a band I have a true affection for any day. Step forward The Albert, The Green Door, Concorde II, Patterns and The Coalition in Brighton and Water Rats, The Borderline, Marquee II and The 229 Club in London. Proper atmospheric venues.

Gig Dilemmas

As age creeps in the bladder goes on a work to rule basis. Loo visits at gigs need to be carefully planned. Whoever the artist nearly all have a nailed on toilet track.

I give you:

The Vibrators Troops Of Tomorrow.

999 Feelin' Alright With The Crew .

Tom Robinson War Baby.

Secret Affair Crumble Gunn or Soho Strut.

UK Subs She's Not There. {rarely played).

Paul Weller. He offers numerous options. He knowingly delights in exposing his audiences to extended versions of the likes of Walk On Gilded Splinters or Up In Suzie's Room and with Porcelain Gods we seem to have a self- titled call to the urinals!

The 'One Hit Wonder' Artist's Chart Of Merit.

Many acts are rightfully branded throwaway one hit wonders and dismissed as a result. For some this is totally justified (Mr Blobby, Match Stalk Men, Grandma We Love You, Jilted John, Shadd Up A Ya Face etc).

For some acts this is very unfair. These are the guys who have great bodies of work but for whom the great British record buying public only picked up on one tune and as a result they only troubled the chart on very rare occasions. Not to be confused with the shit noted these were so much more.

10. The Motors. Airport is always remembered but the follow up Forget About You also made the Top 20. But what about the likes of Dancing The Night Away and That's what John Said?

9.The Adverts. Gary Gilmore's Eyes. Other great singles included No Time To Be 21, Bored Teenagers plus two albums the first of which was great.

8.Classix Nouveaux. If ever a band deserved chart success it was this hard working lot from Wimbledon. Their only top 40 was the dreadful Is It A Dream. What about Guilty, Tokyo, Forever And A Day, Never Again? Also three top quality albums.

7.The Saints. The amazing I'm Stranded failed to chart. The follow up This Perfect Day scraped into the Top 40 . Quality albums followed amid numerous line- up changes.

6.Killing Joke. Love Like Blood was Top twenty. This was nothing compared to the likes of Requiem, Eighties, Follow The Leaders, Are You Receiving. Numerous great albums.

5. The Vapors. OK Turning Japanese was catchy and still gets regular airings on the TV whenever anything remotely oriental is being covered but they were far more than this. Their debut single Prisoners is exceptional as were News At Ten, Waiting For the Weekened and Spiders. Two brilliant albums in New Clear Days and the darker follow up Magnets. Seriously under-rated.

4. The Vibrators Automatic Lover. A Top 40 'hit'. This was a great tune but what about the likes of Baby Baby, London Girls, Judy Says, Baby Blue Eyes, Disco In Moscow? Numerous great albums.

3. 999. Homicide again scraped into the Top 40 but (apart from I'm Alive and Feelin Alright With The Crew) this band were responsible for a wealth of great singles such as Nasty Nasty.

2. The Chords. Maybe Tomorrow. A storming track but matched by others

in Something's Missing, In My Street, and the equally sublime British Way Of Life. One cracking album the best of the Mod Revival period.

2b. The Icicle Works. Known only for their psychedelic inspired Top 20 hit Love Is A Wonderful Colour this band were so much more. Other cracking commercial 45s included Hollow Horse, Who Do You Want For Your Love. Evangeline , Melanie and the imperious Understanding Jane. Added to this they released 5 fantastic albums. One hit wonders my arse!

1. Magazine. Shot By Both Sides. A blistering effort that stalled at number 40. Rhythm Of Cruelty and the four singles from the Soap era were truly magnificent. Four quality albums in addition.

ABBA.

At school in 1980 there was a pretty camp chap called Mark S. He adored ABBA. Although derided at the time like many others I now see their full worth and for that reason I have to offer my favourite three ABBA tracks.

3.Hasta Manana. I remember it from the late seventies but refused to admit I liked it.

2. Eagle. If ever a track has to be described as epic then this is it. Brilliantly structured.

1.When I Kissed The Teacher. Possibly a little borderline in context it is a fantastic track and apparently one of Benny's favourites so I can't be wrong.

Bands to reform, preferably on the same bill.

3. Slade. To get Noddy, Jim, Don and Dave together for one last time would be a momentous occasion but for it to work Noddy's voice would have to be up to it.

The greatest of all the Glam bands without a doubt (although The Sweet ran them close) and amazingly all are still alive!

Come on Noddy you stubborn old git!

2. XTC. Too much inter-songwriter rivalry between Messrs Partridge and Moulding for it ever to occur and of course the stage fright may possibly still be an issue but if this band had continued playing live at their prime I am sure they could have been bigger than The Beatles (and how I would have loved that!).

Apart from Go2 their albums were all gems (especially Skylarking).They would probably sell out most large UK venues even now such is the ever loyal following.

THE JAM .Only to be considered under the exceptional circumstances. I.E an approving Weller (extremely unlikely), a good cause and no friction in the camp. A considerable number of hatchets would have to be buried.

Brucey would jump (quite literally) at it but once again, probably rightly, it's never going to happen. Liklihood of occurance. Nil. With a rational head we should remember them for what they were, the greatest live band in Britain and 'the best f*****g band in the world ' and leave it at that but oh if only… .. it would wipe December 2nd 1982 from my memory once and for all.

Theoretically it could happen. All members are still active.

Irritating Jam Faux Pas: Mistakes made by the media and so called fans alike.
Eaton Rifles
Sound Effects
Rick Butler

THE ETON RIFLES, SOUND AFFECTS and
RICK BUCKLER. PLEASE.
DRIVES YOU FUCKING MAD.

Q13. What relevance does the respective hemisphere of your country have on an international Rugby Union Match?

Come in number 176 your time is up

Trivia Quiz Answers

1. The Sweet. Offered it by Chin/Chap but apparently wanted to write their own A Side hence Mud got the gig and a monster hit it was.

2. Horror Bags Bones, Claws, Ribs, Fangs and Bats (never seen the latter).

3. Frys : Chocolate Cream, Peppermint Cream, Orange Cream and 5 Centres. Note in later years all the fruit flavours were released as individual bars. Similar to the limited edition coloured vinyls of the 70s.

4. 1974 World Cup Group Match Scotland 2 Zaire 0. Lorrimer and Jordan.

5. The Tot range. Jelly Tots (jelly buttons), Tiger Tots (mini Licquorice allsorts), Candy Tots (mini dolly mixtures) and Teddy Tots (Jap cubes)

6. Weller jokingly said that The Jam should have digs above The Rainbow (Finsbury Park) as they played there so often. Digs for gigs.

7. Adam And The Ants. Roxy Music. The Vibrators.

8. False his real name is Barry Green.

9.The Vapors-Guildford, Merton Parkas -Merton (Wimbledon accepted) Skids-Dunfermline, Icicle Works- Liverpool, Magazine-Manchester and XTC Swindon.

10. Wales. Red with yellow and green tramlines design.

11. Vicks Sinex

12A Yes Invariably. 12B False. It was a Triumph Dolomite Registration POK 79R and after the Capri they went for the Triumph TR7.

13. Absolutely nothing at all. It's all pretentious rugga bollocks (they call a groin strain a testicular injury or taking a penalty 'going poles'). Another way that they unsuccessfully try to inflate the importance of Egg Chasing.

The hemisphere has no relevance to the game or indeed any sport at all but it is a mightily posh word so it's banded about continually and features in virtually every Rugga conversation.

BBC. Please.The vast majority of us don't care . Similarly with The Commonwealth Games. Aside from Adam Peaty's grandmother who gives a fuck?

My Desert Island Discs:

You know the score. Eight tracks, one book and one luxury item. Here we go.

8.The Monkees. What Am I Doin' Hanging 'Round. Pure classy 1960s pop. Knocks spots off any Beatles track.

7.Toss up between Secret Affair. Seen That Movie Too (A track from the LP Behind Closed Doors), very moving or Chris Pope- Peace Of Mind. A stormer.

6. The Icicle Works. Understanding Jane. One of the best thumping rock

tracks ever written. Should have been massive hit but of course missed out.

5. The Sweet. Fox On The Run. Infuriatingly catchy and self- penned.

4. Magazine. Definitive Gaze. Pure post punk brilliance.

3.The Clash. Tommy Gun. Manic punk brilliance in three minutes.

2.Slade. How Does It Feel. A hauntingly brilliant track from the best band of the early seventies.

1. XTC. The Mayor Of Simpleton. Find me a more perfect pop single.

Book: Giles Smith. Lost In Music. I have read three times and it gets better with every read. Transmits you seamlessly into the punk/post punk period with an enduring wit. Quite brilliant.

Luxury Item: How about a record player (Solar powered)!

NO MORE HEROES ANYMORE: Luckily there were many in the 70s/80s.
Music:

Andy Partridge (XTC). Quintessential eccentric English genius

Paul Weller. An angry articulate man way ahead of his time.

Howard Devoto (Magazine) See Partridge comments above. Hugely underrated.

Jim Lea (Slade). The brains behind the operation musically and lyrically.

Joe Strummer. Coolness personified.

Sport:
Alan Knott. Impish wicket keeper who often paired so well with Tony 'pretty adjacent ' Greig . Loved his Green slash Slazenger bat.
Ian Botham. The ultimate awe inspiring all- rounder. Flintoff was not fit to clean his boots.
Tony Adams. Began his long illustrious career at the start of the 1980s (Sunderland at Home 1983). A titan. Rightly known as Mr Arsenal.
Jimmy Connors. A fiery obnoxious character despised (at the time) by John McEnroe. True grit.

Media:
Mike Read (DJ not Run Around). A brave Radio 1 breakfast show DJ who championed virtually all the bands I loved (and still does). The likes of The Icicle Works, XTC. Classix Nouveaux, The Jam, The Vapors and even 999 all got regular airings on the breakfast show.
David Coleman. 'Poterfield one nil' A genius.

Ralph. Commie obsessed neighbour of Harry Boyle in Wait Til Ya Father Gets Home. Gloriously politically incorrect.

Ritchie Benaud. 'Bawled 'im' . Flawless.

Eddie Shoestring. The coolest TV detective of all time.

Jon Pertwee. The coolest Dr Who of them all who encountered the evilest of monsters.

I have included a number of asides along the way but there remains a number of issues which confuse, irritate and frustrate me. Apologies if the odd one has been mentioned in passing before but I am self- proof reading and can't be arsed to trawl my way through the pages again.

This is a traditional Woolworth's style pick and mix of the asides I haven't fitted in.

- Why have the BBC resorted to dumbing down with regards to programme linkers? They used to be a cut above ITV with an air of class. Unfortunately no longer the case

- Still with the BBC annually they celebrate the Minority Sports Personality Of The Year (strangely nearly always the winner comes from one of the few sports that the BBC have coverage rights over) but in addition why do they persist with a programme that should have been retired years ago.

A Question Of Minority Sport. A tired old format which lost its sparkle following the departure of anchor-man David Coleman back in the late 1970s. It normally features a selection of athletes, swimmers and cyclists many of whom I would not recognise if they were sitting next to me on a bus.

During Football World Cup periods why do companies decide to align themselves to football when there is clearly no connection? Amongst many in 2022 we had a 19 year old female lawyer knocking a 1970s style black and white football around the office encouraging you to make a few decisions before the second half started. She didn't strike me as having any interest in football whatsoever. These are the same type of companies that disassociated themselves from the game in the hooligan days of the early 1980s.

- Why do so many UK citizens struggle so much with their own language? There are no such words as 'anythink', 'somethink' 'nothink' 'preformance'and 'precentage'. It's why my spell check is burning up now. Others claim they have 'brought somethink' when they have purchased an item. Embarrassingly the foreign football pundits speak better English than the likes of Shearer, Keown and Savage.

- Double Barrelled names. These used to be a sign of a privileged background.

Nowadays it is little more than a chav badge of honour.

Often the result of a couple of spectrums declaring undying love for one another after a heavy night in Spoons, a whirlwind 'romance' and a shotgun wedding where both names are taken on board before their first kid arrives a couple of months later.

Then reality sets in, the novelty wears off and the rows begin. In no time at all you are left with a kid with two names, one parent and a face destined to grace the Crime Watch Wall Of Shame in fifteen years time. Bleak but true.

- Whilst on the subject of Crime Watch why do people who hold up Jewellers insist on running from the premises and screeching away in a car. It rather attracts attention which is surely the last thing you want to do. Then they post their antics on ' sowshall media bruv'.tMorons.
- What's the point in ironing sheets and pillow cases?
- Why does my wife buy Multi -Purpose Wipes and supplements with floor wipes, kitchen wipes and bath room wipes? Jesus.
- Why have The FA totally destroyed the aura of Wembley in demolishing the twin towers, sacrificing those beloved stanchions and playing FA Cup Semi Finals at the home of the final?

Why do the contestants on Bullseye look uncannily like characters out of the children's game Guess Who?

- Why do so many drivers fail to use their indicators?
- The validity of the travel sickness pill.

Back in the early 1970s myself and Sid suffered terribly from car travel sickness. The solution came in the form of Joy Rides. These were a bright pink pill that tasted so appalling that they had you retching on the spot.

The parents used to put them inside a grape to soften the blow. It didn't. Effectively it just meant you were sick before the engine started up rather than on the journey itself. Utterly pointless. As a result I still detest grapes.

- A capital I does not have a dot on it.
- Chelsea FC (sorry Shauny Boy but it's got to be said). This club epitomises everything that is wrong with modern day football. They have no concept of longevity. Success must be instant. Prior to the injection of Abramovich's ill-gotten funds they were little more than a moderate sized club which occasionally picked up a domestic cup. Playing in front of crowds of under 10,000 with vehicles and disabled cars parked behind the goals they were rightly classed as mediocre in the football world. They did have cracking stanchions though.

Excessive funding over a couple of years pushed them falsely up to the realms of the top table. In the Ambramovich period managers came and went with a ruthless regularity (some following acquisitions of Champions League and FA cup trophies the season before) player prospects were signed for big money and farmed out on or loan or sold if they didn't produce the goods within a couple of months (Salah, De Bruyne, Lukaku, Matic. for example) Often they then attempted to buy back for big money once another club had done all the dirty work. Even 'club legend' Didier Drogba was being hounded by the fans (many calling him Dog Breath) up until the day he finally scored. At one stage they had over thirty players out on loan!

The media call them one of the big clubs. They are not. They are a small club with money. There is a huge difference. Clubs such as Everton, Villa and, dare I say it, Spurs are all far bigger but don't have the financially acquired trophies to show for it. Chelsea are finally being found out for what they are largely due to other clubs having the financial weight that was once limited to Chelski.

Added to the above they are classless. About ten years ago my son was dragged along by one of his Chelsea loving mates to a Chelsea Stadium Tour. I think it took about 25 minutes!. He returned to tell me that when they went into the Visitor's dressing room the guide said ' this is where the losers get changed'.

Sums them up perfectly.

Little has changed over recent years and the recent appointment of a manager in Graham Potter who lost six games on the trot for Brighton surely will not bode well for a club of this type. Will be long gone by the time you read this.

- Man Utd. Inexplicably they still remain the media darlings. Season after season of mis-investment and under-achievement but the media still insist on granting them complete comprehensive coverage. Every FA cup tie involving them has been televised live for about the last 4 years. This weekend a home tie Vs Reading was deemed worthy of live coverage. None of the other big clubs would have had a home game Vs Reading covered live.
- Striking workers. Why do they all use that chant along the lines of ' what do we want, fair pay, when do we want it, now' Unoriginal and childish. Added to that they are always grinning. At least make it look like you don't want to be striking.
- Silver piss is always reassuring.
- Perish the thought but if ever a book or film were released about Mad Vlad surely there could only be one title. It begins with a C has four letters and ends with a T and it's not CLOT.

- What is it with Rishi Sunak's strides? They always appear to be in a perennial state of pre alteration peg up limbo hovering at least 2" above his ankles.
- Woolworths. Covered before but worth another mention. What a strange institution this was. A music department based solely on chart offerings (with the legendary ex chart cheapo bin) caged pick and mix delights , Adidas Beckenbauer rip off football boots and above all a Levis/Wrangler hybrid denim clothing range which went under the name of Lasso.

Arguments with Geoffrey over the suitability of purchasing the Lasso denim trucker jacket with our Christmas money lead to Geoffrey acquiring a parking ticket in Fonnereau Road Ipswich. After turning our pleads down he deemed the fine to be a punishment from God and we were given free reign to acquire the following week.
- That chap who advertises funeral plans for his family 'that sure knows how to party' appears to have moved into the realms of Gold Bullion and Verisure Intruder Alarms lately. A link between protecting his potentially ill-gotten bullion with alarm detection and a tilt towards the worst possible scenario whereby a funeral plan comes into its own should it all go wrong?
- The wisdom of the boss of Wetherspoons?

His outspoken views on the benefits of leaving the European Union were widely advertised particularly in the pubs themselves in which many from Europe were staffing the bars.

In recent months a number of Spoons outlets across the UK have been forced to close with lack of staff often being cited as the issue. For affordable food and drinks they are arguably untouchable. The same accolade can now be quoted in terms of their ability to piss on their own skin on chips (with or without alcoholic drink).
- The most irritating character in 1970s sit-coms is by an ooh aaahh country mile Tristran Fourmile (son of George and Mildred's neighbours the Fourmiles). Precocious brat!
- The acting in the current day-time dirge series Doctors makes the Grange Hill cast seem like potential Academy Award winners. Even 'what's the matter RoLAND!
- Why are cookery/baking programmes so popular in this country when 80% of the population find cooking oven chips a challenge, live courtesy of Deliveroo and buy ready- made Omelettes from the supermarket?
- Do any images of dyed in the wool prog rocker Jethro Tull exist without some bearded hippy standing on one leg playing a flute?
- As touched on before a double negative is only acceptable (and actually es-

sential) in the context of a rock song.
- Many Asda outlets now offer a drycleaning franchise in addition to a McDonalds. One is clearly their target market, the other merely offering the punters the chance to look smart at those forthcoming court appearances?
- The school concept 'Own clothes day' Are uniforms really on a rental basis? Why do the media always refer to 'The Kop' on Liverpool based stories? Kop set for takeover.
- Can Nationwide dumb down their TV adverts anymore?

Those dreamy Top 10 Band logos

FINALE

Naturally thanks are due but I have to say are limited with regards to my family who have ridiculed me from the start. The vast majority of my gratitude goes whole heartedly to Messrs Jon Anderson and Rick Wakeman of Yes (plus my son's Sausage Dog Jerry who accepted my undivided dedication subject to a bit of biscuit bribery).

Without Jon and even more so Rick, there would have been no Punk explosion. Rick was behind the monstrosity that was Tales From Topographic Oceans in 1973. Need I say more?

This was an album release comprising four tracks which lasted between 18 and 23 minutes a piece. To be fair to Rick he was apparently against this particular release but I think still contributed somewhat over-elaborated keyboard elements.

This progressive rock was nothing more than pretentious self-indulgent dog shit but Rick took it a step further with an even more over- elaborate affair. The Myths And Legends Of King Arthur And The Knights Of The Round Table from1975.

Not only was this a 'classic prog rock concept 'album Rick took it to an all new self-indulgent level by having his band perform this dirge live with knights ice skating around the band on pantomime horses. The horrific evidence remains on You Tube! The gap between artiste and consumer was never ever greater than at this point in time.

Admittedly Yes/ Rick Wakeman were not the only culprits (hang you heads Fleetwood Mac, Pink Floyd, King Crimson, Barclay James Harvest, Jethro Tull and the mighty Stackridge) but they were probably the most contemptable of all of them. Their heads were so far up their arses at the time they were almost a shade of Esso Blue (another for the teenagers).

Cue The Clash at the 100 Club, The Electric Ballroom,The Roxy etc.The complete opposite of the above and a real chance for bands of the people to relate at ground level to their people. Given the state of the nation in 1976/77 it had to happen and thank god it did.

Although I was too young to actively participate in these events at the time my senses (working overtime) were awoken to the new phenomena and by 1977/78 I was fully into it.

From that moment my life has been significantly impacted by music and I have taken in upwards of 200 gigs since.

One of the best remains the first.

As noted above this was THE CLASH at The Gaumont (Ipswich) although this was probably due to the impact it had on me (being my first gig albeit in The Circle) rather than the actual quality of the musicianship but that is probably a bit harsh on The Clash (although not on The Kidz Next Door!).

A wide variety of towns have been taken in along the way including Ipswich, Brighton, Coventry, Birmingham, London, Norwich, Redhill, Lewes, West Runton, Cambridge, Guildford even Burgess Hill and the appetite for live music remains intact.

Whenever I return to Ipswich (the parents in law still live there) I like nothing more than drifting around the town and taking in the sites that were once so important to me back in the 1970s/80s.

The Gaumont Theatre remains a venue but is now The Regent. The stage door at the back where I met The Clash is still there but now behind gates/fencing. The Corn Exchange remains as is and still puts on live shit in a similar vein to the likes of Rory Gallagher!

Parrot Records is now some 'trendy' clothing outlet so when my sons pop in I just stand in the area where the two punk sections used to be and dream of those LP covers. They wouldn't understand.

The siting of the small badge shop is a mystery. It appears to have been swallowed up by one of the adjacent shops as no such miniscule recess exists anymore. Town Centre Pub Mannings was around back in the day and it still is today. The only pub I have frequented recently where they will only take cash . No cards. Only Ipswich!

The Ipswich Hot Dog outlets (Westler style portable cooking units) are still in existence and remain under strict local council limitations concerning the Onions due to the smell they emanate! A bit like having a 99 without the flake! Again only Ipswich.

Drug taking and dealing by the local Ipswich and East London hoodlum gangs of course is now rampant and goes unregulated. Ipswich Council seem more concerned with keeping those onions off the streets. Suffice to say it is no longer the quaint countrified town that it used to be but at least that famous accent remains. A Strange Town it remains.

Of course thanks must go to the main protagonists who made music once again a realistic, rational and, most importantly, accessible concept. This, for me, sparked a passion that remains to this day and one that keeps me hunting for the Punk gems rather than the long lost Susan Fassbender LP or offerings from Kevin Kitchen.

Thanks in no particular order have to go to:
TV Smith/The Adverts
The Jam
Doll By Doll/Jackie Leven
999
The Vibrators
UK Subs
The Saints
The Damned
Sex Pistols
XTC
The Chords
The Vapors
Secret Affair
Classix Nouveaux
Cuddly Toys
Gods Toys
The Icicle Works/ Ian McNabb
Magazine
The Dickies
The Members
Buzzcocks
TRB/ Tom Robinson

You may have noticed that I have missed out the band that started it all for me that cold night in Ipswich in January 1980, The Clash. In many ways they were the catalyst that set me on the path to music addiction and I will be forever grateful to them for that.

Long may it continue.

Now play Days (that changed the world)) by Tom Robison

IT SHOULD ALL MAKE SENSE NOW!

Step Taylor – January 2023

No comment Needed.